TROUBLE IN
MONARTO

TROUBLE IN
MONARTO

Thomas James Taylor

Contents

...for Janet

One

I have always trusted my instincts. Call it what you like, gut feeling, sixth sense, whatever, but when the hair on the back of my neck stands to attention and that little red light starts to flash somewhere deep in my head, I've learned through experience that the best place to be is somewhere else.

I had gone to ground in one of Monarto's sleazier districts with a suitcase full of money, which, strictly speaking, I was not legally entitled to. Admittedly I was pretty tired from the events of the past week, and the celebratory drinks of the previous night still dulled my senses, but the truth of it is that I was just too sure of myself. That is until the door of my room began to fly apart under the thunderous roar of automatic gunfire.

Do you know how highland Indonesians catch monkeys? They tie a hollowed-out coconut to a tree. Inside is a banana which the monkey can get only by putting his hand through the hole. He can only get his hand out again if he releases his grip on the banana. They catch more monkeys that way.

Well I ain't no monkey but I sure do sympathise with their dilemma. For a second or more I swear I contemplated risking the rain of death coming through the splintered doorway, to cross the room and retrieve the suitcase from under the bed... the bed I had so recently vacated.

If you have ever been in a similar situation I'm sure you know what a heart-rending experience it is to have to leave something you love behind. But I'm big on self-preservation and what I lack in decisiveness I make up for in planning. I don't simply wander in off the street into any hostelry and ask for a room. From this room, from this building, there were no less than four exits for a man in a hurry, and I was in the biggest kind of hurry. Unfortunately three of my preferred exits were beyond my fastdisintegrating door. I didn't much like what the organism had to do to survive, but I did not argue with my instincts as I snatched up my needle gun from the top of the dresser and hurled myself from the tenth-storey window.

By the time I had acquired some dry clothing, after making good my escape into the harbour, and after a couple of shots of the hair of the dog at a tavern deep in the criminal sector of the docks area, I had made a little headway with the question which had been burning foremost in my mind, namely: Who the hell had tried to make mincemeat out of me? I worked on the problem this way.

To begin with, to know who, one should first ask, *why?* Was it the money? Okay, so maybe it was the money, but who knew I had that amount of cash, and why not simply sneak-go me at gunpoint instead of blowing the *bejesus* out of the place? Answer: it was not a robbery, not in a fit. Someone had tried to do me in!

I had been to Monarto on several prior occasions. It was one of several havens I frequented between projects; a hodgepodge city built and run by crime and corruption, a place where you can get whatever you want if you know the right people, which I did, and if you had plenty of cash money, which was my present problem, because I now only had the money I had crammed into my wallet that morning.

The big-nosed barman walked down to my end of the bar where I had perched myself on a stool next to a sick-looking potted palm.

"Nother one, mister?"

"No, thanks. You got a telephone?"

I phoned Jimmy. . . the kid. He ran an electronics shop on the west side. A good lad. I helped him out a couple of times, as a favour to his mother when he was fighting to break away from life on the streets. He was something of a whiz-kid when it came to things electronic, so I helped him by way of a grub-stake to get started in a small shop on Dunstan Drive. I had also bargained a favour with the local hoodlums to stay off his case, in return for which I promised I wouldn't tear off their arms and beat them with the soggy ends. Unfortunately it's the only language they understand.

The phone at the other end rang a couple of times before the receiver was lifted. A female voice answered: "Harris Electronics. Can I help you?"

"Yeah, is the kid there? Jimmy."

"Who is this?"

"A friend," I replied.

Her voice became suddenly frosty. "Jim is not here at the moment. He's out on a service call."

I had gotten off on the wrong foot. I suspected she was fond of Jimmy and wasn't too keen on mysterious phone-callers asking after him.

"Wait a minute, miss, don't hang up. Like I said, I'm a friend, and of his mother, Joyce. Alex Jaeger, he may have mentioned me?"

"Mr Jaeger, why didn't you say so? Jim will be thrilled to hear from you. I'm Pat, Jim's wife. Let me patch you through to his mobile."

There was some clicking and some waiting, then: "Alex, is that really you?"

"Sure is, kid. Listen, Jimmy, I need your help. . . ."

I waited at a greasy spoon across the road from the hotel where I said I'd meet him. I paid two bucks for a bowl of chilli concarne which I wolfed down while watching from the street-front window for him to arrive. It wasn't that I didn't trust Jimmy, but someone was out to get me and I wasn't about to offer a static target to any would-be assassin, particularly after announcing myself on a line which, conceivably, was being listened in on.

He arrived half an hour and two coffees later. I wouldn't have recognised him but for the fact that he drove a van with HARRIS ELECTRONICS painted across the side.

The kid wasn't a kid any more. He had grown into a sturdylooking man, not unlike his father as I remembered him in the service. The black, curly hair and strong jaw were his main features. I made a mental note to stop calling him the kid.

I gave him a couple of minutes to make his way to the bar and order a drink, then dialled the number for the hotel and asked the barman to page Mr Harris. He came to the phone.

"It's me. Sorry about the game of hide and seek, but I have to be careful. And it might not be a good idea for you to be seen with me right now," I warned him.

"I understand, Alex, but if there's anything I can do, just ask. I owe you."

"Thanks for the offer, buddy. Where did you park the car?"

"It's parked at the corner of Argyle and Opal, the post office carpark.

It's a maroon Interceptor. The key is under the left rear."

"Nice. Thanks, Jim." I hung up.

While I was on the phone I noticed a blue sedan pass by, twice, and the ugly brute behind the wheel seemed to take inordinate interest in Jim's van before eventually pulling into an available parking space two cars behind. I waited until Jim came out onto the street before I made a move.

While he kept his eyes on Jim I moved with a knot of pedestrians along the opposite side of the street, my hand on the butt of my needle gun inside my coat pocket. When Jim climbed into the driver's seat I darted across the road and approached the blue sedan from behind, and drawing level, I fired two shots into the rear tyre. It would be flat before he covered half a mile.

From a few yards back I watched Jim pull away from the curb, expecting the blue sedan to do the same, which, to my surprise it didn't. Instead, half a minute elapsed before ape-features slid across the seat to open the passenger-side door for an elderly lady struggling with a load of shopping. I could see that a paper bag was about to burst open and I raced over to rescue it. I helped her open the door and load up the rear seat.

"Thank-you, young man. You're very kind," she said, and her son was equally as pleasant.

"Not at all," I responded. Turning up my collar and thrusting my hands deep into my pockets, I left the scene of my latest outbreak of paranoia.

The car was where it was supposed to be, along with a few bits and pieces I had asked Jim to throw in. A carry-bag in the boot contained the necessary equipment to knock out most types of burglar alarms, while in the glove box and on the front seat he had left me a cellular phone, a phone book and a street directory, along with a couple of late edition newspapers. As I switched on the radio and searched for a news station I allowed myself a moment's bitterness and cursed whoever was responsible for upsetting my holiday plans in such a despicable manner. Not to mention the loss of a considerable amount of cash. I should have been out wining and dining, romancing, squandering all that lovely loot. *Someone* was definitely going to pay.

I found a news station. The female broadcaster was prattling on about a pack of domestic dogs turned feral, roaming a southern suburb and menacing the local population. Interesting, but not what I was looking for.

I kept an ear cocked to the radio and began scanning the first newspaper for anything concerning open season on tourists in a harbourside hotel earlier in the day. Not that it warranted a mention with all the other bizarre stuff going on. There were the usual number of despots turning their armies against their angry and undernourished citizens; the odd man-made environmental disaster and terrorist actions; crazies causing all manner of mayhem, and the usual smattering of business frauds, government corruption, duplicity, greed, malpractice. Compared to this array of garbage I was more than happy to be a simple, benign outlaw.

My attention was suddenly seized by the present radio news item". . .evidence of further violence between factions of organized crime with heavy gun-fire at the harbourside White Horse hotel today. A police spokesman said that although police arrived quickly on the scene, the perpetrators had already fled the premises. He described the scene as a gangland type shootout."

So, there was strife in the old town, was there? But, so what? It had nothing to do with me, did it? But I had to concede it was the only tangible piece of information I had to work with, and my hunch was that the report wasn't too far from the truth. I would have to go straight to the top to see if there was any connection. Or the bottom, depending on one's perspective of these things. This meant a visit with Guido Spinoza, whom I had come to know from my very first encounter with this city.

Guido owned at least two pubs around town that I knew of, the Sword and Sandal and the Pink Pope, along with a string of pizza delivery outlets. These were mainly window-dressing. People in the know knew that his real business lay in futures, as in *if you don't cut me in on your racket, you got no future!* He also owned a country mansion on twenty acres of land, which was where I was now headed.

The drive in the country gave me a chance to unwind a little. As soon as I left the city limits and began to climb into the surrounding hills I could feel the tension ebb from my body. Shifting down a couple of gears I pushed the pedal hard to the floor. The old girl responded nicely by squatting low on the road as the power surged all the way out to 10,000 rpm's, at which point, with valves threatening mutiny and a trenchant bark emitted from the extractors, I shifted into top gear and floored it again. A glance at the speedometer indicated that I was travelling at over ninety miles per hour as I crested a small rise and passed a somewhat surprised policeman sitting with his speed-camera setup. I smiled serenely and offered a friendly wave, hoping that the picture would turn out nice for him. By the time I passed his buddy, who was leaning against the patrol car about a hundred metres further on, I was accelerating towards one hundred and ten miles per hour with still another gear to spare.

The guy had a sense of humour. He merely pouted his bottom lip and shook his head, once, to indicate he had no intention of playing the game. Commendable, but disappointing. I guess he figured having the photograph of the offending vehicle was enough, which was of no consequence to me. I had taken the precaution of borrowing a set of licence plates at the post office car-park.

Half an hour later I turned off the main road one mile out from a small town called Foster Vale. For a couple of kilometres I passed through a forest of pine trees. The air was cool here, and wonderfully fresh. I was sorely tempted to pull over and take a leisurely stroll in the country air, but I had business to attend to, although I did slow down and enjoy the scenery.

When I emerged from the pine forest, vineyards took over the landscape. Sauvignon on my left and Shiraz to my right, and amongst the vines the bright colours of hats and shirts worn by the pickers stood out amid the sea of green leaves. Those people were earning their money out there in the hot sun. I tooted the horn and waved. Other faces emerged from the vines as they straightened their backs for a moment to observe who the rubber-neck in the flash car was. I caught the eye of a pretty girl wearing faded blue jeans and a khaki shirt, and solicited a smile from her.

Guido's place was hard to miss. It sat like a monolith amid acres of manicured lawn. The idyllic surroundings of the valley had been invaded by this self-bestowed monument to his overdeveloped ego and substantial wealth. Grotesque.

The grounds were surrounded by a twenty metre high wall on which a number of security cameras had been mounted.

I drove up to the main entrance where a pair of white lions sculptured in marble stood sentry at the heavy wrought iron gates. I immediately felt the cold gaze of a camera lens on me. Without moving its lips the nearest lion to me said: "Alex, my boy. How nice of you to come and visit."

The curious thought of Guido being transformed into this limestone Leo as retribution for sins many and various came to mind. I reminded myself of the vulnerable position I had placed myself in by coming here.

"Hello, Guido. What's new?"

Solenoid operated locks clicked and unseen mechanisms whirred as the gates swung inwards on their hinges. "Come in," said the lion.

At the base of the steps at the front of the residence I was met by two besuited, bow-tied henchmen, both of whom must have measured twenty-four inches around the neck. One opened the car door for me while the other surveyed me suspiciously.

"Good afternoon, sir," said the one doing the surveying. "Mr Spinoza asks if you would please deposit any weapons with us before entering the house."

I complied with this *request*, but still had to submit to a thorough frisking before being permitted entry.

Once inside I was led down a long hallway, past a statue of Romulus and Remus and on to a large, well lit room where I was *invited* to make myself comfortable until Mr Spinoza could join me.

When the lackeys left me I amused myself by inspecting the room and its furnishings. Along one wall hung a fine collection of paintings, oils by Sydney Nolan, Peter Snelgar and Pro Hart, while on the opposite wall rows of shelves accommodated books of every description. A reading desk had been positioned at the far end of the room to make use of the sunlight coming in through the glass doors which opened out to a terrace overlooking the landscaped grounds at the rear of the house. I was gazing out through these doors when I heard the door behind me creak on its hinges. Turning, I found Guido entering the room.

Guido is a dwarf. He stood three and a half feet tall in his slippers and red silk dressing-gown as he closed the door behind himself, a glass of wine in one hand and a fat cigar in his mouth. He had aged somewhat since the last time I had seen him. In his mid forties now, I reckoned.

"How do you like my humble abode?" he asked, walking towards me with a wide grin clamped around the double corona.

"It's very impressive."

"The arms business can be quite rewarding, as you know, Alex. Always someone fighting a war somewhere, eh? It payed for all of this, but let's sit out on the terrace and talk in the sunshine. Are you hungry? Or thirsty, perhaps?"

We seated ourselves at a round table beneath an umbrella printed with the Ferrari logo. Guido's chair had been specially built to bring him up to a comfortable position at the table, which left his feet dangling some distance above the paving.

"It's been a long time, Alex. How have you been occupying yourself? Lots of women?" he chuckled.

"No, Guido. I move around quite a lot. You know how I operate."

"Yes. Yes I do. The loner. . . always outside the system. If you could do like me, eh? but of course if you stay too long in one place it is dangerous. But I keep asking you, Alex, why not come and work with me? You have talents I could use, and you could use a steady income. You know I can help with a new identity. I have the connections."

"It wouldn't work, Guido. We have different interests."

"Oh, that's too bad. If you ever decide otherwise. . ."

"I'll keep it in mind," I lied.

The butler arrived with a plate of fresh lobster and two cold beers, and left as unobtrusively as he had come.

"Eat, drink. You are my guest, Alex. It is my pleasure to give you hospitality."

I chewed a piece of meat and washed it down. "So, what's happening around town these days?" It was time to begin steering the conversation.

"There is much happening," he said, raising his eyebrows. "The young people, you know, all on this new drug. Angel wings they call it. Some people bring it here from out of town. People in my city doing business without they ask me. I do what I can to stop them, but if the young people want it," he said, shrugging. "How do I do this?"

"There have been shooting matches," I said by way of statement rather than inquiry.

"These people are very bad," he retorted querulously. "They hurt and kill anyone who opposes. And this drug, this angel drug. Sure I give to the people their cannabis, their hashish. Harmless, but this angel, it is very bad, Alex. They have to be stopped."

I had struck a nerve. Guido was a strange kettle of fish, mostly piranha. His rise to power and millionaire status was a trail littered with corpses. He was totally ruthless. I knew the score but Guido would never admit it, not to me, not even to himself. In his own eyes he was an entrepreneur, a patron of the arts and even a champion of the people. In truth he was a dangerous pint-sized megalomaniac, capable of committing atrocious acts: debauchery, violence and terrorism. My thinking on it was that all this was all based in a deep-rooted inferiority complex, but then I'm no psychiatrist. In short, the man was insane. To threaten his warped self-image was a dangerous business, and I

was beginning to wonder at my own sanity for coming here,
to his own weird and private reality.

"They have to be stopped," I said in absolute agreement,
but it was time to get to the point of my visit. "Did you hear
about the disturbance at White Horse this morning?"

Guido was about to push a large piece of lobster into his
mouth as I said this. I studied his face intently as the morsel
lingered for a brief moment in mid conveyance before
completing the journey.

It was hard to tell with Guido. His eyes and face went
through all the right expressions to suggest that, yes, he
was aware of the incident, but what was I implying?

He continued to chew for a while, washed it down with a
sip of cold beer. The metaphoric penny appeared to drop as he
looked up suddenly. You? It was *you* at the hotel?"

He started to laugh, a high-pitched emanation with a quality
in it I found repugnant. I hoped that perhaps he might choke,
but he managed to recover.

"I'm sorry, Alex," he said, wiping the tears away from
his eyes, "but it strikes me as funny. You'll have to forgive me.
You see, this morning I received a telephone call. . . from
the boss-man of these hoodlums I've been telling you about.
His name is Vincent --- Vincent Zendell. He said to me only
this: we frighten your off man like a scared rabbit and we
have the money. That's what he say. Nothing more, and then
he's hanging up. Did you have some money?"

To me it seemed to add up. A supposed friend of Guido's
arrives surreptitiously on the scene in the midst of an ongoing
conflict between the two of them. A weary or nervous
adversary might well conclude that I had been brought in as a
hired gun, which would certainly fit with Guido's way of
doing things. In response this Zendell character sends a
couple of his goons over to do the job on me. They screw up,
but they do come away with a suitcase --- *my suitcase* ---
containing

two hundred and fifty thousand dollars, in Zendell's mind the fee for putting the hit on him. Hence the gloating phone call.

"Yes, I had some money," I said distractedly, still working with this information, trying to make the pieces fit.

"You see, Alex, I have been wondering about this since before you come here. He must have thought-"

"That you hired me to kill him," I said, completing the sentence for him.

After years of experience involved in clandestine operations with the service, before I had sickened of the whole crummy charade, I learned never to take anything on face value. Was I being confronted with the simple truth here, or, as my subconscious was screaming at me from way deep in my skull, was I overlooking something very simple? I worked on the problem as I drove back to the city.

Two

Whatever it was that was troubling me had not surfaced by the time I reached Monarto, but I had come up with a plan of sorts, which I hoped would furnish me with a little more information about this Zendell character, or, at the very least, provide me with an entertaining night out. I was, after all, meant to be on holidays.

I located what I was looking for in the telephone directory which Jim had so thoughtfully supplied me with. A Salvation Army secondhand clothes store, situated just out of the main shopping area on the north side of the city.

I found a parking space in a laneway on the third tour of the block. I was a couple of hundred yards from the store, but that didn't matter, and I set off along the footpath, whistling like some carefree fool. I had taken little enough exercise since my arrival, apart, that is, from my early-morning swim in the harbour. The thought of it caused me a momentary pang on angst, and clenched jaw muscles put an end to my whistling. Someone was going to pay, I promised myself.

This was a pleasant part of the city. Wide, brick-paved footpaths were shaded intermittently by small elm-trees. Here and there street cafes served reposing citizens coffee and sandwiches in the warm, afternoon sunshine. There was a whole-food barn where people could buy uncontaminated produce (or so the sign promised), a book exchange, a record bar and a tobacconist which had in its display window the biggest damned hookah I had ever seen.

As I neared the Salvation Army store I could hear music issuing from across the street. It came from an old, double storey building which had been renovated and converted into a tavern. Through glass doors, above which its name, *Princess Tavern*, was painted in bold silver letters, I could see that the management was doing a fairly brisk trade. I stood at the curb and watched for a while to assess the patrons as they entered and departed, concluding that this was as likely a place as any to begin my search.

In the store I selected a pair of faded denim jeans, a cotton shirt and a light, military-style leather jacket which buttoned at the waist and at the wrists. Shoes were a problem; put on a pair of someone's half worn out shoes and you'll know exactly what I mean, but I eventually settled for a pair of once white runners in not too bad condition which fitted snugly enough.

An inspection in the mirror showed that I had done all right. The style and colour were suitably inconspicuous for the company I would soon be keeping. I approached the woman at the till and handed her the price tags from the items I had selected. They totalled forty dollars and I flipped open my wallet to pay up, indiscreetly revealing a wad of around thirty, damp one hundred dollar notes. Her eyes grew stalks.

"Please accept this as a donation towards helping the less fortunate," I found myself saying in a magnanimous manner, and handed over a single grey note.

Upon entering the Princess Tavern I attracted the usual cursory perusal from the locals, most of whom were seated at tables in groups of from two to five and roughly equal numbers male to female, though a count would have shown a slightly greater male ratio. I made for the end of the bar where I spotted a vacant stool and ordered a beer.

This tavern was typical of any scattered across the country. A number of punters were gathered around television sets and a TAB window at the far end of the room. Three pool tables, all presently employed and with twenty-cent pieces stacked up along their edges, occupied the space just inside the street-front windows. Behind me the juke-box issued forth noisome rock music while customers indulged in alcohol and amiable conversation.

The atmosphere was cheerful, though redolent with the odour of stale beer and cigarette smoke. When the barmaid arrived with my beer I inquired as to the use of the upper storey and was informed that it was frequently used for bands and discos.

"There's a band on tonight," she volunteered. "Ten bucks a head for male, female no charge, neat casual dress. The band starts at about nine-thirty."

A meat market, I gathered. "Who's playing?" I asked. By way of reply she pointed to a poster on the wall behind me, declaring: *ROSS ROBERTS & THE BLUES CONNECTION.* Appearing Thurs 2nd Feb. Doors open at 8p.m. Bundy 1/2 price till 10 o'clock".

A tall young fellow wearing R.M. Williams boots, jeans, T-shirt and a leather waistcoat had come up beside me with an empty glass in his hand while I had been talking to the barmaid. As I was reading the poster he said, "They're a good band."

I judged him to be in his early thirties. He had long dark hair and his face was pale and clean shaven.

The barmaid returned with my change from a hundred and placed it on the counter, where I let it sit for a time. The tall fellow beside me put his empty glass on the bar. "Nother one thanks, Judy." Then turning to me, he said, "Yeah, they're good. You won't be disappointed."

"I'm looking to score," I said, opting for the bold approach. I sipped my beer, waiting for a response. During the intervening silence he glanced at my money on the bar, than back to me for a closer inspection. His beer arrived, which he paid for from a handful of coins.

"What are you looking for, exactly?"

"Not green," I stated, using the time-honoured method of circumlocution used in such circumstances.

"I don't think I've seen you round here before."

"I gave an easy laugh and looked him square in the eyes. "It's okay, buddy, I'm not *the heat* or anything. I had to skip bail from over West. Things were getting a bit heavy, if you know what I mean. I don't know anybody over here, but I need to score," I related earnestly, inferring that a had an addiction.

He thought for a moment before answering. "If I'm going to help you, and I'm not saying I can, mind, you better tell me what you want."

"Angel wings," I said. "Can you help me with that? There's a finder's fee in it for you," I added.

Replacing his glass on the bar, he said, "How much you looking for?"

"A hundred for the moment. More if it works out."

"Hang about," he said, "and I'll see what I can do for you."

I watched as he ambled across the room and sat at a table

occupied by a couple I guessed to be in their late twenties. The guy was of stocky build, with short blond hair and dressed in a leather jacket, slacks and thongs. The girl was attractive: long, brown hair, faded, threadbare jeans, white lace blouse under a black denim jacket. My representative leaned across the table to begin negotiations.

While I peeked by way of the mirror behind the bar, they talked furtively among themselves, casting occasional glances in my direction. After a couple of minutes of this I was reasonably confident that a successful connection had been made. It only takes a very short time to say no, so I figured they were now working out the details.

I watched as my man received instructions, then, giving a final nod to *Stocky*, he stood and began threading his way between the tables, back to where I waited at the bar.

"If you can be back here tonight, you'll be able to get on," he said as soon as he had propped at my elbow. "The guy will be here at nine. It's the best I can do, there's nothing else around at the present."

"Nine o'clock will be fine. Who do I see?"
"Don't worry about that. I'll be here to bring it over to you. The guy's a bit *toey*, as you might expect."

"Yeah, I can understand that. It pays to be careful," I agreed amiably, sliding a twenty along the bar to him as I pocketed the rest. "See you tonight."

I had five hours to kill before I had to be back for my appointment at the tavern, so when I returned to the car I picked up the phone and called Jim and Pat, to see if they would like to join me for dinner at a restaurant of their choice ... *my shout*. We arranged to meet at six-thirty, which gave me plenty of time to find a motel room where I could clean up and even squeeze in an hour's nap.

We met at a seafood restaurant over on the west side. I arrived first and was sipping black coffee at a table near the back of the room when they found me.

Up close Jim's resemblance to his father was even more striking than I had first noticed. We shook hands and stood there grinning at each other like a couple of fools awhile before he remembered to introduce his wife, a svelte brunette with wide, brown eyes. Her name was Pat.

"Pleased to meet you at last, Mr Jaeger."

"Pleased to meet you, too, Pat. But do call me Alex. Shall I order some wine with dinner?" I asked, offering her the chair opposite me.

I ordered a bottle of the best white in the house to get the ball rolling, and soon we were chatting away like old friends, which in Jim's case was fairly well true.

Pat proved delightful company, intelligent and vivacious. She kept pressing me to tell her about Jim before she had met him at night school, where they had both taken a course in business management. I obliged, to Jim's occasional discomfort, with a couple of anecdotes of the trouble he had managed to get himself into as a lad, and a story his father had told me, of his first experience with alcohol - a story related to me while on early morning patrol near the Cambodian border.

By the time our main course arrived at the table I found it necessary to order another bottle of wine. Pat had the grilled barramundi while Jim and I opted for the snapper, and between mouthfuls we continued to find plenty to talk about.

When Pat began quizzing me about my time in South-East Asia and, later, as a mercenary in Central America, Jim tactfully guided her around the subject. He had learned from Jack, his father, that it was a time neither of us cared particularly to recall.

Jack had died in the jungles of Cambodia because of a *potential* political embarrassment. We had been cut off by a large group of advancing enemy soldiers, then abandoned; left for dead by command for no other reason than to save some jumped-up general a red face.

A grim expression must have crossed my face as I remembered.

"Is anything wrong?" Pat asked, her own face clouded in concern.

"A touch of heartburn," I said, recovering quickly. Not accustomed to eating so well, but I refuse to waste it." I shoved in another mouthful.

The coffee arrived right on cue - just as we pushed back our plates and were commenting on the fine meal. Jim produced two panatellas from his coat pocket. "I remember how you and dad used to like a cigar with your coffee, and I find that I've developed a liking for them, myself."

I was deeply moved by this simple gesture. The kid must have been around ten years old when Jack and I used to sit at the family table after a meal, discussing the problems of the world over a coffee and a cigar. I suddenly missed my old friend very much.

We lit up and leaned back in our chairs, savouring the moment. Pat sat quietly regarding the two of us - evidently the poignancy of this ritual was not lost on her.

Breaking the silence I said to Jim: "You've done very well for yourself. A lovely wife and a successful business. Your father would be very proud."

"Jim is so grateful for the way you helped him and his mother over the years. And so am I, Alex. The business is doing fine, as you say. Won't you let us repay you in some way?"

"All I've done is help out with a few dollars here and there," I said, feeling uncomfortable. "Jim's success is totally a result of his own ability and determination. You mustn't, either of you, feel obligated in any way."

"You could at least come around for a home-cooked meal," she said, looking to Jim for support.

"Yes, Alex, absolutely. You must come to our home. Any time you want."

"Thank-you, I'd love to come around, but it may be a little while. Things are a bit iffy at the present. I'm still not sure what kind of soup I'm in."

"I'm glad you brought it up," said Jim, leaning forward and placing his thick forearms on the table. "I've been dying to ask you what's going on."

Pat elbowed him sharply in the ribs. "Jim, don't be so inquisitive."

"It's okay," I soothed. "I was waiting until now to fill you in on the situation."

I was grinning broadly at the both of them. Jim was trying not to look surprised at the jab he had received from his wife, and I could tell that Pat was just as eager to learn what was going on as Jim, only she was feigning cool restraint.

I related the day's events to them. Straight facts, without embellishment or interpretation. I felt my subconscious kick in and begin to function of its own accord as I proceeded deeper into my account. At one stage I was describing my conversation with Guido, and had gotten past the part about Zendell's telephone message when I realised I had not reported hard fact, but hearsay. I stopped and corrected myself. "Guido *said* he had a telephone call from Zendell. . ."

I could hear myself continuing with the account to Pat and Jim, but my fore-brain was becoming increasingly interested with what was happening immediately behind it; fragments of the day's experiences rising out of a mass of data like cream separating from milk. I watched again as Guido's hand conveyed a chunk of white meat, halted involuntarily at the mention of the White Horse, a furtive look in his eyes, *and then* his face went through all the right movements. I heard him say, *this angel, it is very bad. . . They have to be stopped.*

It didn't come in a blinding flash, what Buddhists might describe as satori, but rather like the house lights coming up slowly in a picture theatre until you begin to notice the tatty upholstery, the grubby carpets and the chewing-gum stuck to the backs of seats. Guido had been lying to me, I could feel it in my bones.

"You're lucky to be alive," said Pat, when I had brought them up to the present. "You could have been killed."

Wham! It struck like a hammer blow inside my thick skull. That was *it*, the one dimly perceived inconsistency I was looking for and which had eluded me all day. Not *could* have been killed --- *should* have been killed. Any killer worth their salt would have had me cold. As hung-over as I was this morning, and expecting no trouble, I had hesitated long enough for a kid with a pea-shooter to have hit me.

My attention returned to the present and my immediate surroundings. "Jim, give that lady a cigar."

Three

It was ten minutes before nine when I pulled up across the street from the Princess Tavern. The upstairs room was colorfully lit and the support band were churning out a spirited rendition of *Rocky Mountain Way* as I locked up the car and crossed the street to the front bar.

The barroom was crowded and abuzz with chatter as I made my way along the length of the room in search of my tall, pale friend. It was *he* who spotted me first. He caught my eye with a wave as I swung my gaze toward the far corner and the TAB window.

"Damn crowded," I observed after negotiating the intervening distance.

"Always is on Thursday night. You got the dough?"
"Yeah." I pulled the grey note from my jeans pocket and pushed it into his palm. His other hand went to the pocket of his leather waistcoat and withdrew a piece of glossy magazine paper which had been folded into a tiny envelope.
"Here you go," he said, passing it to me secretively.

I took it from him by reflex, but this was not the way I had intended it to go down.

"What?" I thought you were supposed to meet the guy at nine?"

"So, he got here early. What's the problem?"

The problem was that I wanted to be here when the delivery was made. I was then going to tail the guy and see if I could trace the money back to the supplier. . . presumably, a certain mister Vincent Zendell.

"How long ago?" I asked urgently.

"Just before I saw you. A minute ago, why?"

"Is he still here?" I snapped, annoyed at the possibility of having blown the whole night for the sake of a minute or so's tardiness.

His eyes covered the room in a long, slow arc, his height giving him a definite advantage. Meanwhile, I stood gritting my teeth in expectancy. I noticed him do a double take as he looked towards the door leading to the car-park. "Missed them," he said.

I scanned the crowd nearest the doorway. People were coming and going. Strangers. A couple entering, two guys leaving, behind them a girl also leaving. I recognised her. The same one who had been at the table with the blond, stocky guy.

"The girl?" I asked, keeping my eyes on her, but no reply was volunteered.

There was no time to spare. I grabbed both of his pinkies and twisted. His eyes widened and his face paled even more, if that were possible.

"The girl?" I repeated with a snarl, and this time he nodded his head enthusiastically,

A fusillade of colourful metaphors accompanied my hurried exit; *some* highly original. I managed to return to my car in time to see a white Commodore emerge from the pub car-park, the girl in the passenger seat and *Stocky* behind the wheel. I pulled out behind them as they swung right and out onto the street.

Their next stop after the Princess was the Pyramid Hotel, only five minutes away. Here the girl went inside while Stocky remained in the car. She was back inside ten minutes, and then it was on to the next delivery.

I was on a winner. I followed them all over the city and occasionally into nearby suburbs where some drops were made at private residences. The girl never stayed long, just long enough for the buyers to check the goods and hand over the money, I figured.

Considerable finesse had to be exercised in view of the fact they would be vigilant for police, or even desperate junkies looking to plunder their consignment. It was particularly tricky around the suburbs where the traffic thinned to almost zero on the quiet side streets, but all I needed to do was keep them more or less in sight.

I followed them into the heart to the city again, then out to the north side, an area they had already covered. I guessed we were nearing the end of the night's activities. I had been following them for almost three hours and I had counted twenty eight drops. Amusing myself with some estimations, I reckoned they were carrying at very least ten thousand dollars.

Still heading north on the main road out of the city, they drove for ten miles before turning into a catchpenny motel by the name of The Old Coach. Conceding the possibility that this might be yet another delivery, I pulled up across the road and surveyed the grounds while I waited for any further development.

An old Cobb and Co. stage-coach sat on a concrete pad in front of the office building, and behind the office the owner's residence, what might have once been a staging-post and roadside inn, judging by the rustic colonial architecture.

Out the back among the pine-trees I counted five cabins. The grounds were poorly lit and I couldn't make out any detail, although two cabins were showing light in their windows. Besides the electric lights, the only other sign that the twentieth century had reached this place was the cool-drink machine out front of the office.

Fifteen minutes passed. Too long. None of the previous stops had taken this long. They were either shacked up for the night or this was where the money would change hands. I excluded the former: anybody with ten thousand bucks in their kick would surely find something a bit more up-market than this flea pit.

I retrieved my needle gun from under the seat and, with great relief, climbed out of the car and stretched my cramped legs. I was about to commence some serious lurking about in the dark in search of bad guys. Things were definitely looking up.

Entering the property fifty metres from the main entrance, I slipped into the shadows beneath the trees. The sound of the traffic on the main road and the covering of pine needles over the ground made it unnecessary for me to concern myself with being overly light footed. I simply strolled among the shadows, directly up to the first of the lighted cabins.

Half a dozen motorcycles were lined up in front of the verandah, and snatches of gruff conversation penetrated the din of rock music. While I circled the cabin looking for the white Commodore, I found that the back door was partially open.

Now I don't normally hold with the invasion of people's privacy, but in making a thorough job of my search I think I had a valid excuse. What I found was a social get-together; five members of *Satan's Messengers* (it was emblazoned across their backs) and their womenfolk, a card game, some drinking and a spot of Heavy Metal to enhance the mood. A tattooed pig dressed as a highway patrol cop and the naked guy tied to a bed-post was entirely their own business. The Commodore was not in the vicinity, so I headed for the next cabin along, which was nestled between a pair of towering pines at the opposite corner of the grounds.

At three-quarter distance I spotted the Commodore parked on the far side of the cabin, and I came quietly up to a window on the side from which I approached. The sound of a television came from within, but a heavy blind was drawn over the window and I couldn't get a see in. When I moved to the rear window I found that the curtains there had been pulled across, but where they almost joined at the middle they did afford a reasonable view if I tilted my head to the side.

Stocky was standing at a wooden table counting out nice little piles of money, securing them with elastic bands and stuffing them into a calico bag. The girl was out of sight but I could hear the sound of running water and the clink of cutlery at the kitchen sink.

Stocky looked in that direction and sneered contemptuously. "You use too much of that stuff. If you *must* do that, go into the bathroom. You people make me want to puke."

She didn't answer, but the water was turned off and a moment later she sauntered out of the room carrying a glass of water and some stuff I couldn't make out on top a magazine.

"And if you come out of there looking like a zombie, you can find your own way home," he shouted after her.

I spent the next few minutes watching him counting out notes into thousand-dollar lots, until the glare of headlights sent long, black shadows moving across the motel grounds. The lights neared the cabin and shone through the curtains in the front window. The motor was switched off.

Stocky shouted to the girl. "Hurry up and get out of there, will you! They're here. Get the door while I finish up."

I heard three car doors thump shut, and soon after came a knock at the door.

"Get the bloody door, bitch!" He yelled.

The girl emerged from the bathroom, still in the process of slipping her jacket on, and went to the door. She drew back the heavy bolt and began to pull the door ajar. She hadn't quite moved out of the way when it flew back in her face, catapulting her backwards to land sprawled on the floor. Stocky looked up, startled, he reached for something in his breast pocket as two men entered swiftly. Both were armed, one with a shotgun, the other with a large hand-gun. A flame and a loud report issued from the muzzle of the shotgun. The blast took Stocky in the face and chest, and a stray pellet shattered a square of glass just above my head.

I raced down the side of the cabin and peeked around the corner, catching a glimpse of a big guy keeping watch. Stocky had bought it, that was for sure, but the girl was still in big trouble, so I didn't waste any time weighing the pros and cons of sorting these animals out. I fired two needles in quick succession at the watch, as far as I could tell, hitting with both. The initial shock of being hit by one of these little beauties will stun a man for a second, and by the time he realises he's still okay, the sting takes effect and it's all over. He had hardly hit the ground by the time I covered the seven metres to the front door and stood flat against the wall... I took a peek inside.

The guy nearest to me had his back turned and was standing over the girl. The other one was busy at the table, bagging up the money. Four needles issued forth, each accompanied by a tiny popping sound of compressed air being released, and both were down for the count.

The girl's legs were pinned under the weight of the first and she was desperately trying to escape from under him. As I entered she ceased the struggle and looked up fearfully.

"It's okay, you're alright now," I said, pushing the needle gun under my belt. "It's over," . . .but I don't think she believed me.

I freed her legs and guided her over to the couch in front of the television. "Sit quietly while I clean up this mess."

The big bugger outside must have weighed over twenty stone, I nearly gave myself a hernia stuffing him into the back seat of the car. I would have preferred him inside the cabin, but that was the best I could manage.

I wondered if the proprietor had heard the shotgun blast, and was he calling the police right now? I had to assume so, but Satan's Messengers didn't seem to be interested.

I went back inside and inspected Stocky for any sign of life. There was none, which was just as well. Most of his face was gone.

I remembered then how he had reached for his breast pocket when the men had stormed in, and reaching behind his left lapel I retrieved a .45 automatic. Checking the clip I found it to be full.

"I'm going to leave you alone for a short while," I said to the girl as I pocketed the .45 and snatched the calico bag from the table. "Only for a minute or two."

I walked over to the couch and knelt down beside her. Her hands covered her face while her elbows rested on her knees, but she was watching me through her fingers. I guessed she must be in shock.

"Do you understand? Don't move. I'll be back with a car to get us away from here."

"Are they all dead?" she asked, just above a whisper.

"No. I put 'em to sleep. What's your name?"

"I'm Alex. Just hang on here for a tick, Janie. Okay?"

I wanted to ask her who these people were, but I was pretty sure she didn't know either, and this wasn't the time for questions. I would have to take one of these bums prisoner to get the information I needed.

I brought the car in quickly, without headlights, then loaded the crud who had killed Stocky into the floor space between the front and rear seats, covering him with a blanket off of one of the beds in the cabin.

When I returned for the girl I found her stretched out on the couch, watching television! Without looking up, she said: "Hey, this is one of the old Perry Mason episodes. It's great. I used to watch it all the time when I was little."

I was flabbergasted. Her partner in crime was lying on the floor with his face blown off; she had probably narrowly escaped death, herself, and here she was casually watching Perry Mason reruns!

"The Case of the Smiling Sphinx," she informed me.

"I've seen it. The curator did it," I told her, crossing to the television set and turning it off. "Now come along, Janie. We've got to get out of here, pronto! The police are probably already on their way. Guns primed and hoping to shoot something."

We drove in silence for a while --- while she gathered her wits and while I tried to figure out what to do next. I needed somewhere to stash my prisoner until he came around, and somewhere comfortable to talk to the girl.

Three police cars sped past us going in the opposite direction, sirens wailing and lights flashing. If they had taken any longer I might have had to pull over at the next public phone and called them *myself.*

Janie pulled a packet of cigarettes and a lighter from her pocket and lit up. After a couple of tokes she turned sideways in her seat and looked at me for a while. I was trying to concentrate on the driving, but I could feel her gaze boring into me.

"Who the hell are you?" she said, finally breaking the silence. "I mean, *what* are you. . . and what were you doing at the motel?"

"I can't answer those questions right now, but I assure you there's a very good reason why I can't." I looked over to her then back to the road.

"Oh, yeah?"

There was something unnerving about this girl.

"I want to talk to you about the drugs." I quickly raised my palm to halt the interjection I knew was coming. "And don't worry, I promise you I have nothing to do with the law, and I don't mean you any harm. The thing is, before I explain myself I need you to answer some questions for me, without first being influenced by what you know about me. I know it sounds strange but there's a perfectly good reason for it."

She continued to stare at me for a few seconds longer, took a drag on her cigarette then turned back to watch the road. "Is Clay dead?".

"If you mean your friend. . . Yes, I'm afraid so."

"He was a pig," she said flatly.

I was as curious as hell but I didn't want to start quizzing her yet.

"Look, I've got a motel room not too far from here, where we can go and sort a few things out, if you're agreeable that is?" She twisted around and reached over to the back seat.

"What are you doing?" I asked.

"You're right, this bastard really is asleep." She sat back down in her seat, took another drag on her cigarette and tossed it out the window. "Well, if we're going back to your room, can we pick up something to drink on the way?"

Four

It was one-thirty in the morning when we arrived at my motel room. I was beginning to feel the effects of the long day and I thought how nice it would be if I could just lie down and catch a few zees. I looked at my prisoner, supine on the floor, and I had a strong urge to kick him. I kicked him.

"You feel better now?" Janie was at the breakfast bar fixing the drinks.

"Yes," I lied. "You certainly recovered fast." She screwed the lid down on the bottle of Scotch, brought the glasses to the coffee table, ice rattling, and sat at the centre of the couch. "From what?"

"Uh?" I was busy binding my prisoner's arms behind his back with his neck tie. "From your shock," I answered, wondering what I could use on his feet. "Would you pass me a wire coat-hanger from out of the closet, please, Janie?"

"That wasn't shock. That was *whacked.* I had just put away a hundred-dollar blast when those bastards came barging in through the door. I could hardly stand up!"

I crossed his ankles and bound them with the coat-hanger. "That ought to hold him," I said, taking my drink and seating myself where I could talk to Janie and keep an eye on him.

"You could have dropped a bomb on that place and I wouldn't have batted an eyelid," she said.

I took a sip of Scotch and leaned back as it warmed a path on the way to my stomach. "Angel wings?"

"Yeah, angel wings... trilonite, the blue stuff."

"Is your eye sore?" I noticed a red mark under her left eye where the door must have caught her. "I'll get some ice for it, if you like."

"No. It's okay, really. You wanted to ask me some questions, didn't you?"

"Yes. I want to know as much as you can tell me about your operation. Particularly, where the stuff comes from and where the money goes. Start with the beginning of your run, tonight."

She sipped some Scotch from her glass and lit a cigarette. "You aren't anything to do with the law, right?"

I shook my head.

She hesitated a while longer before deciding. "Okay. We do the run three times a week. Mondays, Thursdays and Saturdays, and it works like this.

"Clay and me go to the Princess at around three in the afternoon.

We get a phone-call there, telling us when and where to pick up the car. The message might go: white Commodore, LJC 870, 7p.m. at Sid's Pizza Bar - which is what it was today - and so we met there at seven, took the car and-"

"How?" I cut in.

"How what?"

"How did you take the car? Was there a key?"

"Clay has got the key." She flicked her ash and took another sip from her glass. "He gets the key at the post office, in an envelope addressed to him. Okay? We take the car, the stuff's in the boot along with the list of drops; where, how much, etc. It's all very cloak and dagger, don't you think?"

"It's quite a sophisticated arrangement," I agreed. "How did you become involved in this?"

"Clay approached me one day a couple of months back and asked me if I wanted to earn some money. I didn't know him from a bar of soap, but I listened to his offer and decided to give it a try. Two hundred bucks a time and free dope was a good offer, considering I was out of work and struggling at the time. I guess he checked me out before he made the offer."

It made sense. "Okay, you've got the car and the drugs and the list. . ."

"Yeah, but the next thing we do before we start the round is go to a phone-box and call a number which is written at the top of the list, to let them know we picked up the car and to find out where to take the money when we've finished."

"I was wondering about that. I don't suppose you remember the number?"

"Eight-five-two-six-three-nine-nine-one," she quickly rattled off.

"That is very good," I said, genuinely impressed. I went over to the telephone, dialed for an outside line, then the number she had given me. It rang ten times before someone answered.

"Hello, is this Paddy's Fish Market?" I inquired.

"This ain't nowhere, buddy," came the reply. "You've just rung the telephone-box on Beaufort Street."

I thanked whoever it was and put down the receiver.

Janie was smiling over the top of her glass as I returned to my chair. "Public telephone, right?"

"Right. You got any idea who you work for?
"Can't help you there, I'm afraid," she said, proffering her empty glass at arm's length. "Please?"
I took it from her, drained my own glass and went to the bar.
"Who pays you?" I asked over my shoulder.
"Clay did. He was in tight with them. I wasn't allowed to ask questions. He always told me it was a health risk and that I was better off not knowing."

I carried the drinks back to the table and resumed my position. I wasn't learning a great deal and I was feeling decidedly low. Looking down at the silent third member of this little get-together, I said, "How do you suppose these guys knew where you were taking the money?"

"We got a call at the Princess telling us there had been a change in plan, to go out to the Old Coach, cabin five, the key would be in the door, same as usual. It's happened that way before, so we didn't think anything of it, but that's obviously how we were set up. Someone who knew how we worked."

"Was the Princess on the list?"

"As a matter of fact, no, it wasn't."

"But that's where you got the call. Ergo, whoever organised the rip-off had to have been informed that you would be there, or that you had been seen arriving."

"Yeah, hey, that's right." She thought for a moment. I bet it was that son-of-a-bitch, Jacko," she announced with renewed vigour. "That bastard would sell his own grandmother if there was dope involved. He was the only one who knew we were going back there."

"You mean the guy who played middle man for me?"
She nodded.

"You're probably right," I said, "but tell me something. There was thousands of dollars worth of drugs in your car and the place wasn't on the list. Why did you stop for a measly hundred-dollar deal?"

"It wasn't just a hundred. Jacko ordered two hundred bucks worth, himself. We always carry some extra for situations like that. To tell you the truth, I might not have worried about it. I can't stand Jacko, but he said you were hurting and you didn't know anybody in these parts. I felt sorry for you. I had to argue with Clay to get him to stop by." She smiled coyly. "I wanted to talk to you but you weren't there when we arrived, and Clay was in such a damned hurry.

"Anyway, you said you'd tell me who you are if I answered your questions."

"Maybe I haven't finished asking my questions?"

"Like what?"

"Like have you heard of anyone by the name of Vincent Zendell?"

"Sure. Who hasn't? He recently took over the biggest used-car outlet in the city. He also owns a night-club cum cassino over on Pier Street. Word has it, he's linked to organised crime. Or at least that's what I hear."

There was a snort followed by a groan in the vicinity of my left sneaker. I kicked again, and tossed the remainder of my drink in his face.

"Wake up, you crud," I said in my nastiest tone, and found it hurt my throat.

He blinked furiously in effort to clear the stinging alcohol from his eyes. I had to psyche this guy out while he was still disorientated, or I might have been forced to do something I really didn't want to do.

Standing, I retrieved the .45 automatic from under the cushion and grabbing him by the lapels of his jacket with my free hand, dragged him across the floor and slammed him against the wall. He was fully awake now, and I think I had his attention.

Waving the gun in front of his watering eyes, I said, "All right, you get one shot at this mister shotgun man. One chance, you hear me?" I cracked him on the knee with the gun butt, which must have hurt considerably. He nodded his head and grunted.

"Right answer, you live. Wrong answer, not so good." I shoved the muzzle of the gun under his chin. "Who do you work for?" I ground out the words for effect.

"Zendell," he blurted out.

"And the money you tried to rip off?" I brought my face down close to his, wearing what I hoped was a threatening expression.

"Whose money is it, mister shotgun man?"

He swallowed hard under the pressure of the muzzle. "Spinoza.Spinoza's money."

They just didn't make tough guys how they used to.

I left Zendell's goon asleep on a park bench with a note pinned to his jacket charging him with Stocky's demise, then called the police. All they had to do was match his fingerprints to those on the murder weapon and his days as a gangster were at an end. . . . And good riddance.

When I returned, Janie listened attentively as I gave her the explanation I had promised. At the conclusion of my discourse I leaned back in the couch beside her, feeling relaxed for the first time since the bizarre events of the day had begun.

"So Guido staged the attack on you and blamed it on Zendell, expecting you to go after him?"

"That's the guts of it. . . but why?"

"Isn't it obvious?" Janie replied, making an expansive hand gesture. "He wanted Zendell dead while distancing himself as much as possible from the act."

"Yes, that is the obvious answer, and not an unreasonable assumption, but there are certain subtleties. Remember, he explained the attack on me as a case of mistaken identity. That, together with the fact that he chose to involve *me*, would ensure that any act of vengeance wouldn't involve blood-letting. He knows that's not my style."

"But what about what happened tonight? Murder. And the shootings around the city? They're involved in a war, we hear about gunfights every day in the news, and Guido Spinoza as good as admitted it to you!"

"Interesting, isn't it? That they're out there killing one another, or at least their hirelings are, and yet Guido exhibits a lack of desire for Zendell's actual extermination. And the biggest curiosity of the whole thing is that Guido has the resources to squash Vincent Zendell like he would an annoying insect. That snake-in-the-grass tried to enlist me to *worry* him, not to kill." I thought about it for a while, until Janie asked, "What would you have done if you had believed Guido's story?"

"I would have made life very uncomfortable for Mr Zendell until I had regained possession of the money, and left him with something to remember me by, but it's that runt Spinoza who's accountable to me now.

"You're not seriously thinking of tangling with *him*, are you?" she said wide-eyed. "Are you crazy or something?"

"Or something, probably." I put my glass down beside the half empty bottle on the table. "Your turn to pour the drinks. "How much money do you suppose you have in there?" I nodded towards the calico bag sitting on the bar.

She looked at me with suspicion showing in her eyes. Hesitantly, she said, "About eighteen thousand. Why?"

"Don't worry, I'm not laying claim to it. I'm only suggesting you take it and get the hell away from here. Head east and lose yourself in one of the bigger cities."

She sipped her drink, studying me closely over the rim of the glass with those simmering brown eyes of hers. As her mind worked on my suggestion I found myself admiring her sultry good looks; the way her long brown hair softly framed the her face, the way her lips curled slightly at the edges. *NO!* I cautioned myself. She was a crazy, mixed-up junkie and I had one hell of a situation on my hands. I had been shot at, robbed, set-up and involved in a murder, all in the same day. I certainly wasn't going to involve myself with this young woman, not on any account.

"What would I do in another city." There was a note of dejection in her voice. "I don't like the idea of being alone in a new environment."

"Well it's not a healthy proposition staying around here. How long do you think it will take the police to tie you in with Clay? You've been seen together on a regular basis for the last two months, but the police are the least of your problems. You were witness to a murder, which will likely get you immunity against criminal prosecution for drug trafficking, if you testify against Zendell's men, but do you think he will let you get away with that? You're in a spot, Janie. You can bet that eighteen thousand he'll have his men scouring the streets for you by morning."

"Let them scour," she said defiantly. "I can disappear in this city as well as I can anywhere else."

"You're stoned. You're not thinking clearly."

"Stoned or not, I'm not leaving."

"You're crazy," I told her. She was being illogical and totally unreasonable.

"*I'm* crazy? You're the one who thinks he can go up against Guido Spinoza.

I laughed at that. It was a valid point.

"There's another option," she said evenly, once again fixing me with that steady gaze. "We could team up."

I stopped laughing.

Five

I woke on the couch with a pillow under my head and a blanket thrown over me, but without the faintest recollection of how I came to be in that position.

Janie was curled up under the covers of the double bed. I had intended letting her sleep on while I showered and shaved, but as I somewhat groggily swung my feet to the floor and climbed to my feet she raised her head from the pillow. "I hope you slept all right. I thought it best to leave you where you were."

"Fine," I said, trying to rub the stiffness from my neck.

She pushed herself to a sitting position, demurely pulling the covers about her, and I noticed her face and neck were wet with perspiration.

"You okay?" I asked.

"I feel as though I've been hit by a number nine bus. But then you don't look as though you'd win any prizes this morning, either."

"Thanks." I made a mental note: no more boozing until this situation was resolved.

She brushed at the strands of damp hair around her face and neck with her fingers. "I wanted to wake you earlier." There was a tremulous quality to her voice, betraying effort of control. "Do you still have that trilonite you scored last night?"

I had forgotten completely about it; excusable, I told myself, in light of the night's activities - and a quick search of my pockets came up with the small envelope. I turned it over between my fingers.

Again her voice quavered: "I'm afraid I have quite a habit." I went over to her and sat on the edge of the bed, handed it to her, saying, "You really ought to try and do something about getting off this stuff."

As she reached to take possession I saw the puncture marks and bruising along the inside of her forearm where she had been injecting herself.

"I tried to kick it about three months ago, but I couldn't do it."

"Isn't there a clinic or something?"

"Ha. That's a laugh. Yeah, I tried the clinic. All those damned book-learned experts asking their inane questions and treating me like I was something that just crawled out of the sewer."

As I watched, Janie took one of the motel brochures from the bedside table and placed it on her lap. Onto it she emptied the contents of the envelope, deftly working it into a line. The envelope she rolled into a short tube which she used to sniff the blue powder. It was done in seconds.

"I was hanging out, bad. Hadn't had a taste for about thirty six hours because my supplier got busted two days before, and no one would do me any credit. I'd lost my job a week before. The clinic was the only option open to me without resorting to stealing, but those jerks didn't bother to mention to me, until after all their probing and poking, that there was a six to eight weeks waiting period. What was I supposed to do?"

"What *did* you do?"

Her eyes left mine, to watch where her fingers twisted the small piece of paper into a knot. Shrugging, she said, "I did what a lot of girls do in that situation. I needed the money to keep up the supply." In an irritated gesture she flicked the twisted-up paper away and looked up at me in defiance. "Does that shock you?"

"It doesn't shock me. No. Survival is the name of the game."

She leaned back into the pillows and studied my face for a moment, and I could tell by the diminished size of her pupils that the drug had taken affect. She said, "I'm glad you understand, Alex. There's a lot who wouldn't."

"Don't let it bother you. . . what other people think. It's what *you* think that counts. Would you consider going to a clinic, now? The way things are at present, it would make a lot of sense. We could find you a private hospital somewhere. Out in the country, maybe.

You can afford it, now." I said, indicating the bag of loot sitting on the breakfast bar. "We can book you in under a false name. They'd never find you. What do you say?"

She didn't reply, only reached for the packet of cigarettes beside the bed and lit one while contemplating my proposal. Her dark eyes glowered at me, matching the red, glowing tip of her cigarette in intensity as she drew on it, blew smoke in my direction.

I held her gaze, wondering what was going on in her mind.

"I was awake for hours this morning," she said, "thinking about my options. That bag of money and a quick fix were high on the list for a while there."

"What stopped you?"
She pondered awhile before saying: "That's more money than I've ever had at one time, it represents the prospect of

freedom. I guess I just didn't trust myself not to blow it. I've got to get myself together. A million dollars wouldn't make my life any better."

"You'll go to a private clinic then?"
"All right. Yes. I'll do it."
"That's great, Janie." I had a strong urge to reach over and touch her reassuringly, but, to be honest, I wasn't all that sure that *that* was my only motive. I went with the reassuring smile instead. "It's a good decision."
 I let Janie use the bathroom first, while I made myself a cup of terrible motel coffee and set my mind to work on my own problems, and how I was going to solve them.

Half an hour later we were driving along Ocean Road, heading towards Semaphore where Jim's shop was situated. The day was bright and warm, and the streets were busy with morning shoppers paying inflated prices for cheap, cunningly displayed merchandise. A group of unemployed youths hung-out in front of an amusement parlour. None of them seemed to be particularly amused to me.

I had been keeping an eye out for a doctor's surgery while Janie sat, unnaturally quiet, in the seat beside me, and before we had covered five kilometres I spotted what I was looking for.

The surgery was an old, red-brick building maintaining a precarious existence between *Megamart* on one side, and *Giant Hardware* on the other. I pulled up alongside the curb and killed the engine. Janie seemed a bit surprised, until she looked out and saw the sign. She pushed open her door and got out without a word.

"You all right?" I asked as we approached the threshold.
There was no reply.

Entering, we found a dingy, badly ventilated waiting room. At least there was no one there before us, only a dowdy, middle-aged woman sitting behind the reception counter, sipping coffee and thumbing through a year-old copy of *House and Home*, which she put aside as we approached the counter.

"Yes?"

"We would like to see the doctor," I said, wondering why else she thought we had chosen to walk through this particular door. We were led along a corridor to a door labelled: CONSULTING ROOM. Beneath this was the doctor's name, Dr Robert Mainwaring, followed by half the letters of the alphabet, proclaiming the doctor's qualifications. Had we chanced to hit the mother lode? The Grand Pooh-Bah of the medical profession?While this curious thought scampered through my mind, the receptionist tapped lightly on the door, then pushed it ajar.

The contrast to what I had seen so far surprised me; a well-lit room, conspicuously well maintained, with all sorts of medical paraphernalia contained within. Microscopes, bell-jars, surgical instruments laid out in sterilisation baths, the mandatory eye-chart hanging on the wall, an examination table and a large cabinet, its shelves full of esoteric gadgets, the use of which I could only guess at. And beside the overflowing book shelves, a human skeleton suspended from a steel frame.

"Alas poor Yorick," came the richly-timbered voice with a broad Scottish accent.

Dr Mainwaring was a large-framed, portly old gentleman wearing a dark-blue suit; very much of the *old school* ilk. He sat behind a mahogany desk exuding an aura of calm assurance. Removing the bifocals from where they were perched on the end of his bulbous nose, he placed them beside the ashtray where his rosewood pipe trailed the last wisp of blue smoke.

"It proves what the sign on the door says I am." he chuckled, nodding towards the skeleton. He closed the ancient tome he had been studying at his desk and laboured to his feet, a twinge of rheumatism making its presence felt, judging by the fleeting grimace which upset his countenance.

"Do put yourselves at ease, and tell me how I may help you," he said, looking from Janie's face to mine.

When we had seated ourselves in the well-padded chairs provided, he lowered himself back into his own chair and seemed, through instinct, but more likely through the skill of a practiced eye, to direct his attention to Janie.

She looked uncomfortable in the chair, sitting stiffly upright with her hands folded and resting on her lap. She turned to me and imparted a thin-lipped smile that told me she wanted me to explain. It was Mainwaring, however, who instigated the proceedings.

"How long have you been using trilonite, Miss...?"

"Stuart. Janie Stuart," said Janie. "About twelve months, but how did you know?"

Mainwaring had retrieved his glasses and was toying with them between his big hands. "It's not so difficult, Miss Stuart, or may I call you Janie?"

"Janie, is fine."

"Your pupils are abnormally contracted and your eyes are slightly glassy." He leaned across his desk and pointed with his glasses. Those white spots on your fingernails show a calcium deficiency, and now that I look closely I can see a spot of blood on the sleeve of your bonny white blouse. You use intravenously. You're the only one in the room not wearing a jacket, and yet there is perspiration on your brow."

Janie had moved to cover the spot on her sleeve with one hand, now she wiped nervously at her forehead.

"I could have guessed heroin, but I happen to know that trilonite is the more common in use these days."

I wondered what the old boy would look like in a deerstalker and with one of those long, drooping pipes protruding from his mouth.

"It's a nasty business," he concluded
I caught myself staring at two grey tufts of nasal hair in the wake of his explanation. "A private clinic, Doctor. Can you recommend one?

"Aye, there's one hereabouts." Mainwaring's chair creaked loudly under his weight as he leaned forward and punched a button on his intercom. "Would you call Doctor Phillips at Rushbrook House, dear." Then to me and Janie he said, "It's a picturesque place out in the countryside, and well staffed, too. I think you'll like it. Lots of fresh air and plenty of space to move around. Not like here in the city, eh? Doctor Phillips is a personal friend. I'll tell him to take especial care of you."

"It sounds fine," I said, turning to Janie. "What do you think?"

She nodded resolutely. "Yes."

In a moment the receptionist's voice came over the intercom: "Doctor Phillips is on line two, Doctor.

Mainwaring pushed the appropriate button and lifted the receiver: "Hello Gus. Robert Mainwaring here. . . I'm well, thank-you. I have a young lass with me now. Miss Stuart, trilonite addiction. She would like to come out to your clinic for a couple of weeks. . . Oh? Yes, I see. All right Gus, I'll get back to you. All right. Yes, goodbye."

Doctor Mainwaring grunted in annoyance as he replaced the receiver.

"Can you hold out for three more days, Janie? It's the first available opening, I'm afraid."

If Janie was disappointed it didn't show in her face. To Mainwaring's question she merely shrugged.

"I'll write you a prescription for codeine phosphate. It'll help."

He replaced his glasses on the end of his thrombotic hooter and began scrawling on a prescription pad. "And some diazapam, I think, to help you relax. I'll get Mrs Mainwaring to book you in for Monday, lla.m. And I'll write you out a referral before you leave."

He also gave Janie a cursory examination and attended to those terrible bruises on her arms while, at my request, he told me as much as he knew about trilonite, which turned out to be considerably more than I had bargained for.

The drug had appeared on the local market around eighteen months ago, replacing the heroin which had suspiciously dried up at about the same time. Users found no problem in switching from one to the other, and in fact it cost them much less to maintain their addiction using the new drug. Lucky them! It was fast becoming the new buzz drug of the times, replacing amphetamine, cocaine, crack cocaine, heroin and the like. And the stuff was something of an enigma. Under chemical analysis it was revealed that highly specialised laboratory procedures needed to be undertaken in production of the drug.

The production of the morphine-based heroin hybrid, which constituted the main body of the drug, was a relatively simple operation, but it also contained a hitherto unseen molecular structure, one which required highly specialised equipment and a great deal of specialist skill to produce. What the action of this newly designed molecule was, was unknown!

Mainwaring's professional curiosity had been piqued at the arrival on the scene of this new substance, as no doubt had been the curiosity of the boffins whose job it was to find an answer. In his enthusiasm to give me all the facts, he embarked on a lengthy dissertation about neurons, chemical receptors, molecular keys and endocrine function, much of which passed straight over my head, athough I got the general idea. I figured the old boy was entering the twilight zone, anyhow. He probably saw himself back at the good old Alma Mata, standing at the lectern delivering a lecture to a bunch of keen-minded, fresh-faced academic types who still believed the world was a nice place. He was a smart old codger. There was no doubt of that. I was getting a pretty fair picture of the situation. Someone was dumping huge amounts of money to put a drug that was obviously expensive to produce onto the streets. The stuff efficiently superseded all the other drugs of addiction and contained a factor X, an unknown bit which took eggheads and lots of money to produce. Why? And that someone, as things were shaping up, was more than likely mister philanthropy himself. Guido Spinoza.

The thoughts and images being conjured in my mind were only spectral, but this whole affair was taking on an altogether more sinister appearance than I cared to admit.

When the Doctor had finished attending to Janie's wounds we headed back to the car. I was keen to see Jim and initiate the plan I had conceived over the cup of lousy motel coffee earlier, but upon departing the surgery my growling stomach reminded me it was time to eat.

I found a shopping mall half a mile down the road, with a café and a chemist where Janie could get her prescription filled. There was also a department store and a couple of boutiques which Janie immediately zeroed in on.

"You get something to eat if you want," she said. "I'm going to do some shopping. I need a new outfit. I can't wear this stuff around for the next three days." She counted out five hundred dollars from the calico bag which sat behind her seat. "Might as well enjoy being wealthy, right?" she beamed.

"Right," I agreed, and she left me sitting behind the wheel, smiling after her.

The cafe served up a hearty plate of scrambled eggs, toast and bacon which I devoured with gusto. I decided to buy a morning paper from across the way and returned with it to peruse while I finished with a cappuccino while waiting leisurely for Janie to find me.

The first five pages confirmed that the world was in its usual state of madness, so I turned to the *funnies* in order to lighten my mood. I checked my horoscope and was warned by Astra, Lady of Light, to *"beware sharp objects, get rich quick schemes and seafood"*. On the up side, I could find *"an ally from an unexpected quarter"*.

I sneered in self-reproach for bothering to read such drivel. I folded the paper and caught sight of an interesting headline. *"Bikie shoot-out at Old Coach."* I read on: *"The body of an unidentified man, along with two unconscious men was found in a cabin at the Old Coach Motel when reports of gun-fire were reported to police in the early hours of this morning. Members of the Satan's Messengers biker gang are being held for questioning."*

Tough break for the girls and boys, I mused. Bad press breeds bad press.

Janie appeared at my table, a milk shake in one hand, three shopping bags in the other. She was wearing new blue jeans, a black, low-cut tank top, a lightweight silver jacket and tan coloured, knee-high leather boots.

"How do I look?" She spun slowly in a full circle for effect.

"You look good," I understated.

"I bought something for you, too," she said, placing the bags on a vacant chair. She rummaged through one bag then another. "Ah, here it is."

From the bag she withdrew a grey, woollen sports jacket. Finely woven and obviously expensive. I liked it.

"Try it on," she insisted enthusiastically. I did, and it fit perfectly.

"It looks good on you," she said, happily tugging here and smoothing there to straighten out any wrinkles. "Do you like it?"

"It's very nice, Janie. Thank-you."

We continued our journey in renewed spirits, if for the most part in comfortable silence, both of us preoccupied with our private thoughts. For my own part I wondered about the man called Vincent Zendell, just how, exactly, did he fit into all of this? All I really knew about him was that he was a rival of Guido Spinoza's, and that his methods were somewhat crude. What was it Janie had told me? He owned a night-club and casino on Pier Street, and he had taken over a used-car business. Yes, that was it.

The fact that he was a rival to Guido seemed to be his most endearing quality, possibly a useful one, but there was still the anomaly I had pointed out to Janie during our discussion of the previous night, and it continued to bother me. Why had Guido allowed him to establish himself to such an extent as to become any sort of a threat at all? I knew well enough that Guido considered this city to be his own personal dominion, and indeed, with the number of corrupt government officials, cops and union bosses he had in his pocket, his claim bore considerable weight. Zendell had to be serving some purpose otherwise Guido simply wouldn't allow him to continue breathing. On this point I was certain.

Six

Harris Electronics was situated on Reef Street, a quiet byway in the seaside suburb of Semaphore, south-west of the city. Pat was busy with a customer as we entered the shop, explaining the operation of an echo-sounder and assuring him that her husband would install it for him at a nominal fee. Leaving him to think it over she came over to greet us.

"Alex, how nice to see you again. And friend?" she asked playfully.

I introduced Pat and Janie to one another and asked after Jim. "You'll find him out the back, there." She pointed towards the doorway behind the sales counter. "Go on through, I'll be out when I get a spare moment."

We found Jim sitting on a high stool, bent over his work bench, soldering connections on a circuit-board.

"Glad to see you're hard at it," I said in order to gain his attention.

He swung around to see who had interrupted his industry. "Alex. Well, this is a surprise. Come on in."

He replaced the soldering iron in its wire cradle and switched it off. "To what do I owe the pleasure?" He said this to me, but his attention was with Janie who stood beside me, insouciantly inspecting the mass of equipment piled about the room.

"I'd like you to meet a friend of mine. This is Janie."

"Pleased to meet you Janie." Jim said, offering his hand.

"Hello Jim."

As they shook hands Jim gave me one of those you-sly-old-dog looks which I did my best to ignore.

"What do you know about tapping telephones?" I asked without further preamble.

"Not legal," he replied.

"Neither are police scanners or radar detectors, both of which I can see from where I stand, wise guy. You making your own here? Not good for business, if you get caught."

He shrugged and employed a boyish smile. "Supply and demand. It's what they taught me at that school you helped pay for."

Damned if he didn't remind me of his old man at that moment. His mannerisms especially.

"I want you to rig me up a phone-tapping device. Can you do that?"

"I guess so." He paused a moment. "Whose phone?"

"Guido's, of course."

"Of course. The place with the high walls, security guards and closed circuit monitors."

"That's the one. But I won't have to go inside the walls for this. There's no overhead lines entering the property. There ought to be an underground junction box outside the wall. I only have to deal with the cameras."

"Okay," he said. "It shouldn't be a major problem. I've got a friend who works with the telephone company, at head office. I'll get him to fax me an installations plan of the property. I expect you'll be doing this at night, so you will want to know the exact location."

"Now you're talking." He was beginning to get into the spirit of things. "What can you rig up?"

"Anything you want. How sophisticated does it have to be?"

"A simple unmanned listening-post was what I had in mind," I told him.

He thought for a moment. "Hang on a second," he said, and went out to the shop. He returned carrying a couple of micro cassette recorders, each the size of a cigarette packet. As he placed them on the bench, he said, "A character like Spinoza would probably have two or three separate in-lines; one or two for business, one private. Two recorders, pulse-activated, can handle that easy enough, It's a doddle, but you've got to get the connections right, Alex. If there's three or more in-lines it's not going to be easy to do in the dark, especially if you have to work quickly." He continued on in this vein, throwing in such vagaries as voltage feedback, differential phasing which would tip Guido that his phone was being bugged, and anything else he could conceive which would complicate matter for me. His motive was comically transparent.

I looked to Janie, who sat on a packing crate smoking a cigarette, to see if she had detected what Jim was up to. She nodded confirmation.

I raised my hand, halting him mid-sentence. "All right, Einstein. You want to give us a hand to connect this gismo?"

"You asking?"

"It's either that or listen to your interminable techno-babble for the rest of the day."

A sheepish grin crossed his face. "I was only trying to-" But we both broke into laughter before he could complete the half-baked rebuttal.

"You boys enjoying yourselves?" Pat stood in the doorway, hands on hips, one eyebrow cocked in feigned disapproval. "While you two have been swapping bawdy jokes, I've been making a two thousand dollar sale."

"Well done," I said. "You sold the echo-sounder?" "Do fish swim?" she rejoined, obviously very pleased with herself.

She caught sight of the cassette-recorders on the bench and adopted a weary martyr tone. "Jim. . . you haven't been looting your own store again? They're the last in stock."

"Alex has a small job he'd like me to help him with, hon," he said, dropping me right in it.

"It's nothing, much," I told Pat. Then checking my watch, "My goodness, is that the time? Why don't you explain it to Pat while Janie and I go see a man about a bus. Can you have things ready by tonight?"

"Sure." He glanced furtively to his wife, then back to me. "No problem."

"How about you and Janie come to our house for dinner tonight?" Pat suggested. "Or is it only back rooms that are conducive to hatching clandestine plots?"

I made a mental note not to involve Jim any further. . . *after tonight.*

"Do you have anything on tonight?" I asked Janie, giving her the opportunity to decline if she felt uncomfortable about it.

"I'd love to," she said to Pat. "I'll bring the wine, shall I? Red or white?"

*

It was an old, yellow school bus with a seating capacity of perhaps forty-five. I had noticed it during our drive out to Semaphore. With the *"4-Sale"* sign plastered to its side, it presented itself as an interesting solution to the problem of the security cameras at *Villa Vulgar*, as I had come to call Guido's country mansion.

It was parked in the front yard of a dilapidated timber and fibre board dwelling in the quasi-industrial suburb of Monroe which straddled the arterial road running south from Monarto.

The whole district was in a state of decay. Within its bounds there were quite a few factories, many now defunct, but some continued to spew smoke and fumes into the atmosphere in the production of metal, plastic and rubber goods, coating everything with a fine, grey precipitant and giving a sombre, even desolate air to the entire vicinity.

Janie and I climbed the steps of the verandah and I rapped on the rickety screen-door which threatened to part company with its hinges at any moment. The main door was open, affording a dim view into a passageway running through to the rear of the house.

"Anybody home?" I called.

I was still peering into the murky interior when Janie nudged me with her elbow. To my right a man's head --- long brown hair and full beard --- protruded through a pair of filthy floral curtains in the open window. He looked to be about forty years-of-age, and the way he squinted in the daylight suggested we had just woken him.

"Whad'ya want?" His voice sounded like he had been gargling caustic soda.

"I'm interested in your bus," I explained, while beside me Janie had a bout of the giggles.

The disembodied head remained motionless, as did the features of his face while the eyes studied the two of us. His eyes, I now noticed, were blue and brown: *one of each!*

"Go ahead and check it out," he rasped. "There aren't any keys, the ignition switch is under the driver's seat. I'll be out in a sec."

I started the motor and was surprised to hear no knocks or rattles. It actually ran very smoothly.

The owner arrived and stood outside the concertina doors, all six feet eight inches of him, if I was any judge. His height made him appear slim, but he looked strong. He wore a denim jacket, no shirt, tattered jeans and elastic-sided work boots. He carried a slight paunch, probably from drinking too much beer. Taking a good draught from the can he had in his hand, he said, "Take her for a run" . . .and squeezing in past Janie he took the seat adjacent to me. Janie took the seat behind me and I did as he suggested.

Finding reverse gear, I backed out of the yard and started off down the street, soon to learn that despite the rough exterior, mechanically it was in very good shape. It drove like it was on rails, and the motor fairly purred.

The big guy sat quietly the whole time with his clodhoppers up on the windscreen ledge and sipping steadily his breakfast.

When I had taken a wide, circuitous route through the neighbourhood and parked back in his front yard, I asked him to operate the lights and indicators while I checked that they functioned.

"Okay," I said, coming back to the doorway, and he cut the motor.

"So what do you think?" he asked.

"I'd like to hire it for the night."

He looked at me suspiciously, and I didn't blame him for that. I should have informed him of my intention from the outset.

"*Hire?* Well. . ." He drained the beer and crushed the can in a large hand. "I need another beer. Let's go inside and discuss this."

We followed him inside, and as I walked along the passageway I noticed that the lounge room was entirely devoid of furniture, but in the centre of the room stood a gleaming, black and sparkling chrome motorcycle.

"Nice bike," I commented.

"You know what it is?" he asked.

"Thousand c.c. Vincent Black Shadow. A Classic."

"Damn near an antique," he added. "Nineteen-fifty, C-series. Better fork design than the earlier models."

The kitchen contained a table and four odd chairs. Alongside the sink sat an ice chest, which he flipped open and from it fished out a beer.

"I'm squatting here, as you may have gathered. Have a seat. Anyone want a beer? They're cold!"

We sat and accepted the beers.

"You want to hire the bus, do you? Well, that's interesting. I never thought of hiring it out." He seated himself at the table and tore the tab off his can.

We followed suit. "Cheers," I said.

Janie suggested we introduce ourselves. "I'm Janie, and this is Alex."

"Adrian, but everyone calls me Took."

"Do you live here all alone, Took?" Janie asked, surveying the kitchen.

"Yep." He nodded saturninely. "Been in this hole for three months while I worked on the bus. Gonna sell it and take off. Up North, maybe. Might even take my ass over to South-East

Asia." He swept his tangled locks back from his face. "I could live pretty good over there on the proceeds I can get from the sale of the bus and the bike. This country's ratshit now, anyway. It doesn't have a soul any more, if you know what I mean."

"I do," said Janie. "I know *just* what you mean."
Took gulped down another mouthful of beer and plonked the can down hard on the table, then looked me squarely in the eye. "The only way I can let you take the bus for the night, is if I come along as the driver. I've put too much time and effort into her to risk any damage being done. Whoever buys it can drive it over a cliff, for all I care, but I'm not letting it out of my sight until I have the money I worked for in hand. My fee, by the way, is a hundred dollars. . .plus petrol."

This complicated matters somewhat, and things were already complicated enough.

"What did you want it for, anyway? You and your pals going on a pub-crawl?"

"No, not a pub-crawl." He waited patiently while I searched for the explanation. "It's a round trip of around sixty miles. Out to Foster Vale and back, that's all. No risk to your vehicle, I promise."

Took seemed amused. "You're having trouble telling me exactly what you want it for, Alex. Just how dodgy is it? because I could sure use some money right now, but I have no intention of seeing the inside of another prison cell.

"It was for non-*p*ayment of alimony, in case you're wondering. My ex is a real bitch."
I told him as much as he needed to know for the purpose of convincing him that there was no risk to his bus. Well, not much anyway, if all went well.

His recent spate of isolation had primed him for the small adventure my plan offered, and I do believe he would have been in it for the relief of boredom, alone. I agreed to the hundred dollars, *plus petrol*, and I gave him Pat and Jim's address before we left.

He promised he would be there to pick us up at seven, sharp.

Seven

Jim succeeded in obtaining the fax from his friend at the telephone company. It revealed the location of the junction box, roadside, ten metres out and almost in line with the front gates of Guido's residence, and it showed that he was right about the number of lines running in. There were three. He had also assembled the bugging gadget I had asked for: a neat, black package a hundred centimetres square and thirty centimetres thick, with half a dozen coloured wires protruding from it.

At the dinner table I jokingly commented that he might add this to the other sideline products he had in his shop. I realised I had made a mistake when Pat's expression betrayed disapproval; and I also had a feeling that there had been words about his involvement before Janie and I had arrived.

If this was the case, Jim only added to her displeasure by paying rather too much attention to my dusky companion, a situation Janie innocently augmented in her endeavour to entertain our hosts. She displayed a natural gregariousness I had not previously seen in her, and as I updated Jim and Pat on the recent course of events, she filled in with details and colourful embellishments of her own. As Janie's background grew more and more clear to Pat I noticed her attempts at concealing her feelings become less successful.

Where Jim's past included contact with what might be described as the seamier side of life, she had no such experience to draw on, and showed signs of internal conflict with her middle-class upbringing.

Janie, as promised, had brought along the wine. She sipped away at her glass continually, and while she genially replenished all our glasses, I noticed that it was her own glass which received the greater portion. At one juncture she produced her bottle of codeine tablets, dispensed three into the palm of her hand and swallowed them with a sip of wine. It wasn't until then that I realized it had been some ten hours since she had used the last of the trilonite.

Still oblivious to Pat's coolness towards her, or so I thought, Janie continued in a lively manner, now about Took, in whom she confessed a special interest.

"He's a weird guy, sort of solitary, you know? But there's something about him I can't quite put my finger on. A calmness. Yeah, that's it, there's an aura of calmness around him, and you should see his eyes, they're fantastic. One blue and one brown. I've never seen that before. He's got this motorcycle he keeps inside the house. A Vincent something. You should see it. I bet he just climbs on that thing and takes off any time he feels like it. I wish I could do that."

Pat's reply to this was, "Why don't you?"
Janie ignored the barb and answered ingenuously. "Maybe I will, one day. I forget what it's like to be really free. I know it sounds silly, but the idea scares me a bit."

"I'm sure you would do very well, Janie," Jim replied. "You should travel. Travelling broadens one's horizons. Isn't that what they say?"

"Yes, they do say that don't they." She refilled her wineglass, took a sip and topped it up again.

Pat, in her despair, took to gulping wine, herself, and when the two bottles Janie had brought along expired, she went to the larder and emerged with two more.

To everyone's surprise, she said, "I'm coming with you."

I was more surprised than the others because she was looking directly at me when she said it. I think she blamed me because Jim was taking an interest in Janie. So what could I say? I had given her my assurance that there was absolutely no risk. The only reason I had done so, however, was to enlist Jim's assistance with as little disruption on the domestic front as possible.

"Of course you're coming, Pat. The more the merrier."

At two minutes before seven Took banged on the front door: still resembling a wild man in denim.

"You guys ready?" he asked. "If you're not, it's okay. I'll wait out here 'till you are."

The five of us piled on board. Took behind the wheel, Jim and Pat in the passenger seat at the front of the bus, and Janie and myself behind the driver.

The girls had decided to bring the wine along. Jim carried a small haversack with a few tools and the black box in it, and I had my needle gun, just in case. Thus prepared, we set forth.

When everyone had settled into the journey and Took was clear on which route to take, I leaned back into my seat and turned to Janie. "How are you feeling?"

"Not so good," she replied meekly. "Can I lean my head on you?"

"Of course you can, I replied, and she snuggled up to me and rested her head on my shoulder. "You did well over dinner," I told her. "I'm afraid I didn't realise it was going to be so difficult for you. I'm sorry I dragged you into it."

"That's okay, Alex. I wanted to come. It helps keep my mind off it.

"They're nice people, both of them. Pat is just a bit possessive of her husband, that's all. It's a natural instinct for a woman when there's another female around. She'll get over it."

In less than an hour we were driving along the narrow road between the vineyards just out from Villa Vulgar. Our timing was pretty good; it was about ten minutes before sundown. I directed Took to pull in at the side of the road while we waited for twilight. He had a last look at the plan so he could pull up directly over top of the junction box, and I put on a baseball cap, pulling the peak over my eyes to hide my face from the security cameras.

Pat, by this time quite affected by the wine, insisted on drawing a mustache on me with her eyeliner pencil. It looked rather incongruous but it pleased her so much I let it remain.

When the sun touched the horizon, I removed the pressure cap from the radiator and we ran the engine until it was close to boiling, then drove the last half mile to our objective.

As we neared the perimeter wall of Villa Vulgar, white steam was gushing from the radiator.

"Okay, Took, just this side of the centre of the entrance and five metres off the edge of the road. Over a bit. Slowly. Can you see it yet?"

Took shook his head. Metre-high grass grew along the verge, making the job difficult. And the poor light didn't help matters.

"Put your headlights on," I suggested. We could not afford to miss it. We would look a mite suspicious if we overshot the mark and had to reverse up to find it.

We rolled slowly forwards. "There!" Jim pointed. "Got it," Took concurred, and middled the bus over the concrete cover.

Jim was first off and slipped down the blind side of the bus with his bag of tricks. Halfway along, he got down on his stomach and rolled underneath. The rest of us congregated at the front of the bus to gawk at the steam, milling about scratching our heads and remonstrating our frustration in a perfunctory fashion.

The wall-mounted floodlights suddenly lit up, and I noticed one of the cameras swing around to point in our direction. The lights weren't having a great effect in this half-light, as I knew they wouldn't. Whoever was sitting in front of the security monitors at the moment would have no chance of getting a clear look at any of our faces. All he would see would be a group of frustrated travellers waiting for the radiator to cool.

Janie lit a cigarette and sat in the grass with her bottle of wine. Pat and Took followed her example while I disappeared down the side of the bus to see how Jim was getting on.

He had the lid off the junction box and the excess cable pulled out in front of him, cutting along the outer casing to expose the wires within.

"Everything okay there?" I asked. "Yeah, not a problem. This shouldn't take long," he answered without looking up from what he was doing.

At that moment a gruff voice issued from the opposite side of the bus. "Hey, you lot. You can't park here!"

Lowering my head to ground level I saw a pair of grey trouser legs, a pair of military type boots and two pairs of doggy paws standing behind the gate.

"Company" I told Jim. "Stay with it."

As I came around to the front of the bus I got a look at the guard: a pugnacious-looking individual with a cudgel at his hip and a Pit Bull at the end of a short leash.

Took had already responded to the challenge. He walked a couple of paces towards the gate and pointed back over his shoulder to the bus. "Boiled radiator, man. Got to let it cool off a bit."

"Move it, fellah. You're on private property." The dog, picking up his handler's tone, growled menacingly as if to emphasise the remark.

"If you understand anything about mechanics," Took tried again, "you must realise that that would be rather unwise. The pistons are above normal operating temperatures, right? So they're probably expanded tight in the cylinders. It could bust a ring or something if I move it before it cools."

"Listen you hippy freak or whatever you are, if you don't get that piece of shit out of there, immediately, I'm going to kick your sorry ass. Now move it."

I walked up to Took's side. "Calm down, mister *(shit-head)* I added quietly, for Took's benefit. "Do you know where the pickers' campsite is? We're driving them into town tonight, for a bit of a shindig. You know, barbecue, beer, live music and all that?"

But it didn't work. He pulled out a small device from his pocket and pressed a button. The gates opened part way, then he reached over to unfasten the leash.

I called for the girls to get back on the bus, hoping that would satisfy this cretin. It didn't. The leash snapped free and the dog sprang forward. It was time to retreat.

I made a dash for the bus, expecting Took to do the same. I had taken a number of strides in that direction when I turned and looked over my shoulder, only to see Took standing his ground, the pit bull closing fast.

I really did not want to use my needle gun. I might just as well have written *Alex Jaeger Was Here* in letters ten feet high across Guido's wall. I decided to hold off and see if Took knew what he was doing. I then witnessed one of the most extraordinary things I have ever seen.

He was crouched, feet apart and leaning slightly forward, poised on the balls of his feet. A yard before the dog made its leap, Took let go a shriek which might have given a banshee cause for alarm. It surprised the animal into a fraction of a second's hesitation, causing it to misjudge its last stride and leave the ground awkwardly. Took lunged under the arc of the Pit Bull's trajectory, meeting it mid flight with the force of their combined weight and speed. There was a snap and an anguished yelp as they fell to the ground. Then Took was quickly on his feet again, standing over the incapacitated animal.

The girls cheered and hooted from the windows of the bus, and I was so amazed at what I'd seen, I almost forgot to warn Took of the on-rushing security guard.

His eyes were wide with rage as he flew at Took, and whatever it was he was trying to say, remained strangled in his throat.

Took's long leg whipped out with blinding speed, the toe of his size twelve clodhopper impacting into the man's solar plexus as he attempted to bludgeon Took with his up-raised cudgel.

Took adroitly leaned away from the impending blow, allowing his assailant to pass and fall in an untidy heap.

"Do you need a hand?" I asked as the dust settled. Took's eyes were wild-looking, but his voice was calm. "A bloke spends three months working on a bus, and *he* calls it a piece of shit."

"Perhaps he'll be more sensative to people's feelings in future," I suggested.

The drive back to Pat and Jim's house was a joyous one. Jim had successfully completed his task and Pat seemed to have enjoyed the outing immensely, although she was to have a change of attitude when she woke in the morning with a fearsome hangover and recollections of the previous evening came back to her; but Took was the hero of the night, and when we arrived back at the house Pat insisted that he come inside and relax for a while before departing.

When quizzed about his mind-boggling display at the gates of Villa Vulgar, Took replied, "It seemed like the thing to do at the time. The dog was only doing what it was trained to do. I hadn't intended to kill it."

"But what did you do?" Pat asked, her voice still pitched high with excitement.

"I think I broke its neck. I should have broken the guard's neck and kicked the dog in the guts." He seemed despondent.

"You didn't have a lot of choice," I said, consolingly. "I'm damn glad to have had you along with us." I made a mental note to pay him a healthy bonus.

Pat had pulled yet another bottle of wine from the pantry, and she and Janie were getting on famously by this time, so I took her aside to the kitchen and explained about Janie's battle with drug addiction, telling her of the arrangements with Mainwaring to get her into a clinic. "But," I added, "it's going to be tough for her over the next few days. She'll need support from friends."

To this revelation, Pat was extremely sympathetic. "Oh, you poor girl," she crooned to Janie, when she re-entered the lounge room.

"Why didn't you tell me you were ill?" . . .and she flung her arm around Janie's shoulders in an alcohol-affected display of sympathy and concern, which I expected would wear off by morning.

Before Pat fell asleep on the couch she had agreed to put Janie up for the night in their guest-room while I attended to another piece of business. It would be quite late by the time I was through, so I decided on heading back to my motel room for a night's sleep afterwards, in my bed, this time.

Janie was unimpressed at the prospect of being left behind on this one, she confided to me in the kitchen while swallowing two more codeine tablets and a couple of valium.

"I'm not going to be able to sleep tonight anyway," she protested.

"Why can't I come along with you?"

"Because I don't know what to expect from Zendell," I calmly explained. "I don't want you within a mile of that bastard. I'm sorry, kiddo. I know you're feeling lousy, but I'm afraid it's impossible. . . *this* time."

She must have noted the resolve in my voice and she remained silent for a while. Then with a sudden turn of her head which tossed her dark locks over her shoulder, she glared angrily at me.

"Do what you damn well like. You can get yourself killed for all I care. And if you do, I want that money, here, with me."

"It's your money," I replied somewhat lamely. I knew she was hurting and I felt powerless to help, but I had to catch up with Zendell, tonight. Almost thirty-six hours had elapsed since my hotel door had been shredded by gunfire and my money stolen. I liked to work fast --- fast enough to catch people off balance, and I was not even halfway towards having this thing sorted out. I could not allow this girl to get under my skin. Besides, I told myself, I was doing as much as I could to help her. . . wasn't I?

"We all have our problems," I said to her, and immediately wished I hadn't. She turned her back on me and no more was said.

Eight

There were two reasons why I wanted to meet Zendell, foremost being the possibility that I could enlist him and his resources against Guido. The chances of this eventuality were, I had to admit, slim, but attractive; in fact, irresistible, to my way of thinking. That I, the guy Guido had tried to manipulate into nobbling his competitor, should combine with his competitor and repay his contemptible arrogance with the slap in the face he deserved, appealed just as much to my sense of humour as it did to my appreciation of irony and justice. Ideally, the *coup de grace* would be to simultaneously land a crippling blow to Zendell's operations; a thug of lesser stature than Spinoza, perhaps, but just as deserving of being taught a lesson as that pint-sized parasite.

Simple curiosity was the second reason. What did he look like? How did he talk? What was his game, this new kid on the block? . . .and more to the point, why was he still in business? The answer to this last question would have to wait. I wanted to gain his confidence, not spook him with a lot of probing questions.

It was going to be hard enough to gain any credibility with him; after all, a man in his position was bound to be highly suspicious of a stranger walking in off the street with a story like the one I had to tell. In fact, the only probable good I could see coming out of this improvised excursion was that I might stir up some action, anything which might present itself as an opening, a way of striking at the vitals of the beast.

In a way I was almost glad circumstances had contrived to cast me in the role I now played. I had to admit I wasn't entirely comfortable with the idea of drifting around with a suitcase full of money, looking for ways to fritter it away, no matter how much I tried to convince myself to the contrary. No. *This* was the sort of thing I thrived on, the hunt, the risk-taking, the playing of the game. It was the only thing which ever satisfied the fire burning within.

The fuel? I had often wondered what it was I burned. Perhaps, deep down, I knew the answer, and perhaps deep down was where I wanted the answer to stay. The men in my unit used to say I had a death-wish, a condition my Commanding Officers were only too glad to utilize, but to hell with all that. Some things are best forgotten. Sometimes it doesn't do to fathom too deeply the depths of one's own mind, not when you have buried there a host of unwanted memories. *There* there be demons.

I swung onto Pier Street in downtown Monarto. I had once heard it referred to as the biggest remand yard in the state. Not so much a joke as a wry statement of fact. I supposed every large city in just about every country in the world had a street like this one.

Being Friday night there was plenty of activity in the pubs, clubs and discotheques which lined both sides of the street as I drove amid the slow-moving traffic. It occurred to met as I moved westwards, away from the central business district and towards the docks, that the businesses appeared to classify themselves in a kind of diminishing running scale; a symbolic representation of society's diverse appetites. Beginning with department stores, travel agents, theatres, cinemas, amusement parlours, cafes and pizza bars, it continued on to girlie shows, betting shops, sleazy bars and brothels. From the *day people*, who were lucky enough to have jobs and were out for a night's entertainment, to the *twilight people*, those who were to one side of recognized, mainstream society. Their response to a failing economy and their second-placed position in the pecking order, to pursue the occasional and ephemeral bouts of merry-making which chance and circumstance offered; to the *night people*, who roamed the streets in search of solace, perhaps in the form of a friend and a conversation in a barroom some place, perhaps found only in intoxication, then to return to whatever shelter meager finances could afford; to the *people "of" the night,* for whom the day held nothing but the stark light of a pitiless reality, and among whom lurked a predatory breed who laid in wait for easy prey, to inflict on them whatever brand of treachery they practiced. Here on this one city street existed a revealing cross-section of a modern city of the technological era, and it was both illuminating and alarming to see it as I did at that moment.

Beyond my reverie I spotted the pink neons which announced *Swank's Night Club & Casino,* above this the disjointed movements of a neon dancer, gyrating crazily atop a spinning roulette wheel.

By the time I found a parking spot I was at least a hundred metres past the building, but I was lucky even to get that. If I was forced to park down a side-street, the odds of my car being stripped, stolen or merely broken into were quite good. As it was I was still concerned that I might return to find it gone, so I approached a group of likely-looking lads who sat nearby at a sidewalk table, sharing a bottle of something which was labeled Cola, while they ogled passing women.

The red Interceptor had already caught their collective eye, so to allay my apprehension I asked if they wouldn't mind keeping an eye on it for me if they were going to be there for a while. I tore a twenty-dollar note in half and offered it to them, promising the other half when I returned. They were suitably impressed with this cliche gesture, which, I felt sure, they had all seen at one time or another on some late-night television rerun; and to the cries of "Yeah, sure mister, we'll watch your car for you," we struck the deal.

I made my way back along the footpath until I came level with Swank's on the opposite side of the street. It was three storeys high, with glass-enclosed balconies on the second and third levels. I noted the fire-escape on the eastern side of the building. Not that I was expecting trouble, it was merely second nature for me to make such observations. The last landing of the steel staircase was only about fifteen feet up. I had jumped from much higher, I recalled, and turned my attention to the pair of besuited, bow-tied muscleheads under the marquee at the main entrance... No problem. I patted my inside breast pocket and felt a reassuring presence, took a deep breath of carbon monoxide and whatever other poisons filled the foul-smelling air, and set off across the street.

I followed a pair of punk rockers who might have passed as macabre clowns visiting from another galaxy, and watched them pass inside the building before me. As I neared the threshold, however, musclehead number one pulled me up short.

"Excuse me, sir, but you can't come in here with jeans on."

"Listen, buddy," I began after a moment's hesitation. "I've been called down here to lend a hand with your fucked up sound system. . .as a special favour to Vinnie," I threw in for good measure. "I ain't got no time and no inclination to be changing my duds. Get him on the blower if you have a problem with that, but hurry it up, I've only got half an hour before I'm due back at the *Muttonhead* gig."

I think it was the Vinnie thing that did it, but as I was blocking the doorway and attracting some attention, they let me pass.

The ground floor was given over to a disco setup, with lots of noise and flashing lights - what I imagined an epileptic brain cell might look like from the inside - so I climbed the stairs to the second floor.

Here I discovered a plush lounge bar where a jazz band played on a bandstand at the far end of the room. Patrons either danced or sat at tables, sipping cocktails or beer while the band played an improvised version of Lennon and McCartney's *"A Day in the Life"*. A blue neon sign above the bar read: The Blue Room. Apart from the dance floor in front of the bandstand, the floor was covered with expensive blue carpet. The walls were painted light blue, and on them were hung poster-size photographs of famous musicians, past and present, in gold leaf frames. The ceiling was the same dark-blue colour as the carpet, and from it hung elaborate crystal chandeliers which cast a soft light throughout. I stayed until the end of the song and climbed the stairs again.

Here I found the casino. Craps, baccarat, roulette, blackjack, two-up, it was all here; and weren't the punters having fun! I thought I would test my luck before getting down to business with Zendell, whom I guessed was behind one of the closed doors up on the mezzanine level.

I walked around the blackjack tables, watching to see which one, if any, was paying out. None of them were, for a while, but after five or so minutes I noticed a croupier at one of the tables push across a couple of payouts. No one else seemed to have noticed, so I went over and occupied a spare stool beside a young Vietnamese chap wearing a sports coat and *jeans!*

"How come they let you in here wearing jeans?" I asked him.

"I come here all the time," he replied through a huge smile.

I returned a similar smile. "Oh. That explains it."

"What's the limit?" I asked the barbie-doll croupier.

"A hundred dollars on this table, sir. Shall I deal you in this hand?"

"You bet," I said, and placed a hundred on the table for her to convert into chips.

I started the first game with a ten dollar chip. I was dealt a lousy nine, first card, and paid ten dollars for the second: a five. The woman at the end sat pat. *I-come-here-all-the-time* busted going for a five-card trick. It was my turn. I was on fourteen and needed a six or a seven. I bought another card for ten dollars, a six, and I sat on twenty.

The dealer flipped her second card, a nine, which put her at seventeen. The rotten bitch then drew a four, smiled sweetly at me and said, "Bad luck, sir."

If this was going to be an indication of how my meeting with Zendell was going to go, I was not impressed. I bought another thirty dollars worth of chips to bring me back to the even hundred. I was determined to crack it this time. If I won the hand I would apply the same brazen tactic to Zendell. If I lost, I would tread carefully with him.

This time I put a fifty-dollar chip up front, and was dealt a jack. I put the remaining fifty on the next card. When she dealt me the ace of spades, and busted trying to beat the others, I accepted it as a good omen, took my two hundred winnings and split while I was ahead.

Back in the *Blue Room*, I ordered a soft drink at the bar and borrowed a pen and a sheet of paper to write the following note:

Mr. Zendell: It seems you and I have a common acquaintance in Guido Spinoza. It could be to our mutual benefit if you would care to join me in the Blue Room for a chat.

I signed my name and passed it to the bartender who agreed to see that it was delivered right away, and to direct Mr Zendell to my table when he arrived.

I found a vacant table by the eastern wall which was reasonably close to the fire escape, but not so close to the band as to make conversation difficult; and there I sat, facing towards the bar to watch what developed.

The band finished its rendering of *Season of the Witch* and was part way through something called *Strange Cactus* when I caught sight of them entering the room from the casino upstairs.

The one with the bow-tie took up his position at the foot of the stairs while the other, dressed in a sharply-tailored black suit and wearing a white carnation in his lapel, went directly to the bar and waved my note at the bartender. The bartender pointed in my direction and, I presume, gave him my description. I watched with interest as he approached.

He walked with the bearing of a confident man, a young man of about twenty five or so years, I decided when he had gotten closer. His face was angular, almost handsome in a predatory sort of way; olive-brown skin and short, jet-black hair combed severely backwards from his face. He was a man of slight build and around five nine or ten in height, well groomed and precise in appearance. Slick like a snake. Yes, I decided. . . Vinnie the Viper.

I stood as he neared my table, and over his shoulder I noticed that his minder had moved along the wall in order to facilitate an unobstructed view of proceedings.

"Mr Zendell?"

He gave a curt nod and seated himself immediately. "What is this all about, Mr Jaeger?" he said, tossing my note on the table between us.

I wasn't about to let him take charge of this meeting. This was *my* show. "I'm surprised to be talking to such a young man, Mr Zendell. You must be ambitious, or you've had some lucky breaks at least, what with your car yard and all."

He made no attempt to disguise his annoyance and fixed me with a beady-eyed stare. "If this is a shakedown of some sort you'll be leaving this place in pieces," he hissed, and I do believed he would have liked that.

"On the contrary, Mr Zendell." I made a slow, deliberate sweep of the room with my eyes. "As my note suggests, quite clearly, I have come here to make a proposal which should be to our mutual benefit. And, in the spirit of fairness," I said, feeling suddenly inspired, "I should explain to you that I have people here of my own, and any attempt by your henchmen to spoil our little *tete-atete* could only result in an awful scene. It would be a shame to upset these good people's evening. It really is very pleasant here. You are to be congratulated."

He made a cursory check of the room, then looked back to me.

"I don't see anyone."

"They're very professional," I replied.

He smiled pleasantly, and I got the impression he could be quite charming if he put his mind to it.

"So let's hear this proposal of your's, Mr Jaeger, but please do be brief. I have other matters to attend to."

He was an arrogant devil. I took my time, sipping my drink and clearing my throat before delivering my opener.

"The heart of the matter, Mr Zendell, lies in the fact that you and I are both being caused a certain amount of aggravation by one Guido Spinoza, and I think we could serve each other very well by combining our energies and our resources to fix it so he doesn't bother either of us any more."

Zendell was watching me coolly, but I can tell when I have gained someone's interest, and he was very interested.

"I don't know what *your* problem is," he parried, "but what makes you think that I have any grievance with Mr Spinoza? He happens to be a highly respected member of the community."

To this remark I chuckled derisively. "Respected? Oh yes, I suppose he is. In different ways by different people, I think it would be fair to say. It doesn't necessarily follow that because a person is treated with respect, they are deserving of it. And as for being a member of the community, I find it hard to imagine that he has ever been a member of any community."

"What am I to think when a man comes into my club with wild accusations like this? I don't know you, Mr Jaeger. I have never met you before tonight, or even heard of you. What do you expect me to say? For instance, and let us treat this hypothetically, if your insinuations applied I would be a fool to discuss anything of this nature with a complete stranger. You could be the police." He leaned back in his chair and delivered another smile. "Is that not true?"

"That's true," I conceded. "I could be a copper and I could be wired for sound. But I'm not, and if it makes you feel any easier, we can continue this conversation as a hypothetical exercise. That would rule out any chance of entrapment, wouldn't it?"

"I think perhaps you are mad," he responded, "but even madmen can be interesting, so I will listen to a madman's tale because it amuses me."

"That's a very interesting manoeuvre, Mr Zendell. I can live with that."

He was understandably concerned, and at the same time keen to learn just how much I knew about him, regardless of my identity.

I was aware that my position was a bit chancy. Guys like him don't like people like me knowing too much about their business. It's a good way to end up face down in the bay.

I had to ask myself how much I wanted to enlist his help. Not that much, was the answer I quickly arrived at. I would set the cat amongst the pigeons and leave. His concern about this being a set up, and my audacious lie about having back up would stay his hand this time, I hoped. There was still an outside chance that something might come from this meeting, so I had to play this scene with conviction. I would give him enough to strike "copper" from his list. . . with a little checking.

Zendell had pulled out a gold cigarette case and lit up while I weighed these things up.

"Okay," I said. "Here it is on a platter for you. Yesterday morning my room was sprayed with gunfire, forcing me to make a rather ignominious exit through my window, and in doing so, leaving a substantial amount of money behind. Now that's as may be, and as I am now aware, nothing to do with you, but here's the interesting part. Knowing Guido as well as I do I went out to visit him later that day, to see if he had any clues about who might have perpetrated this despicable act, and do you know whose name he came up with?"

Zendell was beginning to look uneasy, but he remained silent.

"Yours, Mr Zendell. How do you like them apples? Now, like I say, I know it wasn't your doing, but I do know that you and he are having, how can I put it, territorial disputes?"

His composure was once again under control and, smiling, he replied: "That is a very interesting story, Mr Jaeger. Or should I say, a very inventive one? I would be very interested to know how you conclude that he and I are having these alleged disputes."

"I don't care to disclose that. You must allow me to have some secrets. The thing which ought to concern you the most at this juncture is that he tried to set you up, because the thing which concerns me is that he tried to play me for a patsy. You see? It makes perfect sense for us to ally ourselves."

Zendell's eyes indicated plenty of cerebral activity. Which way was he going to turn? I wondered. He could well have been deciding in which part of the bay he was going to have my body dumped.

"Supposing I believe that Mr Spinoza said such a thing to you," he said, at last. "Why would he direct you, particularly, against someone like me?"

"Because," I snapped, growing weary of the game, "he is a conniving, twisted little man who gets his jollies from manipulating people, *anybody*, and if that's news to you, you don't know shit from champagne and you're way out of your league. The reason he used *me,* particularly, was because he knows my form. He probably had me checked out years ago, when we first met, and he's been waiting for the right set of circumstances to wind me up ever since. I guess I just turned up in town at the right time, seeing as how you two are worrying each other like a couple of terriers over the same bone. So why don't you stop with the charade? You know I know the score. You supply me with the information I need, using whatever resources you have at your disposal, and I'll bring his dirty little empire down around his ears. You won't even have to get your hands dirty." *And I'll hang you out to dry, too!* I thought to myself.

Nine

It had gone quite well. Better than expected, at any rate. I left him with my phone number and he said he might call me in a day or two, to see if my delusions had cleared up. He actually maintained the act right to the end.

By the time I got back to the car and paid the lads with the other half of the twenty, it was nearly eleven o'clock. My next objective was to drive to my motel and clock up a good eight hours sleep. This, however, was not to be.

Less than half a mile from my destination the mobile phone on the seat beside me began its shrill cicada impersonation. It was Took at the other end.

"Hi, Took. You guys still partying over there?"

"No, man." There was the note of concern in his voice, and the smug feeling of self-satisfaction I had from the night's work began to wane.

"Something wrong?" I asked, my motel now within sight.

I was steering with one hand while the other held the phone to my earl, so when a car came flying out from a side street ahead of me, spun, side-swiped a car in an adjacent lane and flipped over on its roof, I had to drop the phone in order to avoid it, *and* the patrol car which just as dangerously emerged from the same street, lights flashing and siren blaring. Cars swerved and skidded erratically, narrowly missing one another until everything came to a screeching halt. Other sirens could be heard perfectly demonstrating the *Doppler effect* as they converged on the scene.

I retrieved the phone from under my feet. "Took, you still there?"

"I'm ringing from a phone booth on Clara Street, Richmond. Janie's up the street at number fifty two, it's one of her friend's house."

"What the hell is she doing there?" I asked as I watched two youths climb out of the up-turned car and make a dash for it.

"Janie called a taxi after you left. She reckoned she couldn't stay cooped up all night and had to get out."

A policeman made a flying tackle at one of the youths, bringing him down on the median strip. The other kid was leaping gazelle-like from bonnet to bonnet over the tangle of cars, and heading my way.

". . . . . tried to talk her out of it but what could I do?" Took continued.

Two shots rang out as the kid bounded onto my bonnet and ran across the roof.

"Jesus Christ!" I exclaimed, reflexively ducking for cover. "I'm sorry, Alex. I really did try-"

"No, not you, Took. What did you say again?"

While I watched two coppers kick the stuffing out of one kid, and while the other made his desperate bid for freedom somewhere behind me, I got the rest of the details from Took.

Janie had told him that she had to get out for a while, but Took didn't buy it. She had retrieved the money from the car before I left, I remembered, and Took was wise to this, too. It put him in an awkward position. He felt responsible for taking care of *my woman*, as he put it, and told her that if she insisted on going out to score dope, he had no right to stop her but he was coming along. And that's where he was now; except, now, she didn't want to leave, and he didn't want to leave her there, out of the sense of responsibility for her safety, and out of a sense of loyalty to me, I suspected. The only thing he could think of to do was to ring Harris Electronics' after hours number, getting Jim out of bed, and ask him what he should do. Jim gave him my mobile number. The poor guy didn't know if he was doing the right thing or if it might be construed as interfering.

"Took," I said, "you did exactly the right thing. I'm indebted to you once more." The car in front of me managed to make a tight left turn and move off down the side street. "I'll be there in fifteen minutes," I told him, and terminated the call.

I drove to Richmond, blaming myself for this turn of events. It was I who had told Pat that Janie was going to need the support of friends while she battled her addiction, and it was I who left her in a strange house with people she had only just met that day, knowing full well she was ill. I could have let her come along. She could have found something to do while I played my silly mind games with Zendell. What an insensitive clod I had been.

I had to stop, once, to use the directory, being unfamiliar with this section of town, but I got there in good time.

Driving along Clara Street I spotted the telephone booth Took must have used to call me, and I counted down the numbers of the rundown council houses to fifty-two, and parked across the street from it. It looked like all the rest, except that there were more cars parked near it than the others --- some of the local junkies over for a Friday night session, I guessed.

The street was deserted and the whole neighbourhood very still as I locked the car and started towards the house. The sound of two small, staccato explosions broke the silence, followed immediately by screams. The door of number fifty two swung open and a third shot sounded.

I tried to push against the flow of panicky guests all attempting to escape through the door at the same time. I had to drag the first couple out and wait for agonizing seconds before I could enter.

The first thing I saw as I entered were two bodies sprawled and motionless on the living room floor. One of them was Took. There were three others in the room, frightened bystanders, so I rushed on through. Entering the kitchen I caught sight of a man with a gun exiting through the back door. I charged after him and caught him on the back steps with a flying kick, striking him between the shoulder blades. The pistol flew from his grip as he pitched forwards into the yard, and I was on him immediately to deliver the hard edge of my hand below his right ear.

"Where's Janie?" I called back into the house. I called again but there was no reply. I checked the yard and found no sign. Thinking she might be down behind the furniture somewhere inside I went back into the house and searched each room. The only thing I found was her new silver jacket thrown over the back of a lounge chair, and her bag. I put both articles by the door to collect on the way out.

Took struggled to his hands and knees in an effort to stand, and I helped him to the couch.

"Took, where is she?"

There was a gash on the side of his head and blood flowing down his collar. "Not here? . . .don't know." He didn't sound too good.

"Get me a damp towel. A clean one," I snapped at a girl with long, blond hair. "Whose place is this?"

"Mine," she answered, moving hesitantly towards the kitchen.

When she returned with the towel I folded it and applied it to Took's wound and placed his hand over it. "Hold it firm, buddy. It'll staunch the bleeding."

To the blond girl, I said, "Did Janie get away? What happened?"

Her eyes were still wide with shock. She tried to utter something but it stayed trapped in her throat.

I checked out the other guy, who lay motionless on the floor. He was dead, a bullet wound in the middle of his chest.

Took leaned back in the couch. "There was a knock at the door. They barged in and looked everyone over. Then went for Janie. Everyone was zonked out on that angel wings stuff. Janie too, but she recognized them, I think. I went for one of them but the other must have clobbered me with something. That's as much as I can tell you, I'm afraid. I was too slow, Alex. I'm sorry."

The owner had gotten herself together by this time. She continued with the account.

"Janie pulled a gun from her bag and shot the one who hit your friend. That's him on the floor," she said without looking at the body. "She fired at the other one as well, then ran out the back. The other was armed, too. He shot at her, there, you can see where the bullet hit beside the door."

"Then she's not hurt. Only three shots" I remarked, more for my own benefit than anyone else's.

They would be Zendell's men, sure enough. There was no need to interrogate the one in the yard. And I didn't have to guess at the circumstances surrounding this event.

"Who else used the phone booth tonight? Took, did you notice?"

The owner looked over to the other two people who occupied the room with us, whom I had ignored until now. A chap with shoulder-length brown hair and goatee beard, and his girlfriend, an attractive brunette with a guilty look on her face.

"How much is the bounty?" I snarled accusingly. What are they offering? Money? Drugs?"

"You didn't!" gasped the owner. She stared at them in disbelief.

"Con? Francine?"

"How much, Con?" I got up from crouching beside Took, glowering. "Don't keep me waiting," I warned.

Con cowered against the wall as I approached. "I never knew this would happen," he blurted out.

I kept coming at him.

"Five grams," he bleated.

"She's our friend, you bastard," gasped the outraged owner, and she flew at him from across the room, assailing him with a flurry of slashing nails and open-handed blows.

His girlfriend, Francine, called out, "I made the call. Leave him alone.". . . and the thrashing ceased.

"I'll leave you lot to sort it out then," I said, picking up Janie's belongings and moving to assist Took to the car. They would have a lot of explaining to do when the police arrived.

I figured Janie wouldn't be too far away so I drove slowly around the area in the hope that she might recognize the car and come out of hiding, if hiding was what she was doing. She may have been lucky enough to hail a passing motorist and get a lift out of the area. Still, I had to make a search.

Took was recovering from his bump on the head. He was a bit dazed, but otherwise okay. I owed him. Most of all, an explanation.

"She was a loose end in a murder committed by some of Zendell's men," I replied to his question. "She was there when it happened. Janie can finger them, so Zendell put the word out on the street. A five gram reward for any junkie who can report Janie's whereabouts. By the way, check the glove compartment and tell me if there's a .45 automatic in there."

He opened it. "Nope, not here."

"We know where she got the gun, then. Borrowed it when she came to the car to get her money. At least she had the sense to do that much. It saved her life."

We spent forty minutes scouring the area, and had just decided to give it away --- thinking she must have headed back to Pat's place --- when a car drew up alongside us and sounded its horn. We both looked across to see a uniformed copper behind the wheel of an unmarked car, and a plain clothes cop in the passenger seat, waving for us to pull over.

"I don't believe this," I said to Took. "We'll have to try and brass it out."

I pulled over to the curb and they pulled in behind. The driver climbed out while, I supposed, his pal made a radio check on the licence plates. Had the owner of the purloined plates noticed the swap and reported it? My palms were beginning to sweat.

The cop came up and tapped on my window with his torch.

"Good evening, officer," I said, winding down the glass. "Did I do something wrong?"

I glanced in the rear-view mirror when the interior light in the police car winked on, catching my eye. It was quickly turned off again, but not before I noticed the two passengers in the rear seat, an attractive brunette and a young fellow with a goatee beard.

The cop beside me shone his torch through my window at Took. The side of his face was smeared with blood.

I had the car in gear, clutch rising, accelerator flat down and the ignition key twisted right around in a blink of an eye, and she caught immediately, bless her. The cop nearly lost his toes, barely managing to throw himself clear in time.

"Nice bluff," Took commented as we roared away.

I drove like a madman for the first couple of minutes, then settled down to a less noticeable pace along some busy roads, headed for the nearest stretch of coastline.

It was sheer luck we didn't pick up another police patrol. The boys we left behind didn't stand much chance against the superior performance of the Interceptor, but the police radio was sure to be abuzz with incriminating details.

We had to dump the car --- a car Jim had rented for me under his own name --- because it was now connected to a killing.

When we got to the coast I found a dirt track which eventually led us down onto the beach. We drove along the damp sand for a while before pulling up under a section of cliff at the water's edge. I pocketed the keys and my phone, then hot-wired the car while Took retrieved my bag of implements and Janie's bag and coat. We punched a couple of holes in the fuel tank, collecting some of the petrol to splash over the interior.

"Okay, let's do it," I said miserably. "You got a light?"

"I don't smoke, Alex. Why would I have a light?"

We had to arc a battery terminal onto a petrol-soaked rag to get it going, and before too long she was well ablaze. I sent up a quick prayer to *Grunt*, god of high performance automobiles, and we set about making ourselves scarce.

In darkness we had to wade knee deep through the water to round the point which had prevented us from driving any further. Then after clambering over slippery, algae covered rocks we made it to a sandy beach on the other side. We agreed to put a couple of miles between us and the car before leaving the beach, and trudged along at the foot of a line of dunes, south, in the direction of Semaphore.

Took quizzed me continually as we walked under the blazing stars, until he knew almost as much about the situation as I did.

"So the money isn't your primary concern?"

"Not any more it isn't," I replied. "Guido is up to more than his usual brand of villainy, here. I don't know what it is, exactly, but with what Doctor Mainwaring was able to tell me, it smells bad."

Took thought for a while, then said: "I would have thought the natural thing to do with all this is to take what you have to the Feds, or have I missed something?"

"You haven't missed anything, Took, but there *is* something I haven't mentioned. I think Guido is dealing arms for the Government. Arms produced in Government factories and sold on the international black market."

"But how can that be? Ceasing the overseas arms trade was one of the major policies on which this government was elected."

"That's right, but it still goes on, only it's done by more clandestine means these days. Even international arms trade agreements don't count for much. I was in Uganda several years ago, ordered to take a unit across the Tanganyikan border to find a downed C-5A transport en route to Entebbe. My orders were strictly defined: recover a certain brief-case and get out undetected. The case would be sealed, they told me, and if it wasn't sealed when I returned with it, there would be hell to pay. There was no mention of survivors, and unfortunately there were none, but I did find the brief-case amongst the wreckage. It had been ripped open in the crash, and what I saw of the documents as I gathered them up showed that the cargo of small arms, rocket launchers, grenades and anti-personnel mines were bound for Libya, via Entebbe. The weapons were devoid of manufacturers brand, but the documents showed they were produced here, in Australia. Payment was to be made in gold bullion."

Took whistled through his teeth. "I remember all that shit going on over there. The United Nations condemned the hostile activities, and *our* Government made a big show about supporting the embargoes. And yet we were shipping arms to Libya?"

"It goes on all the time. Sometimes it's the Government agencies who deceive the Government, sometimes it's the Government who deceives the people. Guido seems to have found himself a lucrative position in the scheme of things, if my suspicions are correct"

Took put his hand to his head.

"You okay?" I asked.

"Throbbing a bit."

"Okay, let's take a break," I suggested, and we sat at the base of a dune to allow his head settle.

After listening to the sounds of the breakers for a time, Took said, "So you reckon he can't be touched through legal avenues?"

"As soon as I made any attempt in that direction, alarm bells would begin to ring in the secret corridors of power. I don't have a big enough can-opener for that can of worms. It wouldn't matter who I took my information to. I'm *persona non grata* in this country. Too easily discredited, and I don't have any solid proof to back all this up with in any case."

"Persona non grata, why?"

"Because I deserted the Australian army after we moved into Cambodia. Later I was fighting in South America alongside so-called rebels, against a puppet government installed by Uncle Sam. I was later identified and targeted by U.S. intelligence and had to flee, turning up in Africa six months later to sign on as a mercenary when they were recruiting over there. Since arriving back here I've not been able to work, open a bank account or even hold a driver's licence. I have to live completely outside the system.

"Guido knows all this, too. That's why he blatantly brags to me about his shifty enterprises. Especially the arms dealing, which he claims is how he financed Villa Vulgar. I can't harm him without putting my own head in the noose, and besides that, if he is sanctioned by the Government to covertly trade arms for them, then his other sideline, the drug trade, is also being allowed to continue as concession for services rendered."

Took rubbed his head. "My head is spinning, and it's got nothing to do with this lump on my head. I had no idea of the depth of corruption. It's mind-boggling."

"It takes a little getting used to," I agreed. "It's not an easy thing to come to terms with, knowing it's all just a crummy facade. Unfortunately the average Australian voter has very little idea of what this Government is up to, or what it's capable of doing. If the poor bloody taxpayer only knew where the money was going. . ."

Ten

It was one o'clock in the morning when the cab dropped us off at Jim and Pat's house. There were still a couple of lights on inside, and when we got to the door I discovered a note which Jim had pinned there, inviting us to come straight in if no one was up.

I checked the spare room to see if Janie had made it back, but it was empty. I deposited her things on the bed and carried my toolbag out to the bus where I shoved them beneath the front passenger seat, wondering if I would have occasion to use them, then went back inside.

While Took and I sat quietly waiting for the kettle to boil, Jim appeared in the doorway. "You guys look beat," he observed.

"Maybe you'd prefer a Scotch instead of coffee?"

Neither of us argued as he went to fetch the bottle.

We filled him in on the recent turn of events while we sat around the table sipping our drinks. I handed him the keys to the Interceptor, apologising profusely and explained that if he reported it stolen, there shouldn't be too much of a fuss. I also gave him the money to cover a couple of days hire fee, which he accepted only after I told him it would make me feel better if he took it.

We were a sorry-looking bunch, sitting there passing the bottle around, but there was nothing to do but wait - wait until Janie turned up, the telephone rang, or the sun came up.

By three o'clock, still, nothing had happened. Jim and Took correctly reasoned that a few hours sleep was the best course of action, and although I agreed I knew it would be futile for me to even try.

Jim had his business to attend to in the morning, so I convinced him to go on back to bed. Took, on the other hand, pointed out that he had no such responsibility, and he remained at the table with me.

"She must have found somewhere to hole up," he said, after watching me brood for ten minutes. "Another friend's place, perhaps."

"Or my motel room, or maybe even your place," I added, preferring any course of action rather than none at all.

"It beats the hell out of waiting," he said rising from his chair.

"We'll take the bus."

The air was breathless still and warm as we rumbled along under the yellow illumination of the highway lights, Took hunched in the driver's seat with his forearms resting on the steering wheel, guiding the bus smoothly through the suburbs, occasionally looking over to me from under those woolly locks, to make an optimistic remark about finding Janie.

In less than fifteen minutes we pulled up outside the motel. We disembarked and walked towards my room, searching in the shadows of bushes and alcoves, but there was no sign.

Took made a closer search as I inserted my key into the lock and went inside. The service maid had been in to make the bed and clean up, and there were some breakfast order forms on the coffee table which hadn't been there before we left yesterday morning, but that was all.

I left the key in the door and a note for Janie, in case she turned up later, and started back to the street to join Took who waited beside the door of the bus.

As a last-minute measure I rang the night-bell. The proprietor looked disgruntled as he came to the door in his pyjamas and dressing-gown. He was even less impressed when he realised he didn't have a new customer, but he did confirm that Janie had not been around asking for a spare key to my room.

Took noticed my ill disposition and said nothing as he climbed behind the wheel and got us under way, bound for the old industrial area where his squat was situated. I also remained silent, merely staring through the windscreen at the white lines as they streamed towards us like tracers, to pass beneath the wheels as we rolled through the warm, summer night, all the while thinking of Janie and what shape she might be in.

I remembered how she looked, pinned under Zendell's goon at the Old Coach, frightened but defiant. I recalled the discussion we had in my motel room the next morning, and how pleased she was with the new clothes she bought at the shopping mall, and how she looked in them. I remembered her pout, how nervous she was in Mainwaring's surgery while we arranged for her treatment at the clinic, but she had gone through with it. It must have taken some guts to make that first step. Why hadn't someone taken the time to help her out before this? Such a terrible thing, for someone like her to be fading away in the grip of drug addiction, when her whole life still lay before her.

And how many others were there, just like her, whose lives were being usurped, daily, by this virulent market?

I looked up and recognised the grey, dust-covered streets and buildings which indicated we were nearing our destination, the second and last possibility of finding Janie tonight. Took was the first of either of us to speak on this leg of the search.

"If she isn't here, I guess she'll lay low until morning somewhere. It'll be safer for her to move when there's more people around."

He drove the bus up onto his front yards and left the headlights burning so we could see our way up the steps to the verandah and the front door. The glaring lights cast our black shadows down the hallway in front of us as he pushed open the door.

"Hang on a sec and I'll get some lights working," he said.

He disappeared into the darkness and I heard him make his way to the kitchen. The next thing I heard was the rattling sound you get when trying to start a motor with a piece of cord wrapped around a pulley. On the third attempt the motor roared to life, and soon afterwards Took switched on the kitchen light. When he shut the back door, the noise was reduced to a low drone.

"Flick on a couple of lights," he called.

I flicked all the switches I could find, and soon every room in the house was lit up.

"I'll just go turn off the bus," he said. Then, from the end of the hallway: "There's a couple of beers left in the icebox."

When we had checked the house and found no sign of Janie having been there, we opened the cans I had placed on the table and quenched the thirst Jim's Scotch had given us. Then sat there, looking at one another.

"Where did you get them crazy eyes from, anyway?" I asked for the lack of anything better to say at three-fifty on a Saturday morning.

"*Hiterochromic,* is what it's called. An odd gene somewhere. My father was a Danish sailor, and my mother an Aboriginal tourist guide in the West.

The generator continued to drone in the back yard as we again fell silent, searching for ideas.

I said: "Took, this is driving me crazy."

"Yeah, me too. There must be *something* we can do."

My mood was dark and getting darker. I kept telling myself that Janie could take care of herself, but now the cops were after her as well as Zendell.... *Zendell*, that snake in a suit, I thought, and realised that anger was as much a part of my present malaise as my concern for Janie.

"There is," I said, looking up from my can of beer.

"Is what?"

"Something we can do. We can give Zendell something to think about. Do you know where his car yard is?"

"I sure do," said Took, catching on immediately.

Zendell Motors, as upon our arrival I learned its name to be, covered about a two-acre block, two kilometres east of the centre of the city. It lent itself well to the kind of devastation I had in mind, in that it was sufficiently isolated so that fire would not spread to adjacent properties. Had I any doubts about this I may have had to abandon this particular course of action, or at least modify it appreciably.

I found Took's readiness to assist me in this venture surprising, because he didn't have the same degree of involvement as I did. I was concerned he might consider this a mindless act, but he explained to me his belief in karma, to *his* mind a force transcendent to the criminal law which we were about to run foul of, and he was content to be "an agent of karma", as he put it, if by these means Zendell was to receive a measure of cosmic justice.

I substituted his word *karma* for my word, *come-uppance*, and found that we were in complete agreement. Thus we two cosmic commandos, we agents of karma (or whatever) set about our task.

It was a quick and easy exercise, not to mention satisfying, as we walked along the back two rows of cars, pouring methanol from ten-litre drums we had purchased from an all-night garage on the way over, making sure to cover the tyres as we went. When we came to the showroom, I noticed with delight that movementdetectors were the only form of security within. Movement detectors are aimed at specific areas and leave room for undetectable movement outside their field of vision.

In this knowledge I shattered one of the small ventilation windows situated at floor level, and poured the remainder of the fuel onto the showroom floor, where it spread under the nearest vehicle.

I had come prepared with matches, this time, and after retracing our steps out to the pavement, I ignited the fuel.

Methanol produces an almost invisible flame, and under the surrounding floodlights of the car yard, this was the case. I had to look closely to determine that it was in fact burning.

The rubber tyres and paintwork would be alight before there was any detectable evidence of fire, and by that time we were away, driving to our next target.

It was right on five o'clock and there was the pale glow of impending dawn high in the eastern sky as we entered the street which ran behind Swank's Night Club. Took guided the bus up to the curb and killed the motor as I checked that I had a full range of tools in my bag.

Closing time for the club was five a.m., so we waited there for forty minutes to allow time for tardy patrons and staff to leave the building. I figured after that time the cleaners and whatever security people Zendell hired to stay on would be the only ones left inside.

I was pretty sure Zendell wasn't in there; he would have been informed of the terrible blaze at his car yard by now, and was probably standing, watching the fire brigade pour thousands of litres of water over his charred stock. I mentioned this illusion to Took and we amused ourselves by adding to it with whatever humorous scenarios we could conjure in the growing light.

By the time I stepped out into the warm air, I was once again feeling in high spirits and ready for the job at hand. The rear door opened at my second attempt to raise some attention, and I popped a needle into the grey-uniformed figure which appeared in the opened doorway. Stepping over the guard, I found myself in the kitchen. There was no sign of anyone else about - so far so good. The guard's uniform and the ring of keys attached to his belt were a bonus, I decided, so I dragged him off to the pantry and, moments later, emerged looking as nondescript as anyone else dressed in a grey uniform, cap and black shoes.

A whistling kettle began to shriek. Turning it off I discovered what the guard had been doing before I had disturbed him by knocking at the door... pilfering the pantry. A chicken sandwich lay on a plate beside the kettle.

I helped myself to half and strolled out through a set of swinging doors to enter the discotheque. It just looked like a scruffy room, now that all the dazzle had been turned off and the people had gone home. As I entered the foyer I saw that the lift was on its way down, and I had to hurry up the stairs to evade whoever it was coming down.

I climbed to the Blue Room and, passing through, said good morning to the woman mopping the floor behind the bar. On the third level I passed between the gambling tables and headed on up to the mezzanine deck to look for Zendell's office.

The third door along offered itself as the obvious choice, with elegant gold lettering on the heavy oak door pronouncing: Vincent Zendell, Manager. A quick inspection of the keys I had poached told me that Zendell did not entrust the sleeping watchman with the keys to his office, and for the next half a minute I had to stand outside the door and coax the locks with the set of *Lock Pix* from my bag. Upon first glance into the room I was struck by the size and sheer opulence of it. The furniture was undoubtedly authentic seventeenth century Louis XIV, while the paintings on the walls reflected scenes from the same era. That a crud like Zendell should own such beautiful antiques as these gave me cause to wonder.

I searched under rugs and behind pictures for five minutes, without finding what I was looking for; then, remembering the penchant for secret panels and compartments in the era of Louis XIV, I began again, this time carefully inspecting the larger pieces of furniture.

In the secretaire I discovered a section which rocked slightly as I ran my fingers along the underside of the desk. With a squeeze it depressed, and a blank panel above a row of pigeon-holes popped forward to reveal a secret compartment. Within this compartment I found a leather-bound diary, embossed with delicate silver scrollwork, and flicking through the pages I saw that they were full of personal entries, written by a skilled hand. I pocketed the diary and turned my attention to the wood-panelled walls and the ornate architraves around the doors connecting to a bathroom on the one side, and an adjoining office on the other.

My eyes zeroed in on finger marks well above the light switch at the bathroom entrance, and I chuckled to myself at the obvious blunder on Zendell's part, to leave behind this trace.

The suspect piece of architrave would not respond to my pulling at it, but a firm bump with the heel of my hand produced the desired effect. A section swung out to reveal a set of digital combination keys. I tore the faceplate away using a screwdriver - *these things are child's play* - and pulled out the keyboard, tearing the trailing wires from their plug, and tossed it on the floor. When I closed the circuit within the plug, using nothing more sophisticated than a pair of paper-clips, a large section of the teak panelling slid along to reveal the safe I had been looking for allalong - and I couldn't believe my luck. It was a Davenport, series, with the double combination locks: Expensive and impressivelooking, but for someone who had been doing this sort of thing on a regular basis for as long as I had, it was about as challenging as opening a tin of sardines.

Inside of ten minutes I had drilled two holes, eight inches and ten inches from the left-hand edges, and twenty and one quarter inches from the base. It was then just a matter of inserting a length of steel rod into each of the holes and giving them a good thump with a heavy hammer, which bent the drop-pins out and away from the drawbar mechanism. Accuracy and touch were the main ingredients here, and I knew by the feel and the amount of give behind the rods as I struck them, that I was right on the money. I snapped back the handle and swung open the safe door.

The bound stacks of hundred-dollar bills were the first to go in my bag. The piles of documents held no interest for me, but out of curiosity I did bag the pair of ledgers I discovered sitting on the top shelf.

In one of the two drawers at the bottom of the safe, I found diamond and sapphire jewellery in the form of earings, necklace, rings and brooch; but jewellery is always a problem to get rid of: too easy to trace, unless you remove the stones from their settings. But you never get a good price for them that way, and I never liked to spoil a thing of beauty, so I left them where they were.

In the second drawer was a 9mm Luger with silencer in a black velvet-lined box. This I took, mainly because I didn't consider Vincent Zendell to be a fit character to be in possession of a firearm. I closed the lid and placed it in my bag, tossed the tools in on top and departed the scene.

On the way down to the kitchen to retrieve my clothes, I narrowly avoided a confrontation with a security guard on the stairs, but I heard him trudging up to the cassino as I lightfooted it down from the mezzanine, and managed to hide myself behind a craps table before he reached the top of the stairs. I waited there until he passed by, and snuck out while his back was turned.

It was full daylight when I emerged from the building, and it was already several degrees warmer. It took my tired eyes a while to adjust to the glare, and I suddenly felt the fatigue of a very long day sweep over me.

Took had already nodded off... asleep over the wheel. I had to bang on the door to wake him before I could get in.

"Okay, let's go," I said, climbing aboard.

"How did it go?"

"It went very well," I answered, falling into the seat. "Would you mind driving slowly past the front of the club as we go, please, Took?"

He started the motor, engaged first gear. "Why's that?"

By this time I had the Luger on my lap and was busy screwing the silencer to the end of the barrel.

"What you going to do?" he asked concernedly, as I checked the clip and primed the firing mechanism.

"You'll see."

Took did as I requested, but he didn't seem too comfortable having me sit there opposite him with that evil-looking thing in my hand.

As we rolled along Pier Street to came level with Zendell's club, I aimed carefully out of my side window and fired a volley of three shots.

There was only a *phtt phtt phtt* as the hornets left the muzzle, closely followed by the snapping sound of glass tubes, leaving the Swank's Night Club sign to flash red, early on this Saturday morning, minus the S.

"Took," I said, "I've wanted to do that since I first laid eyes on the place."

Eleven

The burning of a few cars and the larceny of a couple of odds and ends was by no means a major blow to the bad guys, but it sure did a lot to boost flagging morale, and I just knew that between the diary and the ledgers I'd have something with which to bring pressure to bear against Zendell.

Jim was already up and preparing to leave for work when Took and I arrived.

"I've only got a couple of minutes before I have to go," he said as we entered through the kitchen door. "So tell me what you've been up to all morning, apart, that is, from burning car yards."

Took and I looked askance at one another and turned back to Jim.

"It was on the seven o'clock news," he explained, pointing to the transistor radio on the table.

"Much damage?" I asked hopefully.

"A regular inferno, from what I heard."

"The secret agents of karma strike dread into the hearts of evildoers everywhere. . . eh, Took?" I said, slapping him on the back.

I lifted my bag to the table and began stacking the money beside it. Six neatly bound wads of ten thousand per wad. I slid one over to Jim.

"Compliments of Vincent Zendell. Take the day off."

"Can't," he replied earnestly, staring at the loot. "I have customers to look after."

"Yes, of course, but it's yours anyway. Restitution for the trouble I've caused you. Did you report the car stolen yet?"

"Yeah. I've got to go down to the station later and do the paperwork."

"Okay. Good. What time do you knock off today?"

"Midday or so. I'll see you guys when I get back. Took, there are some blankets in the hallway cupboard. Use the couch to sleep on.

Alex, you take the spare room."

I had to remind him to pick up his money before he left, and he stood, wondering what to do with it for a moment before pushing it into his pocket and departing.

I slid two of the bundles across to Took, saying, "And that's for your assistance."

Took was astonished. "Are you kidding? That's twenty grand!"

"So? Take your holiday to South-East Asia. There are no redundancies with this kind of work. I can always get more."

He only looked at it, so I tried again.

"You were the wheel man, the getaway driver, an accomplice. You were taking just as big a risk as me."

"That's true," he said, looking at me serious-like, and he placed his hand on the wad to signify acceptance.

I offered my hand to him across the table. "And by the way, thanks for everything you did last night."

Sleep came quickly, and it came with disturbing images. I stood at the centre of Pier Street. It was night-time, the moon was full and shining directly overhead, drenching everything in a milk-white radiance and steeping every doorway, window and recess in pitchblack shadows. The neighbourhood was utterly deserted.

There came a sudden sensation of expectancy as a light breeze stirred along the street, and from somewhere beyond the shadows I heard the small, clear sound of wind chimes lightly tinkling, and fainter still, the strains of strange, medieval music produced by flute, mandolin and drum.

Along the street moved a macabre procession advancing slowly towards me. Leading it, the neon dancer.

The dancer twirled and flickered red, green, white, as the silent ranks of human forms, bereft of life, their skins a beep blue and their eyes unseeing, followed, as if impelled by some ungodly compulsion.

I kept alongside the column of blue cadavers screaming for them to stop, but they did not hear and I could not make them hear, no matter how hard I tried.

Mindlessly they continued, heedless to my urgent cries, on and on to the end of the street, then to swarm along the pier which jutted out into the bay, and I knew that it was hopeless to try and stop them.

At the end of the pier the neon dancer moved out above the surface of the water, continuing to dance in flickering spasms. Like mesmerized things they flocked and fell, tumbling by the score into the ocean. . . by the hundreds, by the thousand, disappearing without a whimper beneath the ripples.

The neon dancer ceased its dance of death, then flared a brilliant white and assumed a supernatural appearance, an angel with enormous wings, and talons emerged from its toes, a quasi-human face with wild, rolling eyes and lashing tongue. It writhed and clutched at itself in ecstatic paroxysms of malign pleasure. Finally unable to contain these massive surges of whatever unwholesome energies coursed within, it shrieked, then exploded out of existence in a shower of golden sparks.

The sparks cleared to give way to dense, tropical jungle and I know I'm back in Cambodia.

I'm with my unit, pushing through thick undergrowth. The situation is tense, we are following the enemy and they're very close. Each step is slow, deliberate and silent. All senses are at optimum. Nerves are stretched taut.

I lead the unit to the edge of a small clearing where the canopy overhead is thin enough to allow shafts of sunlight to penetrate to the jungle floor. The usual animal noises of the surrounding area have ceased and I give the signal to the others to hunker down and maintain position. I take one slow step forwards to improve my field of vision. As my weight is transferred to that foot, I feel the pressure plate of a jumping-jack mine depress, and I hear the telltale click which tells me I cannot remove my boot without being shredded by flying metal.

There is now a heightened sense of reality, every leaf, every blade of grass is perceived with such intensity that I can see the life process at work within them. The sound of a shiny, black beetle climbing the trunk of a tree is heard with absolute clarity, even the sound of sap rising within the tree is not lost to me.

Hour upon hour I stand there with godlike abilities of perception, experiencing life in the very air surrounding me. I know that the ache in my legs in time will turn to numbness, exhaustion will eventually overtake me and finally, I will fall and be blown into eternity.

I fight with all my strength just to remain and I count the minutes of my life which I will not give up, but which I am powerless to save.

I woke --- woke at the same moment I always do when I have this dream --- when I feel myself collapsing with exhaustion. I felt wrung out even though my watch indicated I had slept for five hours, and as I lay there quietly sorting out my thoughts, the mobile phone on the bedside table began to chirp. To my considerable surprise it was Vincent Zendell.

"Mr Jaeger?"

"Yes."

"I have thought over what you said to me last night and I have decided that we may have reason to discuss the subject further. Can you meet with me this afternoon?"

"You mean, do I want to walk into a trap this afternoon, don't you? Well I suppose I can't blame you for trying, but you'll have to do better than that. Oh, by the way, if any harm comes to the girl I wouldn't want to be in your shoes. Be seeing you, *arsehole*."

He hung up without reply, and I chuckled to myself as I bundled up my clothes and made for the bathroom.

Pat, Jim and Took were seated around the dining-room table when I emerged some twenty minutes later, showered, shaved and somewhat refreshed. On the table before them were the ledgers and diary I had purloined from Zendell's office. Everyone was thoroughly engrossed in their contents as I came in to join them.

I pulled up a chair beside Pat. She looked pale, a result of the wine from the previous evening, I presumed. Jim and Took sat on the opposite side of the table pouring over the diary while Pat studied the ledgers.

"So what do we have?" I ventured.

"What you have, *here*," replied Pat, sliding the ledgers across for me to view more easily, "shows that your Mr Zendell has been dodging around a quarter of a million dollars worth of taxable capital in each of the past two years. Have a look at this for example."

She showed me identical items in both books, headed: *Plumbing Renovations.* In one book the cost was stated as four thousand six hundred dollars, and in the other it was stated as costing seven thousand dollars. She pointed out several other inconsistencies, including door takings, alcohol sales and casino profits.

"One book for himself, one for the tax man. It's about what I expected. How about the diary, chaps? Interesting? Or does young Vinnie lead a dull and uninteresting existence?"

It was Jim who answered. "He is going to be extremely upset when he discovers this missing. And Guido is going to be extremely upset with *him*, when *he* finds out. This is the most bizarre thing."

"Well, come on then, don't keep me in suspense," I said as he flicked back through the pages, not quite sure where to start.

"Zendell and Spinoza are in cahoots."

"What?" This I did not expect.

"Almost three years ago Spinoza bought Swank's night club and put Zendell in charge."

My expression must have reflected my disbelief.

"Here, take a look for yourself," Jim offered, handing the diary over to me. "There's a complete description of the meeting which took place, and the terms of agreement."

Jim named the relevant pages and what I read confirmed what he said. . . and that was only the half of it.

Zendell had stupidly recorded the proceedings of a private meeting he had with Guido after being telephoned and invited out to Villa Vulgar. What transpired was that Guido had given Zendell ownership of Swank's, but only after he had agreed to be a player in a contemptible game of Guido's devising.

The club was offered to Zendell to augment his income, taking it to a level where he could competitively rival Guido in a ruthless campaign to gain control of as many lucrative businesses as possible, lawful businesses already operating in the city of Monarto, and to oppose him, also, in the areas of prostitution, drug trafficking, extortion, loan sharking and the like.

Zendell was already quite well established in the rackets and so, with the club added to his means, a ceiling of five million was put on both players as starting money. The duration of the game was five years, and whoever had the most in cash and assets over and above what each had begun the game with would be declared the winner.

As I read on there was mention of only one primary condition: that neither player extend hostilities to the other's person or place of residence. All other means, it appeared, were fair game.

I had read enough. I looked to each of my companions in turn. To Pat, I said, "You know what's in here?"

"A real life game of Monopoly," she said, giving voice to my exact same thoughts. "It explains the dramatic rise in crime over the same period."

"And why Guido used me like a pawn against Zendell."

"The guy is a sociopath, maybe a psychopath," Took observed.

"Most probably a psychopath," I agreed, "but certainly an evil little shit who is bored with his power and wealth and has to play perverse games to get his kicks."

A dreadful realization struck me. "Jim, you and Pat are going to have to pack a couple of suitcases and leave."

They both looked at me as if I had a skunk on my head.

"I haven't told you about the meeting I had with Zendell last night. That's where I went after our little jaunt in the country. To Swank's, to try and enlist Zendell's help against Guido. I thought they were enemies," I added when they continued to look at me funny. "It didn't go so good, the reasons for that are glaringly obvious now. But I've let the cat out of the bag. By now Zendell will have been in contact with Guido to tell him I've worked out how he's been trying to manipulate me, and that I've twigged to their twisted game of Monopoly."

Pat said it for me: "So now you have Guido Spinoza on your case."

"Ergo, it's probably just a matter of time before he's on *your* case, too," I said, stating the other half of the equation. "If he can get to me through you, he won't think twice about it. I'm sorry, I've screwed things up pretty bad."

"You weren't to know they were in league," said Jim, in an attempt to ease my sense of guilt. But what the hell else could he say?

Took, who had been sitting quietly with a thoughtful look on his face, broke his silence.

"What makes you think Zendell has balls enough to admit to Guido that he kept a diary containing such incriminating stuff? Wouldn't it be smarter for him to say nothing and try to get the diary back himself, before Guido finds out?"

"That's true, Took, but can we risk it? If Zendell goes it alone he may not be able to connect Jim and me, but if Guido gets involved he'll tear the city apart. Anyone he even suspects of having taken a look at this stuff is in real danger. And come to think of it, Zendell may not have the balls *not* to tell Guido."

I watched Jim while he considered his position. Being his father's son, I knew he wouldn't much like the idea of hightailing it, but his first priority had to be Pat's safety.

"It's a murderous game," I said, trying to influence his decision.

"I've already had a call from Zendell today. He tried to sucker me into a trap. It's not safe around here any more, Jim." *And I was the one who made it that way,* I thought to myself.

"Okay," he said. "I'll find somewhere safe for Pat, then I-"
"Don't even think about coming back," I cut in, pre-empting his next words. "You and Pat expressed a desire to pay me back for helping out over the years. This is it, the way for you to square up, the only thing I will ever ask you to do. And believe me, Jim, I know how difficult it is for you. Stay away until this is over. I mean it."

Pat put her hand over the clenched fist I didn't realise I had made.

"We don't blame you for this, so don't blame yourself. There's no need for you to risk your life on our account. Jim and I have saved hard over the years. We've often thought of going over West to start a family away from this terrible place. So there isn't any need for anyone to get hurt."

That had to be the most magnanimous gesture of friendship I had ever had the honour of receiving, but it only served to strengthen my resolve.

"Thank-you Pat. I appreciate what you're saving. It doesn't seem right for people like you to have to move because of cruds like these. If anyone will be moving it'll be them. Preferably to a prison cell where they can discuss, for the next twenty years, where they went wrong."

Took and I drove them to the airport in the bus. It was well within Guido's capability to have police patrols scouring the metropolis in search of their car. If it was found at the airport, he would soon have his people checking passenger lists and questioning airline personnel, and the search would then spread interstate.

We said good-bye out front of the passenger terminal where they bought tickets under assumed names to a destination known only by themselves. Once they arrived and found somewhere to stay Jim would use a telephone answering service to contact me, one at which I could leave a messages should the occasion arise, telling them to come home.

As Took and I drove away from the airport, I said, "This might be a good time of year for you to take that Asian holiday you've been thinking about."

"Monsoons," he replied laconically.

"What do you mean, monsoons?"

"The wet season. Wrong time of year to be heading over there. I don't like the humidity. . . or mosquitoes. Little blighters carry malaria. I'd have to get shots and everything. Nope. I reckon I don't have anything on at present, so I think I'll just hang out with you, if you don't mind."

"Look, you've been a great help, Took, but you don't need to get involved any further. It's not going to be a weekend adventure, you know. Things could get a little hairy."

"It's not a one man job, Alex. Any fool can see that. You might be good," he said, smiling, " but you ain't that good. Besides, if I bailed out now I'd always be wondering."

His last point was a valid one, I conceded. It was one thing for a man to take up a challenge and risk failure, but another thing entirely to walk away from it. I had to give him credit. He was a game one.

I sure was pleased he had chosen to stick around.

"Everything on board?" I asked.

"Everything," he confirmed.

"Then if it's okay with you, we ought to be safe enough bunking at your squat." I pulled out the diary and ledgers from the bag beneath my seat. "But let's find a copying machine first. I think it would be an advantage if Guido was copping some heat from several directions at the same time, don't you?" I had another surge of inspiration and reached for the phone. Before I began punching numbers I gave Took one last chance.

"I'm about to declare war, buddy. You sure you want in?" His only reply was an enigmatic smile. "My thoughts, exactly," I said, and punched Guido's number. It rang twice before the unmistakable sound of Guido's peevish voice answered. I took a breath and delivered my declaration.

"Listen you rat-faced little weasel, you don't intimidate me and you sure as hell don't try and use me like a pawn in one of your demented power games and expect to get away with it. You picked the wrong man, Guido. I'm going to do everyone a favour and kick your arse back under whatever rock you crawled out from!" I waited for a reply.

"That's you, Alex?"

"It is."

"You should have come to work for me when you had the chance. You can't win this. Give it up."

"Suck eggs. You're worried, Guido, and you have good reason to be."

I terminated the call and looked over to Took who seemed amused by my brief invective, saying to him soberly, "You realise, don't you, that we both ought to be certified insane?"

"What makes you think I haven't been?" came his ambiguous reply.

At the public library I made three photo copies of both ledgers, page by page, and likewise with the diary. We then found a secluded corner where Took helped me to compose a letter which we would send, along with the evidence, to the Federal Tax Office, the Federal and the State Attorneys General's Offices, and lastly, Monarto's *Daily News*. To each recipient I named the possessors of the other two copies and the original items. The originals went to the newspaper in case they had a problem with mere copies. I wanted Guido exposed publicly. They were also warned that they may be required to hand over the original articles when the other parties received notice of where they could be found. Whoever sanctioned and protected Guido, in whatever department or agency of the Government they lurked, they were going to be hard pressed to keep a lid on this.

Because it was Saturday I figured it would be at least Tuesday before this action would begin to have any effect. The newspaper would be the first, and later in the week there would be rumblings from on high. It would be interesting, indeed, to see the consequences of that.

Guido's immediate concern would be to disassociate himself as much as possible from Zendell, and to cover up or remove all evidence of his bent game. Well, okay, there wasn't much I could do about that. I had set the wheels in motion and then it would be up to the judicial system to build a suitably damning case against him; and I couldn't even be sure he wouldn't find a way to wriggle out of that. It could, however, give him plenty to think about in the meantime.

I tried to imagine Guido's view of the situation as Took drove us across town. He would be sitting up there in his villa on the hill, behind his five metre high wall, knowing that I was down here in the city somewhere, plotting his ruination. I had to suppose he already knew about the ledgers and diary, but he didn't have the faintest idea of my whereabouts or what I was plotting, and how could he? I had nothing definite in mind myself. He had to be feeling very vulnerable indeed.

What could he do about me? With Pat and Jim safely out of harm's reach there was no other way for him to get at me indirectly. Apart from sending his minions out onto the streets to search for me, there wasn't much he could do. I liked that. Let him sweat. With all his high placed connections and any number of two bit hoods jumping through hoops at his say so, however much money and influence he thought he had, he was powerless to stop a free agent like myself from causing him a lot of grief. . . provided, of course, I continued to avoid detection.

Twelve

We both agreed that until we collected the tapes from Villa Vulgar we were short on useful information to work with. However, in view of the meagre amount of time they had been in place we had to allow a while longer for Guido to make and take calls. Now we could renew our search for Janie.

We began by doubling back to Pat and Jim's house in case she had returned during our absence. There was no sign that she had, so I pinned a note to the door telling her to wait at Took's, and we drove out to Clara Street, Richmond, where we were careful to survey the surrounding area for coppers or goons who may have been on watch. Took parked the bus at the top of the street and I walked down to number fifty two and knocked on the door.

No sound issued from within, but after a few moments I began to get the distinct impression that someone was eyeballing me through the fish-eye lens in the door. I had the Luger stuffed down the back of my jeans and I was ready to use it, but I kept my nervous impulses in check, telling myself that it was only the owner. She was bound to be extremely cautious of knocks at the door after what had happened last night.

I heard the snap lock release and the door opened just enough to reveal part of the blond girl's face.

"It's you!" she said, surprised. Unhooking the latch she opened the door to let me enter.

"You're taking a chance coming here." She locked the door behind me and I followed her through to the lounge room. "The forensic guys were climbing all over this place until a couple of hours ago, but then two D's turned up and told them the investigation was off. They warned me to keep my mouth shut about what happened, in return, they said, they'd overlook the drugs, which was blackmail, pure and simple. They found no drugs! Can you figure that?"

I could, of course, but knowing wasn't going to do her any good if she had any further visits, especially if she had a tendency to run off at the mouth like this.

"I never did get your name. I'm Alex," I said, offering my hand.

"Heidi. Take a seat," she offered.
I sat on the edge of the sofa while she chose an adjacent chair."I was hoping you might be able to help me locate Janie."

"You *and* the pigs," she said wearily. "They questioned me for ages on that one. And, by the way, about you. But they can go screw themselves. Janie is a friend and I know you're Janie's friend. I gave them nothing."

"Thanks, I appreciate it. But can't you think of anywhere she might have gone? . . .bearing in mind that she wouldn't be likely to trust anyone after last night's effort."

"I really wouldn't have any better idea about that than you. There's a lot about Janie I don't know. Excuse me for saying so, but wouldn't she have been in touch with you by now if that's what she wanted?"

"Pertinent point," I agreed, "but it's precisely because she hasn't contacted me that I'm so worried. Janie and I have become what you might call allies, in the short time I've known her, and, as you must well realise by now, she could use a friend she can rely on at the moment. Present company accepted."

"You're not going to tell me what this is about, are you?" She held my gaze for a moment, then smiled. "Well I guess I can live with that. I suppose you have your reasons."

"It's best you don't know, Heidi, believe me."

"I believe you. I'm usually quite a good judge of people, and you strike me as being trustworthy, although I did make a mistake with those two Judases, Francine and Con. I still can't believe they sold Janie out for a measly five grams. I'm curious about that Took guy she was with last night. Who is he?"

"Janie didn't tell you?"

"Only that he was a friend. I left it at that. She wasn't very talkative and she always has been a bit secretive. As long as *I've* known her, anyway. I thought he might be her new boyfriend."

"Only a friend, as she said. He was staying with her while I attended to some business. Did you know she was trying to kick the habit?"

Heidi shrugged. "She mentioned it, I think. We all say that from time to time. I've never known anyone to kick an angel wings habit."

I looked at Heidi's eyes and recognised the same overly contracted pupils Janie had displayed after snorting the drug in my motel room. I hadn't noticed until now how pale she looked, and there was a flat, lifeless quality in her voice.

"You don't use, do you," she said, somehow tuning in on me.

"No."

"You're lucky. I wish I had never started."

"Janie bought some off you last night, didn't she?" I asked, steering the conversation back to the reason I had come here.

"Yeah. She was after enough to see her through 'till Monday, but I didn't have that much to part with. What I gave her would've only lasted the night."

"Then she's probably out looking for more?" I suggested.

"Certainly. I don't think there's any doubt about that."

"So where would she go?"

"She's been dealing for a while now, Alex. She must know of at least a dozen places to score from. It wouldn't be difficult in this town. Even though she has to be careful who she goes to now, it shouldn't take her too long to pick up something from around the traps. I'm sorry I can't be any more helpful than that. If she doesn't want to be found, it makes it very hard. I don't suppose it's worth trying her flat?"

"She wouldn't be that foolish. It's probably being watched."

She crossed to a small writing desk in the corner of the room. "I'll write down the address for you anyway. Not that she ever spent much time there. She gave it to me in case I was ever in the area, but I've never been there."

I accepted the piece of paper she handed me and stood, indicating that it was time for me to go. "Could you just check outside that there's no one watching?"

She accompanied me to the door, unfastened the latch and pulled it ajar. She looked to the right for a moment, then to the left, peering in that direction for some time. When she withdrew her head wearing a concerned expression, I began to worry.

"There's someone watching from the end of the street. He's looking straight at this house."

"You don't recognise Took?"

She made a second observation, her eyes and mouth making three perfect O's as recognition set in. "Oh, yes, it *is* him," she said with a giggle, and opened the door wide. "Good luck," she expressed as I stepped out onto the paving.

I turned and smiled. "Thank you. Take care of yourself, Heidi."

With precious little to go on we took our search to the heart of the city. This we did on Shanks's ponies, zigzag fashion across the central square mile, calling in at hotels and cafes where members of the city's subculture congregated during the afternoons.

There was nothing subtle in our method, we merely strolled into any venue which looked the slightest bit promising and, taking a side of the room each, began asking people if they had seen Janie Stuart.

The most common response to this was, "Who?" In which case, if I thought the person was a prospect, I would furnish them with as succinct a description of Janie as I could construct.

Predictably, reactions split mainly into two groups. Either they were obliging and did their best to assist, even though they were no help whatsoever, or they were suspicious, immediately becoming protective of a girl they had never met, perhaps assuming Took and myself to be a pair of plain-clothes plods with absolutely no idea of how to conduct a discreet investigation.

The result of all this was that we were getting nowhere, and getting there very slowly, but with the foot slogging and the impudent questioning of complete strangers, we continued; there was nothing else for it!

As the afternoon wore on, the atmosphere in the city became choked with a noxious, brown haze which hung in the streets, burning the eyes and lungs, without a breath of a breeze to shift the rotten stuff, and as blanketing cloud moved in from the west, the humidity rose steadily to an uncomfortable level.

We must have tried twenty establishments without a single lead, and I was sorely tempted to give the game away. I was in total accord, therefore, when Took suggested we take a break in the airconditioned saloon bar outside which we stood, wondering where to try next.

We ordered our beers and carried them to a table beside a oneway mirror window with a view of the street, happy to be off our feet and breathing cool, clean air.

There were small groups of people seated at tables around the room, quietly chatting amongst themselves, a couple of solitary drinkers, drinking port wine at the far end of the bar, and a television set mounted on the wall behind the bar, apparently talking to itself.

As I turned my attention away from the television and towards the scenery beyond the window, I chanced to glimpse a clandestine exchange between hands, beneath a table occupied by a group of young men and women. I said nothing to Took, but continued to watch as one young fellow, sporting a waistcoat and a trilby hat, left the table while the other went to the bar to purchase a fresh round of drinks for the table.

"I think we have some candidates, Took."

He followed my line of sight over his left shoulder, noted the party and turned back to me.

"Why's that? They look like a thousand others I've seen today." "That's true, but I think I just saw a sneaky deal go down between that guy at the bar and the one who just left through the front door. I can't be a hundred percent certain, but chances are. . ."

Took drained his glass in one gulp and stood. "I'll get it." He carried his empty glass over to the bar, right away striking up conversation with the young man.

They seemed to be getting on all right by the time the barmaid replenished their glasses, and after paying for them Took accompanied the other to his table. I turned back to the view of the street and applied myself to the matter of retrieving the tapes from Villa Vulgar.

As was the case with the installation, it would again be necessary to fool the cameras, but I didn't like to use the bus a second time. Although it was feasible to lift the tapes quickly and be gone before security came to investigate, it was just too damn obvious to repeat the ploy. It would arouse curiosity and, almost certainly, lead to the discovery of the tampered-with telephone lines; and once Guido had been alerted to the fact, he would know that it was me who had been doing the eavesdropping, and I would lose most of any advantage otherwise gained.

It then occurred to me that there was no need to be delicate with this operation. It wouldn't matter if we tore the cameras off the wall, so long as we weren't seen doing it and if we were out of there with the tapes before the security guard arrived. Then, suddenly, the whole thing fell neatly into place, as I knew it would.

Took ambled over and resumed position his seat at the table.

"How did you do?" I asked anxiously.

"She's okay. At least she was when matey over there saw her at ten o'clock this morning."

I was greatly relieved. Took sipped his beer while he let this news penetrate.

"Janie scored off him at a place called The Sword and Sandal. He said she looked okay, but was acting nervous. He almost wasn't going to go through with the deal because he thought it might have been a set-up, but she told him she was hiding from the cops, so he went through with it."

"So why did he talk to you, if he knew Janie was on the run?" Took smiled. "Have a good look at me, Alex. Do I look dangerous to you?"

He had a point. Took was big, but with his beard, long, unruly hair and hiterochromic eyes, his overall appearance was anything but threatening. It was just conceivable that an enterprising toy manufacturer could model a cuddly toy on the man. The notion made me chuckle.

"I guess not," I conceded. "Did he have any idea of where she was going?"

No, unfortunately. I don't think we're going to have much luck here in the city, though. She'll probably see the note at Jim's and turn up at my place, eventually."

I was about to reply the affirmative when I suddenly realised I was witnessing a very dangerous situation develop out on the street.

The guy in the trilby hat - the guy who I had seen score - made a bad error of judgement while crossing the street. He stepped off the curb on the opposite side and had barely been missed by a car as he made it to the centre of the street, and now he stepped into the path of another car travelling in the opposite direction.

He must be able to see it! was my highly amplified thought as I watched, disbelieving. The driver reacted as quickly as it was possible to react, but the intervening distance was too short, and under full brakes, tyres screeching, the car bounced him from hood to windscreen and threw him into a lamp post not five metres from where we sat.

A scream came from his friends' table, and one of the girls ran towards the exit, yelling back to the others: "Oh, my God. Michael's been hit!"

The stunned driver by this time had left his car and apprehensively moved toward what he must have suspected was an inanimate body. But Michael was having none of it. He struggled to his feet... or foot. One leg was turned at a very unusual angle. With a sizeable gash over his right eye, which poured a copious amount of blood over his face, he hobbled towards the driver, dragging his shattered leg after him.

When the driver gingerly approached and made to give assistance, Michael grabbed him around the throat and began to squeeze, making the man's face turn red and his eyes bug out.

"Was it *Tales from the Crypt* or *The Living Dead* I saw this scene?" I said to Took.

"I thought it was Brain-Suckers from Planet Bizarre. ...I think Young Michael must be made of concrete."

The weirdness continued as Michael's friends and passersby tried to prise his hands from the hapless motorist's neck. It took a minute or two, but he finally succumbed to the grappling hands and the extent of his injuries, not forgetting blood-loss, and soon afterwards both he and the motorist were taken away in a wailing ambulance.

As Michael's friends re-grouped at their table in stunned silence, I explained to Took what I had seen of the incident, emphasizing that I was almost sure Michael had seen the car coming and made no effort to avoid it.

"I don't think that was angel wings your friend sold him, Took. The guy was suicidal and superhuman to do what he did after being bounced off a car and a lamp post."

"You want me to ask?"

"I wish you would," I replied, perplexed. "I want to know what it was he sold Janie."

Took left his beer and went over to their table. I watched as he engaged all of them in quiet discussion. After a couple of minutes, he rose, bade them a friendly farewell and returned to his seat opposite me. He didn't look very pleased.

"Not good news, I'm afraid. It turns out young Michael is a very placid individual... unless it was shock that caused his reaction which I doubt. I've never seen anything like that before. It must have been the drug, and it was from a new batch of angel wings which the guy over there picked up last night."

I pushed my glass away and leaned back in my chair. "The same batch Janie scored from?"

Took nodded and we sat looking at each other, wondering what we could do... if it wasn't already too late to do anything.

On the way back to the bus I called into a gun shop and purchased a short-barrelled, pump-action shotgun and a box of cartridges. The fact that neither of us possessed a firearms licence made no difference, except to the price.

We could have spent the rest of the day trudging all over the city and not get another lead on Janie, so out of desperation and having nothing else to go on, I decided to use the only tangible piece of information I had been given thus far.

The address which Heidi had given me led us to an old, residential section of the city. Here, narrow streets intersected one another at odd angles, and rows of attached and semi-detached dwellings sported low, stone walls with wrought iron gates in frontof tiny yards, each with alike Federation style porches, with carved posts and wooden friezes, and each one built from the same greycoloured stone.

We turned down Janie's street, as quiet and deserted as all the rest, apart, that is, from the black cat which paused in the middle of the street to watch our approach, then turned and ran back in the direction it had come from.

As we drove past Janie's house I saw that the windows were closed and the blinds drawn. From the beams of the porch hung baskets containing pastel-coloured blooms. At my request Took turned left at the end of the street, then left again, to take us along a narrow laneway at the rear of the houses, and we pulled up some twenty metres short of Janie's back yard.

I checked the Luger to see that the safety was on. The needle gun slid easily into a coat pocket. Took picked up the shotgun which lay on the floor beside his seat, pushed five cartridges into the magazine and stood it against the dash beside his left knee.

"Back in five minutes. If you see anything that looks like trouble, honk the horn."

He nodded and pulled the lever to open the door.

I stayed close to the corrugated iron fence which bordered the rear of each property and halted at Janie's gate, distinguishable from the rest of the fence only by the hand-hole cut into the iron to allow the latch to be lifted from the inside. Pushing it open as quietly as possible, I found a concrete-paved yard, barely large enough to accommodate the clothes hoist which stood at its centre, and a wooden bench positioned to catch the afternoon sun. I noticed this peripherally, my attention drawn to the back door which stood halfway open, the splintered wood of the door jam evincing forced entry. My stomach tightened and I selected the Luger.

I moved quickly to the edge of the doorway and, with my back pressed against the wall, listened intently for the slightest sound which might indicate that someone was inside.

I was about to risk a quick glance inside when I noticed the fine gossamer threads across the opening, and a grey spider was busily spinning new strands in the top corner. The web was in the final stages of construction and covered from the stonework above the door to nearly halfway down, maybe an hour or two's work for the little critter, and plenty low enough to have been torn if anyone but a child or a dwarf had passed through here. The intruder was well gone by now, I told myself.

Brushing the web aside I entered the premises and began checking the rooms. Everything was still intact, no sign of disorder, and the television set, video recorder and stereo were where they should have been. I could rule out housebreak.

I moved out of the lounge room, across the hallway and into a bedroom, looking for any sign of disturbance there, then there was a terrible, brain-jarring blow, a flash of brilliant white light inside my skull, and everything went grey as the floor rushed up to meet me. My head whirled and everything went black for a time.

"Oh dear," I heard a recognisable voice utter.

I heard someone groan.

"Are you all right?"

eyes began to focus, Janie was looking down at me.

"How do you feel?"

"Elephants!" I answered, and tried again. "What'd you slug me with?"

"A saxophone. I'm sorry, Alex."

"Am I glad you don't play the piano."

Thirteen

We talked in the kitchen while Took opened cans and emptied them into his one and only cooking pot. I cut thick slices from a loaf of pumpernickel bread while Janie buttered them.

"Like I keep telling you, the stuff wiped my memory. I woke up there when I heard you - someone! - prowling around. I suppose I was so out of my skull that I went home purely through instinct, busted in my own door when I realised I didn't have my key with me, then crashed on top of my bed and slept it off."

This was likely the case. I had already related to her what we had witnessed of the last person we knew to have sampled the new batch of the drug. The only reason Janie had not become suicidal, we figured, was because she had used only a small amount, substantiated by the remaining quantity in the packet she had purchased, and she *"sort of"* remembered snorting a pinch, just enough to relieve her withdrawal symptoms.

She had spent the night in a disused railway carriage in the switching yards, only a mile from Heidi's house, not knowing she had killed the goon and thinking that Took had been killed by the shots which had been fired at her as she fled the premises.

Terrified by what had happened, she huddled in the carriage until she fell asleep. Upon waking, her immediate need had been the drug, which, as we already knew, led her to the meeting at the Sword and Sandal at ten o'clock in the morning, after which it had been her intention to return to Jim and Pat's house. But then the drug took hold.

After our meal I produced the bottles of pills Mainwaring had prescribed for Janie, and placed them on the table before her, saying: "If you don't think these will hold you 'til Monday, we'll go and see the doctor, now, and get something else."

"I'll manage with these," she said after a moment's hesitation. She swallowed two of each, without anything to wash them down, and screwing the tops back on the bottles, smiled mockingly at me. "How's your head?" Her tone was loaded with sarcasm.

Took choked on a morsel of bread, but recovered quickly. He started to say something in a vain effort to distract me.

"This isn't a bloody *game!*" I exploded "Why the hell didn't you just stay put at Jim's place? You nearly got Took killed, you nearly got yourself killed, and we've wasted nearly a whole day searching for you."

I realised I was on my feet and bawling like a drill sergeant. Janie was not phased, though. She, too, was on her feet. I half noticed Took leave the room but I was more taken by the shining fury in Janie's eyes.

"What in hell did you think I was going to do?" she screamed.

"Sit and chat with your bosom friends all night while you go out and play hero? You bastard, don't blame it all on *me*. There was no good reason why I couldn't have gone with you. I was hanging out. I needed something to do to take my mind of it."

There was a tear in the corner of her eye. When she noticed me looking at it she brushed it away furiously, then snatched up a soup dish from the table and hurled it past my left ear to smash against the wall.

"Spinoza is going to kill you, you dumb fuck!!"

That really got to me, and when the table went flying across the kitchen, I was hardly aware it was me who had done it...

"Only if I've got a dead weight junkie like you hanging around my neck!!"

I found Took out in the front room, making some adjustments to the control cables on his bike. He looked over his shoulder as I entered, then resumed what he was doing. "I don't recommend you top a hundred miles per hour for any appreciable amount of time, the con-rods are liable to fail. And don't rev over six thousand two hundred, okay?"

"You're not coming?"

He finished tightening the lock-nut on the clutch cable and tossed the spanners into the tool-box. "I don't think it would be wise to leave her alone, do you?"

I didn't reply, but I had to accept the point. The crazy woman was liable to run off again.

"I'll take her out for a drive in the bus and get some beers while you're gone. Give her a chance to cool down. I'll pick up a tapeplayer from somewhere, too. You can handle the bike all right, can't you?"

"Yeah."

"It'll be dark in an hour. Let's see how you're going to carry the shotgun."

We tried a couple of methods before we sorted it out. Took lent me his leather jacket and we tried it with the gun stuffed up the front, but it was uncomfortable and difficult to steer the bike that way. We tried it with the gun taped to the side of the saddle and, although it was comfortable enough, it was too slow and awkward to retrieve from that position. We settled for having it resting across the handlebars, wrapped in brown paper and lightly taped with gaffer tape: quick to get at and easily pulled free.

The plan was simple enough, although it would have been better with two people. Ride up, blast the cameras - one mounted over the gate and the other at the eastern corner - grab the tapes and ride back. No time for security to act. Whoever manned the monitors would, hopefully, think he had witnessed a simple act of vandalism, perpetrated by a bikie hoon whose face was hidden by a full-face helmet. With any luck Guido would never know it happened.

Took bore down on the kick-starter and the 1000cc motor roared into life, then settled into a steady, thumping idle.

"I'll get it outside for you," he said, pushing it off the stand and selecting first gear.

He rode it through the lounge room doorway, accelerating briskly to slip the tail-end around and angle the bike down the passage, out through the front door onto the verandah and down the steps. All this without his feet leaving the pegs.

"You've done that before," I said appreciatively. I had on the fullface helmet and was pulling on a pair of pigskin gloves.

"Down is easy," he said, popping down the side-stand and dismounting. "Up is the tricky bit."

As I climbed into the saddle and tested the weight of the beast, Took said: "You might need to get some petrol on the way back." He slapped me on the back as I flipped up the side-stand and selected first gear. "Good luck," he said, and I pulled out of the driveway and accelerated off, down the grey dust-covered street.

Fifteen minutes and ten miles later I was once again leaving the outskirts and beginning the climb into the hills. The city still sweltered in the hot, humid conditions, but here the air was cleaner and a touch cooler. I settled into an easy pace and enjoyed the scenery.

I had already forgiven Janie her stupidity. It was even possible I had treated her unfairly. There was no way for me to fully comprehend how it felt to be continually aware of the presence, or absence, of a potent chemical within one's system. Although there was one time, after I had copped a gutful of shrapnel from a mortar shell. I was dosed up with morphine for four days until they could stretcher me out... And more after surgery. The heebie-jeebies I experienced when they cut me off was very unpleasant, I remembered. But trilonite was a different proposition. It appeared to have been designed specifically to produce human dependency.

I passed through a tiny hamlet called Morialta, consisting of a post office and a garage, and turned right where a signpost indicated: Hampstead 9km, Foster Vale 15km.

Maybe I was attaching too much importance to my personal vendetta against Guido, when, down there in the city - and who knew how far the malignancy had spread - peoples lives were being usurped in one of the most despicable ways imaginable. Was it merely money these bastards meant to bleed from the poor fools? I had already established, from the information given me by Mainwaring, that the operation was probably running at a loss, unless, once all the drug users had become hooked on the stuff, the purchase price was suddenly pushed high? Perhaps the chemical configuration was such that no other drug would serve to release its grip on the human organism? A cruel monopoly would be in place to squeeze vast revenue from addicts world wide. Could there be such a merciless organisation?

I chuckled derisively to myself for having posed such a naïve question. And if money was not their main objective, there could, to my mind, be only one other. Control. But to what end?

I let this question pass unanswered as the town of Hampstead came and went, and I began to wonder how it would be if I didn't have all these problems on my plate. I could just keep on riding and not have to worry about a thing. The idea was extremely seductive, and it was with considerable vexation that I brought my mind to the task once more.

I left the main road at the turn-off one mile out of Foster Vale as I had two days ago, when the Interceptor was more than just a pile of blackened metal. Darkness was descending rapidly over the countryside. The blanketing cloud turned red and stayed that way for several minutes after the sun disappeared below the horizon, and pretty soon it was too dark to navigate without the headlight.

I switched it on, but the original 1950 headlamp was not exactly awesome in the candle power department and I was forced to reduce speed in order to negotiate the winding, tree-edged lane.

Soon the vineyard where I had seen the grape-pickers working in the blazing sun came into view. I tried to picture the pretty girl I had seen there, but, inexplicably, Janie's face appeared instead. I muttered a curse beneath the helmet and began rehearsing the retrieval procedure, and before too long the lighted wall of Villa Vulgar appeared out of the darkness.

I rode past the property and pulled up out of range of the cameras to detach the shotgun from the handlebars, then rode into the surrounding illumination, directly under the gaze of the security camera mounted at the eastern corner. Had Took been piloting I could have taken it out while on the move, but, being on my own, I had to come to a standstill before I could use both hands to take aim.

The silence was shattered by the blast, and the big BB pellets tore the camera apart. Satisfied with the result, I pumped a fresh cartridge into the chamber and rode on to the camera above the gate, and dealt with it in identical fashion. Then, parking the bike alongside the junction-box, I lifted the lid and ejected the tapes from the two micro-recorders, zipping them inside a pocket of Took's jacket, replaced the lid and climbed back on the bike.

Dogs had been barking since the first blast, but the whole procedure had taken little more than half a minute. Not until now had I seen any movement beyond the gates: torchlight advancing across the lawn in front of the house; but I was already pulling out onto the road by that time, keenly conscious of the tiny spools of magnetic tape and the information they might contain, zipped inside my pocket.

I travelled as fast as I reasonably could along the narrow, twisting road, but I was confident no one had taken up pursuit. They would still be scratching their heads, wondering what had happened. Until I reached the city limits, however, I continued to feel vulnerable, given that there were few motorcycles besides myself on the road and detection by a police patrol, had word been put out, was one element of this sortie I was unable to do anything about.

I was skirting the city on the eastern side, meaning to connect with the main road south and reach Took's squat that way, when the motor began to splutter. Took had warned me of this, I remembered then, and switched to the reserve tank and kept an eye out for a petrol station. I passed two on my right before coming across one on my side of the road; a combined petrol station, grocery store and video hire. I pulled into the driveway and parked next to a pair of pumps on the outer lane. While standing behind the pumps filling the tank I noticed three youths enter the shop but I paid them no heed. I was somewhat preoccupied being pleased with myself for having had such a successful outing.

The tank filled, I walked into the shop unfolding my wallet, searching for a twenty-dollar note. When I looked up there were three pairs of eyes staring at me. The largest of the youths had the proprietor pulled forward over the counter with a six-inch blade held to his throat, while another was behind the counter, rifling the till. I stopped in my tracks and the four of us stared mutely at each other for a few, elongated seconds.

The one holding the knife showed no sign of nervousness. He sneered and said: "Another donation? Do come in."

I was wondering where the third member of the team was when I felt something sharp and pointy press firmly into my back, sickeningly close to my left kidney, which felt as though it was desperately trying to retreat up behind my rib cage for protection. My skin began to crawl as I kept in check the reaction which once would have been reflex. The blanched, doughy face of the middleaged proprietor told me he was not up to this at all.

"Bring him over here," said the one holding the proprietor.

I yielded to the pressure of the knife and moved forwards, thinking furiously as I neared the counter.

The lad at the till fumbled nervously while trying to stuff the money into the plastic bag, a good deal of the money spilling onto the floor. He couldn't have been more that sixteen. But I didn't much like the look of the leader; his wide, unblinking eyes and cool manner told me he was a nasty piece of work.

I was close now. "Here, you can take the wallet," I said in order to come within striking range.

His eyes followed the bulging wallet as I placed it on top of the counter and, too late, realised his mistake.

My fingers speared up to his eyes. Not a particularly sporting act, but in this case defensible and wonderfully effective. There is only one reaction to this move. Invariably the unfortunate recipient forgets what he ought to be doing and instinctively attempts to protect his eyes from the assault which, annoyingly, has already taken place; and in that moment the proprietor pulled himself back behind the counter.

The move turned me away from the blade at my back, and continuing the movement I spun around to deliver a disabling blow with the heel of my hand under the right ear of my, as yet unseen, aggressor. The tall but slightly-built youth reeled sideways into the potato chip section with a lights-out expression on his dial, and crumpled quietly to the floor.

The unmistakable explosion of a hand-gun rang out, just as I turned to take care of the ringleader. His hands still covered his eyes but the top of his head was smashed like an egg shell, and he fell forward, dead.

Terrified, the boy had dropped the loot and raced past me, making for the door. The proprietor raised the pistol to take aim, fired before I could react. The shot missed, shattering a cool-drink dispenser beside the door. He might have fired a second time, but I was so incensed that he would try and kill a kid that I landed a whistling blow on his chin, and he sank behind the counter, out of sight.

I collected my wallet and my twenty dollars and got out of there. It wouldn't do to be seen by anybody in such a compromising circumstance.

A car pulled up to the pumps as I pulled on the helmet, but they paid me no attention and I was well gone before the grisly discovery was made.

Fourteen

Janie and Took had been on a shopping spree during my absence. I found them in the lounge room, reclining comfortably in new beanbags in front of a new couch, sipping cans of beer, watching a simulcast rock concert on a new television set which sat on a new coffee table, under which a new ghetto-blaster emitted the gutsy guitar-work of Eric Clapton playing Layla.

I stood in the doorway, grinning at both of them. "Excuse me. I must have the wrong house."

Took climbed out of his beanbag, reached over to lower the volume. "We decided to cheer the place up a bit. What do you think?"

"A definite improvement on an empty room," I replied approvingly.

Janie reached into the ice-box behind her head and pulled out a can. "Have a beer." Her words were slurred, the result of mixing her medication with alcohol. "And have a seat," she said, patting the spare beanbag beside her.

I was pleased she had decided to forget the harsh words we had exchanged earlier. I slipped off Took's leather jacket and lowered myself into the seat.

"You got the tapes all right?" Took asked, sliding his beanbag around to facilitate conversation.

I zipped open the pocket of the jacket and produced the items.

"Any trouble?"

"None."

"I've rigged up a bizzo to listen to them." He pointed to a micro recorder jacked into the ghetto-blaster. "Pass them over and I'll wind them back."

As I leaned forward and handed them over to Took, I felt a twinge in my back. "Ehrrg," I said, putting my hand to the sore spot. "I must be getting old.". . .but the shirt was wet where I put my hand.

"You're bleeding!"

Janie reached over and lifted the tail of my shirt while I remained bent over. I twisted around to take a look, and discovered a small puncture mark about half an inch wide and probably as much again deep.

Took fetched a first-aid box he kept in his room, and Janie set to cleaning and dressing the tiny wound.

Pressed to explain how this had occurred, I swept over the incident as briefly as I was allowed, being wholly annoyed with the sordid episode and reducing the number of youths to two, thereby excluding the death of the third.

While Janie threw out the pieces of cotton wool and lint, and repacked the first-aid kit, Took brought the Vincent into the passage, then returned to rewind the tapes.

When we had settled, beers in hand, he started the first tape and resumed his seat.

We soon learned that this tape contained conversations made over the house phones only, not Guido's business or private phone. Such things as grocery orders made by the cook to a store in Foster Vale, and a private call made by a woman, the live-in maid, we imagined, to her mother who did little else but complain to her daughter about the cost of living or the barking dog next door, and: "When are you coming home to visit? It's been so long."

We recognised the daughter's voice again in a couple of later calls, and we learned that she had a telephone betting account with the TAB which she flattened on that particular call. She also had a boyfriend by the name of Wesley, who worked as a boilermaker in the city.

"Oh, Wesley," Janie shamelessly mimicked. "Talk to me dirty. Oooh... talk dirty, darling. I love it when you talk like that."

Janie tossed her head back in laughter. "This is terrible," she exclaimed gleefully. "Wouldn't they just shrivel up and die if they knew? God, I know *I* would."

"Wes, darling," she parodied once more. "Let's knock the old girl off. We can live off the insurance money... our own little love nest far away from all this."

She broke into laughter, again. Bright, girlish laughter which I found very appealing.

"We really shouldn't be doing this," I said through a wide grin.

She turned to me, smiling. "There's no harm, Alex. I'm not really being cruel. I'm not such a wicked girl."

"I know that," I replied.

She continued to hold my gaze, broadening her smile. "Took, let me get you another beer," she said, suddenly turning away. We listened a while longer to similarly inconsequential items, concerned for the most part with the running of the household. With one exception, however, and I realised later that it happened because Jim had expertly wired the two recorders to cover the three telephone lines, and it occurred when all three lines were in use.

We were listening to the chauffeur booking in the Mercedes for a service, when a call from another line came in over top of the conversation. None of us were paying much attention. Took had just begun an anecdote about a woman he knew who had lost her prosthetic leg while hang-gliding, while we kept an ear cocked to the tape. Janie noticed the anomaly first, and raised a hand to interrupt Took's story.

"What's going on here?" she said, puzzled, and we all focused on the new conversation to hear:

". . .in one of your demented power games and expect to get away with it. You picked the wrong man, Guido. I'm going to kick your arse back under whatever rock you crawled out from ..."

"It's you, Alex!" Janie said, wide-eyed and surprised.

". . .when you had a chance. You can't win this. Give it up," came Guido's peevish voice.

". . .suck eggs. You're worried, Guido. And you have good reason to be.

The conversation ended there and Janie looked at me with a mixture of concern and admiration. "You said *that* to Guido Spinoza?"

I shrugged. "It seemed appropriate at the time. I thought it might rattle him, put him under some pressure and force him to make a move he otherwise wouldn't.

"I get it," Janie responded. "Then there may be something . . . he might have made . . . some calls afterwards."

She placed her can of beer beside her beanbag and brought her hands to her face. "Damn it. Two more days," she said wearily.

I realised she was referring to the clinic. Took and I looked helplessly on as withdrawal overtook her.

"Is it too bad?" I heard myself ask inanely. She removed her hands from her face and leaned her head back in the beanbag. "I don't want to feel like this. It's not fair.

"I have to use the bathroom," she said, pushing herself to her feet and leaving the room on unsteady legs. A moment later we heard her retching from along the passage.

I said to Took, "Heidi told me she hasn't known anyone to beat it."

"She's a tough girl. She'll make it if she wants to."

The retching continued for a couple of minutes, then it was quiet, except for the muffled drone of the generator out in the back yard.

Took and I looked at one another for a moment. "You go, Alex. Janie and I had a long talk while you were gone."

Failing to comprehend this strange statement I rose and made for the bathroom. I found her kneeling next to the bowl, slumped sideways against the wall. When she heard me come up behind her she quickly wiped her mouth with a wad of tissue paper, stood and flushed the cistern.

"I'll be all right."

I guided her back to the lounge room, supporting her with my arm across her shoulders and gripping her arm. I could feel small tremors coursing through her body.

"Is there anything I can do?" I asked.

"No. You guys go ahead and check the next tape. I'm going to try and get some sleep for a while."

She nestled into the beanbag and closed her eyes. "Could you find me a blanket, please, Took? I'm cold."

It was at least thirty degrees celsius in the room. A sultry summer evening.

When Took returned with the blanket and placed it over her, she thanked him and said, "It's okay, play the tape. You won't disturb me."

Cheerless now, and being unable to do anything more for her, Took inserted the second of the tapes into the player.

The first couple of calls were business related; managers and accountants from some of Guido's enterprises reporting on the state of his business affairs and making some suggestions how to improve profits in one sector or another.

The third call came from a bank manager, not his own, Took and I determined, who, in total disregard for laws concerning the divulgence of privileged information between a bank and its clients, informed Guido about a wealthy out-of-town businessman who was in the process of negotiating with the bank for a twelve million dollar loan to develop a high-rise property within the city. Guido asked for this person's name. When it was given he told the manager he would be in touch and hung up. I suspected that Guido was going to have the man checked out on behalf of the bank. It could have been a legitimate business arrangement, but with Guido you could never really be sure. Call number four was out-going, to the City of Monarto's Town Planning Department, and it involved a somewhat guarded conversation concerning the possibility of the re-zoning of a certain area --- it was never named --- into a light industrial area. Again I suspected the divulgence of privileged information.

These type of shady exchanges of information along with the occasional phenomenon of the legitimate variety continued to make up the bulk of in- and out-going calls. But interspersed among them came these gems:

Call No. 6

Guido: "Yes?"

Unknown: "Superintendent Marshall here."

Guido: "What can I do for you, Laurie?"

Sup'dnt Marshall: "There was a shooting out at the Old Coach last night. A drug ripoff. One dead.

Guido: "What does that have to do with me?

Sup'dnt Marshall: Two of the perpetrators we found unconscious at the scene. The third, bound and unconscious on a bench in Mill Park at 2:45 this morning. CID charged him with the murder of Clay Blessing. The other two with accessory. They're Vincent Zendell's boys, Mr Spinoza."

Guido: (pause) "Are they likely to talk?"

Sup'dnt Marshall: "Weis, the one who pulled the trigger. CID reckon he's a chance.

Guido: "Arrange an accident. That ought to persuade the others to keep quiet."

Sup'dnt Marshall: "It's difficult. We've had two deaths in custody already this month. The newspapers are stirring up interest.

Guido: "Then get a message to this Weis person. Tell him to keep his trap shut and he'll be looked after. Just make sure he says nothing until him and his pals are in general prison population. Then have his pals do the job. I want to hear no more about it. *Capish?*"

Sup'ndt Marshall: "I'll see to it."

end call.

Call No. 7

Vincent Zendell: "Hello."

Guido: (Sarcastic) "Your boys are in the lock-up, in case you're wondering.

Zendell:(5 seconds silence) "What happened?"

Guido: "You hired morons, is what happened. When are you going to learn? I'm not going to be around forever, Vincent. If one of them had squealed. . ."

Zendell: "I'm sorry, Uncle."

Guido: "I've taken care of it. Don't let there be a next time. You've got to be more careful about who you hire in future. You won't last in this business without good people. It wasn't a bad try, though. I'll give you that. I'll have to be on my toes from now on.

Zendell: "What went wrong? There was only one man and a woman. It should have been a push-over."

Guido: "One of yours went solo? One of mine, perhaps? I don't know, but check it out. Whoever it was walked over your boys and involved the police. And I had forgotten about the girl. Hang on and I'll find her name. You owe me a favour.

Here it is. Jane, or Janie Stuart. Five-five, brown eyes, brunette, lives at 23, McEwen Ave., City. A junkie. Hangs out at the East End. You know what to do, but find out what she knows first.

Zendell: "Yes, Uncle."

Call No. 13

Guido: "Yes?"

Zendell: "Did you send a man by the name of Jaeger after me?

Guido: (Laughs) "All part of the game, Vincent. And good for your education. But you don't have to worry about him, he's not dangerous. He's a burn-out. Ex-soldier who has taken to thieving for a living. (Laughs again) An amusing character. He'll cause you a few problems, nothing more. It's a fair game."

Zendell: "The joke is on *you* this time, Uncle. He worked out that you were using him."

Guido: "How do you know this?"

Zendell: "He walked into my club, not half an hour ago. He wanted me to join him in getting even with you. He thinks I'm trying to move in on your territory. Imagine that, Uncle! A guy like that. . ."

Guido: (Cutting Zendell short) Where is he now?"

Zendell: "I had to let him leave, he had back-up. But I think that I might use him if. . ."

Guido: "Shut up, boy, I'm trying to think. How did he find out I was using him?

Zendell: "I don't know. He wouldn't tell me."

Guido: "Can you contact him?"

Zendell: "Yes. He gave me a contact number."

Guido: "Good. Listen, Vincent, I advise you not to try and make use of this fellow. I may have made a mistake in doing so, myself. Come to think of it he might be the one responsible for the fiasco at the Old Coach. I want you to use that number. Tell him you want another meeting. You know what to do then?"

Zendell: "Yes."

Call No. 17

Guido: "Yes?"

Zendell: "My car yard was torched last night, and my office burgled, here at the club!"

Guido: "It seems Jaeger decided against a partnership after all. (Laughs) How much did he take you for? (Silence). . .Vincent?"

Zendell: (Voice constrained) "The ledgers . . .and my diary."

Guido: (Coldly) "What diary?"

Zendell: "I kept a personal diary. Well hidden. I don't know how he could have found it. He knows everything."

Guido: "You idiot! Why do you cause me so much grief? Did you contact Jaeger, yet?"

Zendell: "I did, but of course he knew it was a trap. I have some news concerning the Old Coach incident, though. It *was* Jaeger who intervened. He took one of my men hostage for a couple of hours. Weis. He denies telling him anything but he is obviously lying. And he had the Stuart girl with him."

Guido: "I want them found. Put everyone you have on it. Then I want you over here, and bring your book-keeper with you.

end call.

Call number twenty was an inquiry from Guido's stockbroker, asking if he wished to purchase shares in a "promising venture" in off-shore oil and gas exploration in Spencer Gulf. Significant only because the conversation was interrupted by a call on Guido's other phone ...*my* call, Took and I concluded, because it was the only time that both lines were busy, and because of the call Guido made immediately afterwards.

Call No. 21

Woman's Voice: "Extension number?"

Guido: "Extension twenty-seven."

Male voice: "Yes?"

Guido: "Cassandra."

Male voice: "One moment, sir. . . On the sound of the pip, please repeat your name, clearly, three times, for voice print verification ... (*peeep!*)

Guido: "Javelin. Javelin. Javelin. (Fine seconds wait.) Basso voice: "This is Cassandra. What is it, Javelin?"

Guido: "I'm getting some interference down here. It's nothing I can't handle but, as a precautionary measure, it would be an advantage to move things along a bit."

Basso voice: "What is the nature of your problem?"

Guido: "A personal affair, not connected with our arrangement.

But if it develops any further I will need to give it my full attention. And as our task *is* close to completion. . ?"

Basso voice: "Very well. I see no reason why we can't bring it forward by two days. Will that suit?"

Guido: "Thank-you, yes. Is the last consignment ready?"

Basso voice: "Hold a minute ... (Prolonged silence) ... The Eastern Star docks tonight, nine o'clock. You can collect when it's unloaded. Bay fourteen, warehouse three. Is that all?"

Guido: "Yes."

end call.

The tape revealed just two more conversations before it fell silent, but neither offered anything of interest. I had already learned plenty, thought.

Guido had the Police Superintendent in his pocket. Zendell turned out to be Guido's nephew, which, alone, explained a few things. Guido was still the murderous, conniving, duplicitous, arrogant little bastard he always was, and Zendell was his apprentice. Oh, and the "burnt-out ex-soldier" thing hadn't gone down too well with me either. But I took solace in the fact that I had stung him fairly well.

Call number twenty-one had been the novelty at the bottom of the cereal box, and it posed more questions than it answered.

"Code names? Voice-verification? Last consignment?" I turned to Took. "The little toad is heavily connected by the sound of things."

"Cassandra," Took said thoughtfully, combing his fingers through his beard and staring into a vacant corner.

"Greek mythology?" I suggested. It was a stab in the dark but Took nodded in agreement.

"Homeric legend, to be precise. Cassandra was taught the secrets of prophecy by Apollo, but he later cursed her so that her prophecies would never be believed. She tried to warn the Trojans about the wooden horse and the fall of Troy, but everyone thought she was mad and so ignored her."

"A disbelieved prophet? A prophet of doom? It doesn't sound good."

"More accurately, these days the name is associated with someone who holds a gloomy view of the social or political future of a country."

"I wonder what the hell we've stumbled on? I don't suppose he picked the name because he liked the sound of it. What about Javelin?"

"A long, pointy thing athletes chuck around," Took replied, and sipped his beer.

"Thank-you, Mr Weisenheimer. I guess it could be an allusion to the spearhead of an operation?"

Janie stirred beneath her blanket and looked around dazedly.

"How long have I been here?"

"About an hour," Took answered.

"Christ, it felt like much more."

"How are you feeling?"

"Terrible." She twisted herself round to lie on her opposite side, began to shiver. "I can't put up with this any longer," she said with her eyes closed. "I've got to go out and score something to get me through. Where are my tablets?"

"I'll get them," said Took, struggling to rise from his beanbag chair. "They're in the kitchen."

When he returned with the tablets and a mug of tea, she sat up and shakily accepted the mug. "My hands feel like dough. Would you give me three of each?" she said to Took.

"You're too ill to be going anywhere," I observed.

"I'm too ill to be lying around here doing nothing," she snapped.

"My skin is crawling and I feel like someone has ripped out my guts and replaced them with broken glass. And it's not going to get any better by my lying around here feeling sorry for myself. I'm going out to score."

"You're not," I found myself saying more forcefully than I had intended. You were lucky to have escaped Zendell's goon squad the last time. You're dead meat if you try it."

"In another couple of hours I won't care". Her voice was unsteady, strained. "It just gets worse, Alex. You don't know what it's like."

She was right, I didn't know what it was like. I suddenly realized that I had been testing her and I had no right to do that. I relented contritely.

"How do I avoid buying the same stuff you bought this morning?"

Janie looked mildly surprised, but more than anything, relieved.

"That stuff was slightly gritty. If it's fine and powdery, it should be okay."

I was about to ask Took, who had been standing quietly watching this exchange with his thumbs hooked in his pockets, if I could borrow his motorcycle. But he pre-empted me.

"No you can't, but in case you haven't thought of it, there's no one combing the streets looking for me... Discounting my wife's lawyers, that is. Tell me where and *I'll* go."

"Thanks, Took," Janie said with affection. "The Sword and Sandal on Albert Street. I'm sorry to be such a nuisance."

He pretended annoyance and smiled ironically. "That's what friends are for."

Janie managed a smile as she slumped back in the beanbag. "It's been a long time since I've had friends like you. I'm grateful to you both."

When Took had been gone for half an hour or so, I turned on the television and switched around the channels, eventually settling on an old, black and white gangster movie. I was unable to relax enough to enjoy it, though; my mind refused to cease throwing up images and pieces of information collected over the past three days, but I left it on as a distraction for Janie.

Her condition worsened. She changed position every few minutes, apparently unable to get comfortable. Complaining of being too hot, she tossed the blanket aside, and because it was a very warm night I thought this only natural. But when she began sweating profusely, I placed my hand over her head and found she was running a very high temperature.

She finally got to her feet and insisted on taking a shower. I put up a token argument to this, but she doggedly persisted and went ahead and showered anyway. I had to assume she had been through this before, and therefore knew what she was doing.

Upon returning to the lounge room she seemed a little better, and her temperature had returned to around normal - if a touch high. But after some twenty minutes, she began to shiver and I had to cover her with the blanket again.

With the shivering came violent tremors which shook her whole body, and at this stage I simply had to succumb. I squeezed in beside her and hugged her close, her head and my shoulder while I instinctively tried to rub some warmth into her body.

Her voice came thickly. "I wanted you to hold me, but I was too afraid to ask."

"Is it always this bad?"

"Yes." She twisted around so that she could look up to me, then took my hand and held my palm against her face. She closed her eyes and with a faint smile nestled into the crook of my arm.

"Don't talk. Just hold me. I'm going to try and get *outof-body* for a while."

After a time the shivering stopped and I felt her begin to relax. A while later the warmth started returning to her body, and her breathing, which had been short and ragged until now, came deeper and more evenly. I looked up at the television screen. Somehow, what I saw there seemed more real to me than my present situation.

Fifteen

Janie's respite was short-lived. The hot and cold sweating symptoms returned after half an hour, this time accompanied by muscle cramping and another bout of vomiting. I didn't understand how the absence of something unnatural to the human body could have such a dramatic effect, but I sure had a better understanding of the consequences every user had to face in the event of being busted, or in some other way being deprived of the substance of their dependence. It wasn't so difficult now, to understand the desperate measures some of these poor *schmucks* took in order to maintain supply.

If the authorities, by some extraordinary piece of good management, succeeded in stopping the supply, there would be thousands throughout the city suffering in the same way Janie was right now. The medication Mainwaring had prescribed certainly didn't appear to be doing very much; and from what I understood of the system, there would be nowhere for them to go for treatment, except, of course, those well-shod enough to afford private care, and that certainly wouldn't count for too many: drugs were the refuge of the downtrodden in this society. My thoughts were interrupted by a cacophonous strain from the television set and an introduction given by a spotty-faced young woman welcoming viewers to *News Update:*

"...Police are baffled by the sudden upsurge in incidents of violence in and around the City of Monarto," she intoned gravely.

"In the twelve-hour period to midnight tonight, police have been called out to twenty one scenes, ranging from murder and suicide to wilful destruction of public and private property, and violent attacks on innocent bystanders.

"One man walked into a hardware store, doused himself with methylated spirits, then set himself alight before the proprietor and patrons could intervene. Others have leapt to their death from high-rise buildings and bridges spanning railways and busy roads.

"Other incidents include a man entering the Clayton Police Station with a machete and attacking police officers before being shot dead... and a woman who hijacked a garbage-compressor truck, driving it into a new shopping mall at Highgate, killing six people and injuring at least a dozen others.

"A crank group going by the name of Organised Urban Resistance Against a Sick Society, or *OUR ASS*, have claimed responsibility, saying their members are prepared to go to any lengths in pursuit of social justice.

"This explanation, however, was totally rejected by a police spokesman just prior to this bulletin. Captain Halliday, of the Police Department's Media Liaison Office, said all attempts were being made to understand the reason behind this outbreak of madness and to contain the situation. He said the police were currently applying the theory that it could be the work of a fanatical religious sect. He also said, when asked to comment on the claims of *O.U.R.A.S.S.*, that they were no more than a bunch of social misfits, eager to capitalise on an unfortunate situation..."

While the topic changed to race relations and deforestation in West Papua, Janie raised her head and reached for the bottle of codeine tablets.

"Would you like me to make you a cup of tea?" I asked.

"A beer," she replied.

I moved to comply, wondering at the advisability of it, when we heard the Vincent accelerating along a street some distance off.

Janie sat up quickly to listen, intent on the sound which she hoped meant relief was imminent. We listened to it accelerate and decelerate among the maze of streets to the bottom of our street, then up to the house, into the driveway and, finally, up the steps and onto the verandah. The motor was turned off and a moment later Took strode into the room.

"It's a bloody circus out there." ...He unzipped a pocket and pulled out a paper bag printed with the red and white logo of DAYLEY PHARMACIST. He held it between thumb and forefinger. To Janie, he said: "It's all in here. You didn't say anything about syringes but I got you some anyway."

Janie was already out of the beanbag and crossing the room on shaky legs. "Took, I'll love you forever. Thank-you."

She accepted the packet and embraced Took, giving him a peck on the cheek, then disappeared down the passageway towards the kitchen.

How has she been?" he asked, pulling off his jacket.

"Not so good."

He tossed his jacket down on the floor and ambled over to the icebox to get a beer. "Want one?"

I nodded. "What's this about a circus?"

"The natives are restless tonight. There's a lot of weird stuff going on in the city."

I accepted the beer. "Thanks. Yeah, I caught it on the television just before you arrived. It has to be the bad dope."

Took leaned up against the wall and took a good draught from his can, burped and wiped beer from his whiskers. "Yeah, I agree, and so do most of the people I talked to. But it seems to have sparked something off. One group I talked to say some of the city's resident loonies are following suit. Like the domino thing, you know? And with so much discontent among so many people, lots are jumping on the bandwagon." He wiped away a trickle of sweat from his cheek. "And this heat doesn't help. People not sleeping, getting irritable. Could be the shit is about to hit the fan." From the kitchen Janie shouted: "Can someone come and give me a hand, please?" There was the note of exasperation in her voice. I found her sitting sideways at the kitchen table, elbows on knees, face in hands; and on the table were a spoon, a syringe and the packet of trilonite. Some of the blue powder had spilled onto the table.

She raised her head and sat back in the chair, holding her trembling hands out in front of her. "I'm shaking so much. You'll have to help me." She smiled, meekly. "It's pathetic, isn't it?"

"What do you want me to do?" I asked, returning the smile.

"If you could just mix it for me. . ."

I came around to her side of the table and scraped the spilled powder into the spoon. "Is that enough?"

"About that much again," she replied.

I tapped out another small quantity from the little, resealable plastic bag until there was what I would estimate as a fair-sized pinch in the spoon... if it had salt and this was a cookery exercise.

"That'll do."

She rose and tore away the plastic packet from the syringe with her teeth, went to the stove where water was boiling in Took's saucepan. She drew water into the barrel, brought it over and squeezed it into the spoon, then handed me the plastic top which had covered the needle. Evidently I was to use this to stir the mixture.

While I did this, Janie took a cigarette from the packet on the bench and tore out a piece of the filter. When the powder had completely dissolved, she dropped the filter into the solution, and placing the tip of the needle on it, I drew the filtered liquid up into the barrel. This done, I handed her the loaded syringe.

Her hands still trembled, and perspiration streamed down the sides of her face. I watched, almost fascinated, as she held it upright and tapped the side to bring the air bubbles to the top, then squeezed the plunger slowly until drops of the narcotic solution dribbled down the needle.

She passed it to me, to hold while she removed her jacket and rolled up her right sleeve, exposing those bruised puncture marks, now much faded and looking appreciably better.

With speed she unbuckled her belt and slipped it free of the loops, looped the end through the buckle and slipped it over her arm, pulling it tight and binding it a couple of times around her bicep. The free end she put between her teeth, then reached to take possession of the syringe. Her eyes met mine for a brief moment, before she moved the instrument to the prominent vein on her arm.

The needle remained poised and trembling over the vein, then slid into it without impedance. She adjusted her grip and pulled back on the plunger, drawing a cloud of deep-red blood, curling in the barrel and mixing with the blue narcotic solution to turn purple. She released the end of the belt from between her teeth and pushed the plunger home.

Withdrawing the syringe she pressed a finger to the puncture mark and sat down, breathed a heavy sigh and, as I watched, all the tension of the last few hours began to disappear from her face.

"A temporary reprieve," she said, emphasising the word temporary. "Jesus... How did I ever get in this mess?"

*

At 3:40 a.m. we left the bus parked on a deserted side-street, out of sight from the docks entrance where two guards, working out of a weather-board hut, checked for authorisation of in- and outgoing vehicles.

Took, as usual, was dressed in jeans, denim jacket and boots, while I, having discarded the cotton shirt I had bought at the Salvation Army shop, had opted for a black T-shirt which I had found amongst a bundle of clothing piled high on a chair in Took's bedroom.

Because dockside security is generally quite good, plan A was to bluff our way through the main gates, rather than plan B, which was to enter surreptitiously and risk being detected by an extremely bored, pistol-toting security guard whose secret desire - *and I've learned this through hair-raising experience -* is to take a few pot-shots at a live target. Plan C, therefore, was to make plan A work.

We strode up to the gates, looking purposeful beneath the glare of the mercury-vapour lamps. The elder of the pair of guards spotted our approach through the window and, setting down a mug of something steaming, stepped out from the gatehouse to confront us.

"What can I do for you boys?"

There was a military bearing about this man, with his at-ease stance, squared shoulders and neatly-trimmed mustache, but his voice suggested an easy-going nature: something I didn't expect. I said: "We're lookin' for work. I hear they're hirin' experienced blokes for unloadin'."

"Dick!" he called over his shoulder to his companion who was perusing a copy of *Tour Australia.* "Are they hiring down at the wharf?"

Dick reached across without taking his eyes from the magazine, picked up the telephone receiver and punched a button.

"Seems busy here this morning," Took said to our security man.

He hooked his thumbs in his belt and half turned to look down the access road, where the headlights of a semi-trailer could be seen approaching from some distance off. "It is, now the strike's over."

"What was it over?" I asked.

"Wages," he chuckled. "What else?"

Security guard Dick leaned out of the doorway with the receiver still in his hand. "You guys paid up members of the union?"

"Yes," we lied in unison. If we were asked to produce our cards here at the gate, the jig was up. It was time to put plan C into action.

"Can I talk to him?" This to security guard Dick. I had to steer away from the subject as quickly as possible.

"One of 'em wants a word," he said into the mouthpiece.

Took began making conversation with the old chap, about the recent spate of sultry weather. The wharf supervisor, or whoever it was on the other end of the line, had apparently assented to talk to me, because security guard Dick was waving me over to the phone.

I took possession of the instrument and started talking: "We're hard workers, mister. Been doin' this sort of thing for years. Got tonnes of experience. Gantry crane, mobile crane, fork-lift or just plain old muscle work. It doesn't matter, anything at all. We just-"

"All right!" came the gruff reply. "I'll give yer a try-out. Hand me back to the gateman."

I did this and went back to join Took, who was watching as the older guard stepped out to halt the approaching semi. "We're in," I told him, slapping him on the shoulder.

A minute later we were issued with passes and given directions to D-wharf, where we were to report to the Wharf Foreman, Klaus Overmeyer.

It was quite a walk, and we paid close attention to each signpost showing warehouse locations. Within sight of our destination and the bustle of activity there, we found the sign which read: Warehouses 1-5, and it pointed left. I checked my watch and saw that it was ten minutes to four.

Took made to turn left, and stopped when he realised I wasn't following. "Hey. It's down here."

"We've got to front the fore-dude," I told him.

"Why?"

"Those security guys. They'll check to see if we turned up. They're like that. They don't like people walking around unaccounted for."

"So what do we do?" he asked, arms akimbo. A roguish smile came to his face. "Never mind. Leave it to me."

The Eastern Star was docked just ahead of us; a rust-bucket which looked as though it should have been cut up for scrap at the turn of the century. Shipboard gantries swung containers down onto the wharf where huge machines, resembling four-legged spiders on wheels, clutched them up under their bellies and rolled away with them, to deliver to the appropriate storage area.

Some wooden crates were being off-loaded by mobile cranes on the wharf, where labourers loaded the smaller ones onto trolleys, the larger ones being carted away on fork-lifts.

We kept clear of all this activity by hugging the wall of the warehouse, lest we be flattened by a five-ton load of electronic toys swinging down out of the dark sky.

We spotted a guy in a white hard hat. He held a clipboard and appeared to be checking goods against an inventory as they whizzed past him into the enormous steel-frame structure, where most of the stuff seemed to be going. It was as bright as day within, and just as bright out here in the arena of activity.

We approached this man, supposing him the be the foreman - besides the white hard hat he was the one doing the least work.

When there was a lull in traffic, Took asked: "You Overmeyer?"

He turned to face us. "You're the new men?

We nodded and he looked us over, sizing us up. "Which one of you wants the fork-lift?"

"I'll take it," Took answered enthusiastically.

We were interrupted by the buzzing of a cellular phone on Overmeyer's hip. He placed it at his ear. "Yes? They're with me now." He grunted and returned the instrument to his hip, and I gave Took my *I-told-you-so* look.

"Okay," he resumed. "Let's see how you handle it. That timber is going aboard as soon as we finish unloading, so we stack it over there." He pointed to a yellow painted section at the edge of the wharf. "You go now."

Took ambled over to the machine and climbed into the seat. He soon had it started and quickly backed away from the timber, lining up the forks as he did so, stopped abruptly, then started in, raising the forks to come level with the base of the top stack. He was handling the thing like an expert, but I knew he had some fool trick in mind.

When Took had the top stack clear of the rest and began to turn with the load, the foreman looked at me and said: "Okay. We find something for you."

He called to a man to take over his tallying, and had only just relinquished his clipboard when an almighty clamour erupted.

Took had backed into a stack of drums, which were now tumbling down like a house of cards. One had split open and was spewing its contents, what looked to be olive oil, all over the work area. The wheels of the fork-lift spun and skidded as Took applied the throttle, twirling the steering wheel one way then the other. He straightened it up. Still in reverse and travelling at a cracking pace, the machine was heading directly towards the edge of the wharf and about twenty fathoms of water, the load of timber, miraculously, still balancing high on the hoist.

I quickly glanced at the foreman beside me... transfixed, eyes wide and mouth agape... then turned back to the spectacle. About five metres from the edge of the wharf, Took jumped clear of the marauding machine, tumbled backwards and came to rest just as the fork-lift struck the six inch thick skirting. The momentum and the weight of the timber held aloft caused the it to pitch backwards and balance precariously on its tail. It hung there tantalisingly, for what seemed like ages, then balance was lost as it pivoted gracefully and toppled over the edge and out of sight, to make a big splash a second or so later.

All work had come to a standstill during this time. It was eerily quiet until Took got to his feet and dusted himself off, then a chorus of whoops, howls and cheers went up from the ranks. His reaction to this was a sheepish grin, then, deciding to milk the moment for all it was worth, he bowed low in three directions and executed expansive hand gestures to his audience.

Foreman Overmeyer snapped out of his bewildered state. His visage darkened from red to scarlet to purple, and he finally exploded with a barrage of Germanic malediction which, although I couldn't understand, was enough to make my hair curl.

Shoving me aside like I wasn't even there, he stalked threateningly towards Took, now breaking into English. "You crazy idiot! You son of a bitch bastard! Get out, go before I kill you with my hands. Get off my wharf!"

Took sidled away, taken aback by the man's rage. When he saw that he wasn't actually going to be physically assaulted, he ambled from the scene. He did, however, make frequent, furtive glances over his shoulder, just to be sure.

"I guess I'll be going, too," I said to the seething foreman, but I doubt he heard me.

Took waited for me around the corner, a wide, dumb smile on his face.

"You're a maniac," I told him, unable to wipe the huge grin from my own face.

We retraced our steps to the signpost which pointed down a laneway, indicating: Warehouse 1-5.

It was no short walk, the warehouses were of monstrous size. At the intersection between 1 and 2 a guard, torch in hand and gun on hip, rounded a corner and walked ahead of us for a while. He was far enough ahead not to notice us, but we lagged well back until he disappeared around the corner of the next intersection.

We entered warehouse number three through a small door at the end of the building and kept to the central aisle as we passed between countless crates, drums and cartons piled high on either side. The floor was sectioned off with yellow painted squares, alongside which grid references were marked; and at every intersecting aisle an overhead sign indicated the number and direction of each bay, whether it be on the right or left hand side of the shed. We started at the higher numbered bays and counted our way down.

Not all of the sections were lit. In those which were it was impossible to see beyond the level of the suspended lamps, but in the unlit sections, we could see as high as the saw-toothed roof. . .Way way up!

At the intersection of bay 19, we had to duck behind a mountain of washing powder cartons to let pass a midget tractor pulling a train of trolleys across our path. At 16, a sneeze alerted us to a man pushing a broom. We lost a couple of minutes waiting forhim to pass, but we made the rest of the way unhindered.

The aisle connecting bay 14 was partially lit from an adjacent storage area. This meant that light spilled from our right as we faced the bay access door. High up to our left, at the top of a stack of shipping crates, was in darkness, and being right next to the roll-up door, it presented itself as the ideal place to conceal ourselves.

Agreed on this we scampered up the side of the stack using the intervening pallets as finger- and toeholds: an unofficial race, Took arriving at the summit before me, which, naturally, I disputed.

Once settled, Took pulled free the Luger with silencer fitted, and my needle gun which were taped to the inside of his denim jacket. Then we waited, in silence for the most part, lying on our stomachs while the minutes ticked slowly by.

We occasionally heard the sounds associated with the handling of goods, and snatches of conversation. There was even a fine rendition of Old Man River, given by one wry individual who used the cavernous structure to good advantage, unaware of his appreciative audience lurking high up in the dusty shadows.

This kind of waiting can be painfully tedious if you don't know how to handle it, and it's a trick of the mind, always, to let you think more time has passed than actually has. My antidote to this is simple. Time does not exist.

I got to pondering the reasons for my having decided to come here. Presumably, all I could expect to find would be a consignment of contraband. Either drugs or weapons. But it was important to Guido, and to this Cassandra character, therefore it was important to me that I find out just exactly what their caper was. And if Guido was answerable to him, chances were I might do Guido considerable damage by putting the kybosh on this deal. I simply could not pass up the opportunity.

I abandoned this line of thought and looked across to Took. He lay with his head resting on his forearms. Although I couldn't see him very clearly in the darkness, I made out the features of his face. His eyes were closed. Was he asleep, I wondered? I wouldn't have put it past him; the man was capable of damn near anything, I'd learned. Unpredictable but totally reliable. I had been very fortunate in gaining his assistance in this affair. Who else would have joined me in such an outrageous venture?

Janie. She showed a lot of courage. What an unlikely collection the three of us made. Or perhaps not. Although each of us had come together from very different walks of life, the one uniting factor we had in common was that, for one reason or another, we all existed outside of the general work-a-day community. Of no great significance, perhaps, considering how the old ideal of a segregated society still lived in the minds of our politicians, but a common thread nevertheless.

At ten minutes to five a fork-lift rumbled into the warehouse from the vicinity of the higher-numbered bays, travelling in our direction. Near the bay 14 intersection it slowed and, appearing from behind a stack of steel shipping crates, swung around the corner carrying a pallet on top of which sat an unmarked wooden crate about a metre and a half, square.

"That'll be it," remarked Took.

The driver, a short, powerful-looking fellow, halted the machine at the bay door and lowered the hoist, depositing the pallet on the concrete floor, then switched off the motor. It looked as though he was going to stay with his merchandise until it was collected. To reinforce this notion, he reached behind his seat and withdrew a magazine, which he spread open over the steering wheel and began thumbing through.

Took looked across to me, expressing the unspoken question while I stared down at the diminutive crate.

This was the object of so much importance ...the reason for code names and clandestine calls? I scratched weaponry from my list of two as I sighted along the narrow barrel of my needle gun and squeezed the trigger.

When he slumped forward into his magazine, I motioned for Took to remain up top while I climbed down to investigate the contents of the crate. When my feet hit the floor I ran over and lifted the dozing docker from the machine, finding him a comfortable spot behind a row of tea-chests. I needed something with which to prise open the lid of the crate. After a quick rummage beneath the seat of the fork-lift, my hand came out clutching a screwdriver, which I waved above my head, indicating to Took that all was well. I rammed the screwdriver into the corner of the crate and heaved. With a squawk, the lid came away, enough for me to get purchase with my fingers and lift the lid.

I looked into the crate and saw what I thought were polystyrene balls, the type used for packing around fragile freight. But when I put my hand in to search for whatever may have lain beneath, I discovered that they were not made of polystyrene at all, but a substance not unlike naphthalene. Moth-balls. And that's exactly what they looked like, except it was odourless.

I drove my arm in up to my shoulder and rooted around. Nothing. I was forced to conclude, therefore, that this moth-ball-like stuff was the bizzo.

At the same moment of me arriving at this axiom, a vehicle pulled up outside, behind the bay door. I listened as it maneuvered up close.

"Don't be too hasty," I said, looking up into the darkness, where I expected Took was experiencing the effects of healthy adrenal glands, as was I.

THUMP! THUMP! . . . Someone banged against the door as I hurriedly pocketed a handful of the stuff and replaced the lid. This done, I went over and pressed the top one of two buttons beside the door, which actuated the electric motor, and the door began to roll up.

When it had cleared the floor by a metre or so, two large specimens ducked underneath and looked around suspiciously... *Why are they always so big?*

The one with the jemmy-bar in his hand went immediately to the crate and lifted the lid to check it's contents, while the other moved me out of the way to place his own thumb on the button, and indicated that I should get behind the controls of the fork-lift.

As the door rose higher, I noted the vehicle they had arrived in: an old, beaten up utility; green and covered with grey dust.

The one with the jemmy-bar seemed satisfied with the crate's contents and hammered the lid back in place. I started the motor and hoisted the load, then rolled forward to the waiting ute.

It was much lower than the vehicles which usually used these facilities, and I found that even with the crate held protruding past the edge of the bay, I couldn't place it in the tray of the ute. I inclined the hoist forward as much as I dared, without the pallet slipping off the fork, and dismounted the fork-lift, saying to Guido's hirelings: "We'll have to ease it off by hand. It doesn't look too heavy."

I jumped into the back of the ute and took the front edge. The others handled the sides, and we slid the pallet forwards until it rested on the floor of the tray.

"What's in here?" I asked, and received cold looks. "Anything breakable?"

"It's not breakable," one of them said after a moment.

"Good," I said, climbing back into the warehouse. "Stand clear and I'll back out from under it."

They obeyed and I tilted the hoist further forward and began to back slowly away. The pallet cleared the tip of the fork and dropped the last twelve inches, the escaping air beneath raising a cloud of dust around the two men.

"There you go, boys. Be seeing ya."

They ignored my impertinence and quickly climbed into the front of the utility, and in a trice they were roaring off along the laneway.

"Hey, Took!" I called up into the shadows. "Come and have a look at this."

By the time Took joined me, I was kneeling on the ground outside the warehouse, inspecting the stuff which had shaken loose from the ute when I dropped the pallet in.

"Come down here and have a look."

He jumped down from the bay and squatted beside me on his haunches.

"What do you make of this stuff?" I said, poking one of the little piles of fine, grey powder.

He looked closely, absently stroking at his beard. "Hey, I know this stuff!" He took a pinch between his fingers and rubbed them together, inspected the resulting blue-grey stain which remained.

"This is the stuff covers my whole neighbourhood."

"And that ute was covered with it," I explained.

Sixteen

It was already light when we arrived back at the squat in Monroe. Janie was sound asleep on the couch, no doubt exhausted by the battle with her illness.

With the promise of another busy day ahead of us, Took and I decided to get some rest before the day became too hot. Took went to his bedroom while I fell into a beanbag beside the couch, my head abuzz with the pieces of disjointed information we had collected over the past twenty four hours. Weariness soon overrode the meandrine wanderings of my mind and sleep swept over me like a vast, grey, rolling fog-bank, the name Cassandra echoing between the hemispheres of my brain.

I dreamt of a snow-covered plain, horizonless. A shimmering, cold, white desert across which a distant voice plaintively called my name; a voice I recognised as Jim's father's. "Jack!" I yelled. "Stay where you are. I'm coming!"

Again the far off voice reached out across the tundra. "Go back. Go back, Alex. There's too many of them. Tell my wife and kid I love them."

"No-o-o-o-o!" I screamed, running in the direction I thought the voice had emanated from.

The snow was knee deep and getting deeper; every step harder to take, as though it were molasses through which I desperately tried to force a trail. . . in vain . . . my energy sapped, I was forced to yield. I wept. . . out of rage and with a terrible weight of impending loss pressing down on me. To lose him a second time was unthinkable. Unbearable.

Snow began to fall. White-out . . . no sense of direction now. The only sound, the rushing blood in my ears and my labouring breath. The snow fell in the form of small, round spheres, gently, as should the most delicate of snow-flakes; the air completely still.

Blue-skinned cadavers encircled me; unwholesome violations of *Nature* . . .a silent, unseeing host.

Overhead appeared a nebulous glow; a luminescent orb coalescing, and within, a moth, brightly coloured. It's name, undoubtedly . . .Cassandra.

It's insect legs grew long, and reaching down into the snow they emerged again supporting from the joints of limbs and from the top of the head a marionette in the likeness of Guido Spinoza, twitching, jerking. And as the moth-leg-strings rose, another puppet emerged from the snow, a simulacrum of Vincent Zendell and beneath this came my own effigy.

TRAVESTY! my very being tried to scream, but no sound came. Fascination held me transfixed as other doll-like images were drawn upwards on moth- leg-strings: Pat, Jim, Janie, Took, Con, Francine, Heidi, Michael and others who were unrecognizable to me.

The leg-strings began to glow . . . green . . . red . . . white . . . and all the figures began to twirl . . .faster, faster, until all became a blur.

The light played garishly on the death-mask faces of those who framed the scene; a ludicrous spectacle within a snow-white arena which dead eyes could not see. The frenzied twirling motion of puppets and strings became a blazing column of light, and within, the neon dancer danced, its flickering epileptic movements profane, tantalising . . . . repugnant.

I awoke. My eyes felt gritty. My face was stuck to the vinyl cover of the beanbag, I painfully discovered as I lifted my head to try and make out the digital clock on the television set. With some effort I focused my eyes. It was 9:18 a.m. The day was already very hot and I felt like shit. I could hear the generator droning at the rear of the house as I rubbed my face and tried to clear the muzziness from my head. I looked over the edge of the couch. Vacant. Janie was already up.

Just then Took appeared in the doorway, fresh out of the shower by the look, with a towel wrapped around his waist. "Not good sleeping weather, is it?"

He seemed bright enough, at least. I mumbled a gruff and unintelligible reply and he left me alone to gather my wits.

I followed Took's example and showered. A cold one. Then pulled on the same jeans I had been wearing for the past three days. Took lent me another clean t-shirt.

Janie was in a plucky mood. She busied herself in the kitchen preparing a breakfast of scrambled eggs, tomatoes, toast and coffee, and over this we discussed the agenda for the day.

"Well, troop," I said, feeling somewhat revived. "I suggest we find out exactly what it is we have here before we go off half cocked, in search of our local trilonite factory."

I was referring to the moth-ball-like substance, a piece of which sat on the table for everyone's inspection, and which I suspected was used in the production of trilonite.

Took ripped the tab from a can of beer and quaffed half of it down in one fluent motion. It wasn't until he had plonked the can down on the table and wiped his mustache that he realised Janie and I were studying him in amusement.

"Medicinal," he said, shrugging.

Janie returned to the subject. "How do we find out what it is?" Then answering her own question: "Chemical analysis, right? We'll take it to a lab."

"It's Sunday." This from Took.

"Oh, yeah, that's right. I forgot. Well what about that doctor I went to? He seemed like a pretty cluey old guy. What was his name again?"

"Mainwaring," I said. "Let's' give him a try."

Took parked the bus in a supermarket car-park and we walked the short distance back to Doctor Mainwaring's surgery. Naturally the place was locked up tight, and a *"closed"* sign hung behind the frosted glass in the door, but set into the brick wall was a brass flange with a button at its centre, and a strip of card in a small plastic window read: *"a.h. emergency only."*

"Well I guess you could call this an emergency," I said, pressing firmly. "I hope he's not out playing golf."

"I don't like being out in the open like this," said Took, looking around apprehensively.

Janie shoved in between Took and myself so that we formed a tight little bunch on the doctor's doorstep. "Me neither."

I was about to make it unanimous when I noticed movement behind the frosted glass. "It's okay, somebody's coming." Mrs Mainwaring, I judged. Too small for the Doctor.

Two slip bolts were snapped back, top and bottom. Then the key latch. The door swung inwards and Mrs Mainwaring stood, holding the door half open. She was in her dressing gown and slippers.

"What is it?" she asked.

"I'm terribly sorry to disturb you on a Sunday," I began deferentially, "but it *is* important. Could we talk to Doctor Mainwaring?"

She didn't seem very enthusiastic about the idea. "How many are you?"

Janie stepped out from behind me. "Only the three of us. Do you remember me from Friday? We came in to see the doctor," she said, grabbing hold of my arm. "And this is our friend, Adrian."

A look of recognition came into her eyes. "Oh, yes. I do remember, now. Janie and . . . ?"

"I'm Alex, Mrs Mainwaring.

"Yes. . . Alex. Well, you had better come on through," she said, stepping aside and opening the door the rest of the way. "How are you coping, dear girl? One more day and you can go to Rushbrook House."

"Oh, not too badly, thank-you. The night-time is the worst, but as you say, just one more day."

She closed the door and led the three of us along a passage. "Robert is in the garden fussing over his azaleas and rhododendrons, or whatever. I've never been any good at remembering all the names. I hope you will excuse the way I'm dressed. We tend not to get many visitors after hours. Or even during business hours, come to think of it."

At the end of the passage she opened a door which led into the private residence. We passed through their living room – well furnished and comfortable-looking – through a cozy dining room where land- and seascapes hung on the walls, and a glass-topped, cedar table stood at the centre of the room. Then through a modest kitchen and out onto the back verandah.

The verandah supported many hanging baskets containing bright blooms, a feature not missed by Janie, and there was a wooden table with a bench seat and a couple of chairs.

There wasn't a lot of space left between the rear of the house and the end of the yard. A bungalow had been built across the back of the narrow block, and between it and the verandah the earth was given over to all kinds of plant-life. Amid this, with water-breaker in hand, stood Mainwaring, dressed in baggy brown trousers, desert boots and a blue singlet.

Mrs Mainwaring marshalled us together under the verandah and stepped out onto the gravel path to inform him of our presence.

"Ooo-hoo! Robert! There's someone here to see you."

His attention thus gained, he looked over in our direction, peering hard to make out who this small gathering might be. Mrs Mainwaring, coming up beside the doctor, spoke hurriedly to him, motioning for him to put down his hose and come meet his visitors.

I was worried that he might resent this intrusion, but with his wife's explanation a smile appeared on his face and he made his way over, wiping his hands on his trousers as he came.

"Ah, Miss Stuart, and friend and friend. Are you having problems?"

Janie quickly allayed his concern, reminded him to call her Janie, and formerly introduced Took, *er* . . . Adrian.

I got to the point of our visit without further ado.

"I have something here which I think might interest you, Doctor."

I pulled one of the *moth-balls* from my pocket to show him. "I strongly suspect it's used in the production of trilonite, but if not, I'd very much like to know what it is."

Mainwaring slapped it out of my hand and it landed on the gravel path. Disregarding me he studied the small, white ball.

After a moment's confused silence, I inquired: "What?"

"Lucky for you, laddie, it's not what it might have been." He nudged it with his desert boot, then knelt down to inspect it more closely. Meanwhile, Took, Janie and myself looked blankly at each other.

"You shouldn't handle substances like this if you don't know what they are, "Mainwaring said gravely. "If it had begun to vaporize when it hit the wet gravel. . ." He looked up at me. "It looks much like sodium cyanide, but it isn't."

I broke from his gaze to turn to the unknown substance. "Look, it's dissolving!" And as we watched it melted away to nothing.

"*Hmmm,*" Mainwaring intoned thoughtfully. "Extremely soluble. I expect you have more?"

"A pocketful."

"Then let us endeavour to unearth what it is you have there." He led us back inside the house and through a door on the opposite side of the passageway to his consulting room. Within, we discovered a lab complete with work bench, sink, gas burners and all the other paraphernalia, including shelves stocked with many glass jars containing, I assumed, drugs, herbs and chemicals.

At his direction I emptied my pocket into a ceramic dish while Janie and Took looked around the room.

"Nice set up," Took remarked.

"You should see his other room. There's lots of stuff in there, too," Janie attested.

"You might say I have more than a passing interest in medicine. Not so much a vocation as an obsession. And it just so happens that the mystery of trilonite, or angel wings, as it is commonly known, is my current project. A very frustrating one, I can tell you. I've been unable to make much headway with it at all." As he talked, Mainwaring used a mortar and pestle to grind a few balls into a powder. He then began distributing small amounts into a row of test-tubes in a rack.

"Why are you so sure this substance is connected with trilonite production, Alex?"

"It's rather a long story, but to cut it short, the man who is distributing the stuff, trilonite, I mean, had this shipped in secretively. Knowing him as I do, I rather suspect he is involved in its manufacture as well."

"It's a fair assumption," Mainwaring commented as he began half filling the test-tubes from a bottle marked "distilled water".

"Extremely soluble, what?"
He lit a gas burner and began heating a test-tube. "How was it packaged?"

"Loose, in a shipping crate."

He boiled the mixture until the test-tube was dry, then held it up to the light between a pair of forceps. "Everyone, have a look at this and tell me what you see."

We obeyed. Like students attending a science class we crowded in and studied the empty test-tube. We stared at it a good while before Took came up with, "Nothing."

"Exactly, said Mainwaring. "Not a trace of residue. Crystalline form but doesn't reconstitute with distillation. Possibly becomes an azeotropic fluid when hydrated."

"No kidding?" I had no idea what that signified.

He partially refilled the test-tube and dropped in a litmus paper, then moved to each of the others, adding one thing or another, making such remarks as, "That's interesting, most unusual," or, one time, *"Pfui!"* He then resorted to the microscope, inspecting each of the solutions and a little of the powder. Finally, he looked up from the eyepiece and reached into his pocket for his pipe, which he lit using the gas burner.

He went back to the first test-tube and inspected the litmus paper.

"Neutral," he muttered, and puffed on-his pipe.

Took, Janie and myself had taken to talking quietly among ourselves while he went about his business. Now we fell silent, feeling sure he was about to impart an explanation of his findings to us. This did not occur however, and when the silence seemed as though it would go on for ever, I ventured the question: "Do you know what it is?"

Mainwaring looked around as if surprised to find others in the room with him. "Did somebody say something?" Janie obliged. "Alex asked if you know what it is."

He blew a plume of smoke into the air, placed his pipe on the bench and thrust his hands into his trouser pockets. "Haven't the foggiest," he replied. "The most confounding substance I've ever come across."

"What is it that's so confounding?" Took asked.

"It reacts, initially, with water, dissolves so totally, in fact, that it is undetectable under the microscope. It is neutral, that is to say, neither acid nor alkali, and it failed to react to any of the tests I put it to. I really need an electron microscope to see what it's doing on a molecular scale. But I think you might be right about it being associated with trilonite, which is now the second most confounding substance I have come across. You will need to take it to the Science Institute where they can conduct a much more sophisticated line of analysis."

"But that will take time, and we don't have a great deal of that. That rat Spinoza has something special planned. And soon! I'm sure of it.

"*Rats!*" Mainwaring expressed loudly.

"I could have put it a little more strongly than that," I replied humourlessly.

"No, that's not what I mean. I have some *lab rats* I keep out the back in the bungalow. As a part of the research I've been conducting I've been adding a regular dose of trilonite to their diet."

"Junkie rats," Took quipped. Then suddenly realising his mistake. . .

"Sorry, Janie. Present company accepted, of course."

The crack bought him a sharp kick to the ankle, then Janie turned back to Mainwaring. "So we try the stuff on the rats?"

"It is the only option I have left. However, if this substance is merely a constituent part of trilonite, we shouldn't expect anything much. But a later blood test may be revealing."

"It's worth a shot," I said. "We've got *F.A.* so far. No offence, Doctor."

"None taken, laddie."

We all pitched in and brought the rats in from the bungalow. Six of them in separate cages marked from *A* to *F*. Two of them being what Mainwaring referred to as *controls*, A and D were drug free. The remaining four had been fed trilonite over a period of between one and four months. We lined up the cages along the bench while Mainwaring mixed a fresh solution of the white stuff.

Took asked, "Has there been any noticeable affect with the ones on the drug?"

"Some," replied the Doctor. "They're not quite as active, and a mite less sociable. Physiologically there was no change, but suspension of the dose for even a short time, say ten hours, and they become decidedly cranky. A common enough manifestation of withdrawal among humans. In a communal cage they seek a quiet corner away from the others, and if another rat comes too close, aggression is the usual outcome. I didn't have the heart to withhold the trilonite for much beyond the ten hours, though." He chuckled. "Some scientist, eh?"

I mentioned to him what Janie's friend, Heidi, had told me. That she hadn't known anyone to beaten the addiction.

"I know how they feel," said Janie, poking her finger into the cage of rat *F* and stroking it behind the ear, which it obviously enjoyed.

"Ooh. . . loook," she crooned. "Poor little thing. Did the man make you hang out? Hey, Doctor. Where'd you get the dope?"

Took gave her a sharp nudge.

Mainwaring smiled. "It's all right, Adrian. It's a fair question. I get it from an addict whom I've been unable to help, or at least, who is unable to help himself. I tried to get a small supply through legal channels, but the authorities insist that enough studies are already being undertaken, and that mine was unnecessary."

"I won't tell anyone," Janie promised.

Mainwaring was ready now. He moved the solution to the bench and drew the liquid up into a pipette. He raised the door of the first cage, reached in and grabbed rat *A*. Lying backwards in the Doctor's grasp, it accepted the liquid without fuss and was soon back in its cage, none the worse. The procedure was repeated with each of the others in quick time.

"If nothing happens over the next few hours," said Mainwaring, "I'll repeat the dose. After that-"

"Doc!" I cut him off. . . Some of the rats had keeled over.

"They're dying!" Janie exclaimed in horror.

In a matter of seconds there were four rats lying dead in their cages. We stood, silent, watching the two remaining rats for over a minute. They remained unaffected.

"Only the subject animals," Mainwaring murmured, and turning to me, said, "Do you remember what I told you about trilonite the last time we met? I mentioned that there is a peculiar structure within the main body of the drug. It's what has baffled everyone so far. A group of molecules that seem to serve no purpose, but which are there nevertheless, and which can only be incorporated into the molecular fabric using highly specialized laboratory procedures."

"Yes," I replied, and suddenly I understood what he was saying.

"An incomplete molecule."

He nodded. "Exactly that. An incomplete molecule, the rest of which is contained here." He indicated the ceramic dish. "The two halves combine within the human body to form a new and virulent substance. Only conjecture at this stage, of course, but it's the most logical hypothesis."

"Chemical warfare against drug addicts," I said, summarizing. "So that's what it's all about. Monopolize the illicit drug market with a cheap, highly addictive and readily available drug which is capable of superseding all other drugs of addiction. Then, when you have everyone hooked... *pfft.*" I snapped my fingers, indicating the finality of it. *"Diabolical."*

Mainwaring broke the brief silence. "We must inform the authorities at once."

"Wait a minute." I grabbed him by the arm as he moved toward the door. "Who do you intend contacting?"

"Why the police, naturally."

"No good," I replied. "Believe me, they're not to be trusted."

He accepted my judgement on this and tried again. "Department of Health, then?"

"If you must, but I'm afraid it may already be too late for them to act. In fact, I'm sure it is. I have to warn you that the moment you advise them of this, you put your life in jeopardy. The people responsible are well connected and, as you see, totally ruthless. Best if you use an assumed name."

"Impossible," said Mainwaring, indignantly. "I would never be taken seriously unless my *bonafides* can be verified. I have a duty."

I put up no further argument, and he left to make his call.

"We've got to warn everyone," Janie said anxiously.

"I agree," Took seconded. "I realise time is short, but we have to warn as many people as we can. If we fail to find Spinoza's operation and this stuff gets through to the streets, we will have saved some, at least, from certain death."

Personally, I would have preferred to begin the search for the manufacturing plant, but Took's reasoning was sound enough. I looked at my watch and saw that it had just gone midday. Roughly eight hours of daylight left.

"Okay, there's time... but we had better go about this as efficiently as possible. I don't want to be blundering around the streets looking for the plant after dark."

"I have an idea on that," Took said. "I know where the ash comes from. It's a smoke-stack about half a mile from my place. And the prevailing wind for the past month or so has been from the west and south-west. So if we work the area east and north-east, we ought to find the bastards somewhere in that section."

"And there's a simple solution to alerting everyone to the danger," Janie added. "The radio! If we can get just one radio station to broadcast a warning, word will spread through the grape-vine. What do you say?"

"I say it's a great idea. Have you guys been taking *smart pills* or something?" I said, affecting a mock look of incredulity. "Okay, let's do it. We've got a long haul in front of us and it's strategy like that we're going to need."

Seventeen

We climbed aboard the bus and Took got us under way, bound for the centre of the city. Janie sat beside me on the front seat, flicking through the pages of the telephone book Jim had supplied me with, making notes of the locations of some of the more popular radio stations in Monarto. I busied myself with studying a map of Monroe in the street directory, and with Took's assistance I marked out the area we would later be combing in search of Guido's trilonite factory.

I did this by marking the position of the smoke-stack and drawing two diverging lines, fan-shape, away from it to the north-east, which compensated for the wind shift Took had mentioned.

The next step was necessarily somewhat of a guess concerning the height of the stack and the distance the ash was likely to travel before it precipitated to the ground. Took wasn't able to say for sure, but between the two of us we decided on a two thousand metre radius as the minimum distance to search in.

I made the fan-shaped zone sufficiently large to account for extra wind shifts between south and west, and although I had expected to be left with rather a large area to cover, I was surprised to find the perimeter encompassed only between three and four square kilometres. The reason for this being that the industrial area did not stretch very much further to the north of the stack. Rectangular in shape, its borders ran west and east. Had the winds followed along this axis the search would have had to take in an area three times the size. If this had been the case we would have needed every bit of remaining daylight in which to conduct the search.

Janie found that three radio stations were situated on a single street on the north side of the city, one of them being the University of Monarto station; popular among many of the counter culture. Approaching as we were from the south, we opted for the most direct route, taking us through the heart of downtown Monarto.

As could be expected during the middle of the day, and especially being Sunday, traffic was minimal, and in any case many of the city dwellers would have taken themselves away from the sweltering heat of the urban environment and made for the seaside, or merely closed all doors and windows and confined themselves to the air-conditioned comfort of their dwellings, were they so lucky.

The air hung motionless in the streets while the surrounding brick, steel and concrete structures radiated heat from all directions. Even with the windows of the bus open there was little relief in our movement as hot air blasted through the interior, as if just released from the belly of a giant furnace. The combination of heat, fatigue and circumstance began to take an enervating toll on all of us, and conversation soon subsided into dumb circumspection.

Janie leaned against the window and closed her eyes. Before long her head was lolling in rhythm to the undulations of the road. Took's weariness was apparent, also. He stooped over the steering wheel with his forearms supporting his weight, staring unblinkingly at the advancing road, his hair flaying about from the open window like angry asps, Medusa-like. And with the monotonous drone of tyres on hot bitumen I sank into the yawning abyss of unconsciousness.

I awoke with a start, feeling myself beginning to topple forwards out of my seat. I looked around dazedly for a moment, trying to ascertain my whereabouts.

"What's going on?" Janie asked groggily.

Took brought the bus to a rapid halt behind a long line of cars, then looked over to us with tired eyes. "Sorry, I lost concentration. Some sort of problem up front."

Fifty metres ahead of us a police car was parked across the intersection. A copper stood beside it, indicating for motorists to wait patiently, doing this with arms raised and patting the air in front of him.

A moment later came the sound of approaching sirens. The wail of fire engines together with the peculiar hee-hawing of a police siren.

I scanned the city skyline. . . "There." I pointed to an inchoate plume of black smoke rising above the next block.

The fire units, when they arrived, consisted of two pumpers and an articulated vehicle with a giant, extendable ladder with a spray nozzle attached, followed by two police cars and an ambulance. When they had negotiated the intersection and sped away down the road in front of us, the copper got into his patrol car to use his radio, presumably to be given further instructions. Minutes passed, during which time frustrated commuters vented their spleens by honking their horns. Finally, he emerged from the patrol car and started directing traffic around to the left, onto the two-lane road which cut across our path.

Merging the three lanes into single file and allowing other crosstown traffic to pass through took considerable time, but eventually we were moving again, and quickly decided on an alternative route to follow.

This route, too, had to be amended however, when, at the next block, we discovered another detour blocking our path. We realised over the next few miles of our circumvolute course that a large area of the city had been sectioned off. Somewhat mystified by the situation, we wondered at the cause of so much confusion, but we were far too preoccupied with our purpose to concern ourselves with this line of speculation for long. Finally getting back on course, we left all thought of the incident behind us.

The employee at the reception desk, a sharply dressed, middle-aged woman with bottle-blond hair and brown eyes, put down the receiver and looked up at the three of us inquiringly. "Yes?" Her voice was bland, cheerless.

The telephone on her desk rang just as I was about to deliver the spiel I had rehearsed on the way over.

"Just a moment, please," she said, turning her back to take the call.

I clamped my mouth shut and looked across to Janie and Took, making no effort to conceal my annoyance.

Fortunately, the call was not a long one. She turned back to us. "Now then. . ."

"It's vital we get a warning out to the population," said Janie, steeling my thunder. "Lives are at risk!"

The woman looked us over, disdain evident in the way she tightened her already too narrow lips. "Who are you people?"

"Never mind all that. We would like to see the Station Manager," I told her. "There's a very deadly substance about to be foisted on a section of the community, and as my friend says, we need to enlist the help of this radio station to alert the public to the danger."

"The Station Manager is out at the moment. In any case, we are not able to broadcast such messages."

"What?" I was truly taken aback. "This isn't any hoax, lady. Thousands of lives are at stake here."

"That's the law," she announced, tersely, but then she decided to continue. "How many crank calls do you think we've had here this morning? You're the first who have actually had the audacity to walk into the building though."

Now she exhibited outright hostility. This was absurd!"What the hell is the matter with you, lady?" I was about
to try again, when, from the corner of my eye, I noticed two figures rounding the corner of the corridor to my left. Turning, I observed a pair of advancing security guard types. She must have *buzzed* them.

"They're threatening to poison the city or something," she told them.
I glared contemptuously at her a moment before addressing the guards. "She's whacko, guys. A misunderstanding, that's all."

"We'll let the police decide," said the nearest, glancing over my shoulder to the receptionist. "Call them."

As she made to comply I looked to Took, and shrugged. He reached over the desk and wrenched the telephone cable from the wall.

"I'm sorry, but we can't let you do that." I struck the nearest guard a cracking blow on the point of his chin. He fell. His companion received my right sneaker in the solar plexus and a chop behind he right ear.

The woman screamed for the briefest moment. Janie silenced her with a resounding backhander.

Mute now, she looked at each of us, a terrified expression in place of the disdainful one she had displayed moments ago. But I wasn't angry any more.

"You're not going to be harmed," I said, discreetly drawing the needle gun from the back of my jeans, and she never saw it coming.

We left the three of them dozing peacefully in a broom closet while we walked on down to the next radio station.

Janie caught me casting her a sideways glance as we strolled along the footpath. . . "What?"

"You surprised me back there. That was quite a smack you gave her."

"Snooty bitch deserved it."

"You might be right about that," I said, chuckling. "It won't do much in the way of changing her attitude, though. You ever do anything like that before?"

"Once or twice," she replied. I guessed she was feigning severity, but she had me guessing.

The next radio station was eight doors down. It inhabited a modern, three storey building with a glass facade. A large banner spread above the entrance proclaimed: PAN-FM, and from unseen speakers issued strident rock music.

"We're going to encounter the same thing here," I said as we stood on the footpath looking up the steps to the glass doors. "Establishment radio. Unlikely to contravene any laws on the strength of a bizarre story delivered by three nobodies fresh off the street. You guys got any ideas?"

"We should have brought the Doctor with us," Took said. "He would have lent credence to our story."

Janie looked at the slip of paper on which she had written the addresses of the radio stations. "We may have better luck at the next one. . . UM-Radio. It's the university station."

UM-Radio was situated on the far corner of the next block along, in a narrow, two storey grey-stone building opposite the University of Monarto campus.

"Okay," I said, standing at the top of the steps. "If we don't have any luck here, we might as well give the game away. We can't afford to waste any more time."

We descended the steps and passed through the doors to enter a small reception area. It was partitioned off from the space behind by blue, free-standing panels. On the walls hung posters advertising forthcoming musical and theatrical events, and a large pin-up board above a row of chrome chairs displayed personal notices and pamphlets.

The desk, beside which stood an imitation potted palm, was vacant, but a bell sat on the desk-top and a card beside it read: Ring for Assistance. I rang, and presently a girl appeared from behind the partition. She was thin, pale, blond; wearing a colourful flower print blouse and blue jeans, and leather sandals which fastened around her ankles with narrow straps.

"Sorry," she said, exhibiting the mug she carried. "Needed a coffee. What can I do for you?" she asked, beaming.

"We wish to get a message out to the community," I said as she put down the the coffee and seated herself behind the desk.

"It's kind of important," Janie added.

"Oh? What kind of message?"

"We have it on good authority that every trilonite user in the city, and possibly beyond, is in danger of being poisoned. I don't think it has hit the streets yet, but the next new batch will almost certainly be lethal."

She engaged me with her clear, blue gaze. "You're not joking."

"I wish I were."

She got up from her chair and rounded the desk. "Follow me."

We followed her behind the blue panels to where a young man and a woman worked at computer terminals amid piles of books and papers. We continued on up a set of narrow stairs and across the top floor where we passed through the heart of the radio station --- two studios, one in use and a production room --- and on to an office at the rear of the building.

Our thin, pale guide knocked on the frosted glass of the office door, then turned to us. "Would you mind waiting for a moment while I explain?"

From behind the door came a loud *"Come in"* and she entered, closing the door behind her.

"I think we might have cracked it," Took commented. "We've made it past the first hurdle, at least."

Janie said, "We've only got to convince whoever is behind that door."

We waited expectantly. . . Presently the door opened and we were ushered in.

Beside a beaten-up desk stood a young man in his mid twenties. He was tall, strong-looking, wearing a short sleeved shirt and blue slacks. His red-orange hair was long and tied back in a short ponytail. There was a vulpine look about his face and his clear, green eyes suggested perspicacity.

"Joe Grummen," he said, offering his hand to each of us in turn. The girl who had led us up here darted off for a moment, shortly to return with an extra chair.

"Thank-you, Gretta," said Joe Grummen, when she had placed it beside the other two. "Please, be seated. Gretta has explained the situation to me." He looked toward the girl who now stood quietly by the door and smiled at her. "I'll fill you in, later." When she had gone, he continued. "This is a community service radio. We'll advertise your gigs and parties, put out a cheerio to friends and loved ones, or even assist in a search for a lost puppy. But this? I've never had to contend with the likes. . ." He paused awhile in thought.

"If we broadcast this warning and it turns out to be a hoax, we can lose our licence. We've had a lot of nutters calling in today, you know."

"I've heard that," I said, resisting the impulse to begin defending our integrity. I had already decided to hijack the station and broadcast the message myself, if he should refuse to aid our cause.

"What's with these crank calls, anyway?"

"Haven't you heard about the riots? It's been on the radio and television all day."

"No. We haven't had the opportunity to catch up with current events. Is that what all the action in the city is about? We were detoured on our way in."

"God, yes. In the city *and* the suburbs. The under-privileged are rising against their oppressors." There was a flicker of fire in his eyes. "Or so, at least, is the word from the street. As far as I can make out, it was a spontaneous thing. The phenomenon began last night."

Joe was leaning forward in his seat, ready to tell the story when he suddenly decided to check his enthusiasm.

"Go ahead," I urged. "I'd like to hear about it."
"Well. . . It was such a small thing. The police were called out to a disturbance at a night-club last night. A bit of a ruckus, apparently, between management and some overenthusiastic punters. By the time the cops arrived it had turned into a

free-for-all. Backup was called in and during the melee a cop shot someone. That's when it turned ugly.

"Someone set light to the place and when they spilled out onto the street, they started busting up local businesses. From there it snowballed. In the confusion the looting started. Somehow word spread. I suspect militant political activists stirred the pot and whipped people into a frenzy, and by dawn the chaos had reached to every poor suburb, and lots have commuted to the city to swell the ranks here. The police say they're stretched to the limit trying to cope with all the new outbreaks. They were bringing in reinforcements from interstate, the last I heard."

I thought for a moment, remembered what Took had told me of his conversations at the Sword and Sandal when he had gone out to get the trilonite for Janie.

"I hear the pressure has been rising in this city for quite some time."

"That's very true," replied Joe Grummen. "This is probably the worst city in the country for unemployment, and the Government has been totally inept in dealing with it. Homelessness and poverty are rife. This sort of thing should not come as a shock to anybody. Perhaps some good will come out of it."

"Perhaps," I mused aloud, and I straightened myself in my chair. "But this is not the point of our visit, and time is getting away from us. Will you broadcast the warning, Joe? I can offer you *some* verification that our claim is valid."

"I would be grateful if you could," he replied earnestly. "I do like this job."

"Then telephone the person who discovered the threat, Doctor Robert Mainwaring. His number will be in the book."

Eight five seven five oh five two two," said Janie. "I've got a memory for numbers," she replied to my questioning look.

Without further discussion Joe Grummen lifted telephone the receiver at his elbow and dialed. After a short wait he had Mainwaring on the line.

Mainwaring did most of the talking, and as he listened Joe's face reflected belief. After a minute he thanked the Doctor for his assistance and replaced the receiver in the cradle.

"That's good enough for me," he said soberly. "I'm still taking a risk, but if I didn't act on what I've just heard I'd deserve to be hung by the balls. Begging your pardon, miss. We'll transmit the warning every fifteen minutes for the rest of the day." He arched his eyebrows. "Or until we're taken off the air for contributing to civil unrest."

Eighteen

Before initiating the grid search of Monroe we returned to the squat. We had decided to maximise efficiency by splitting the search, with Took working alone, riding the Vincent, and Janie and myself using the bus. Working from opposite ends of the search area we would carefully scan every street, working inwards until we met up somewhere near the centre.

I hastily prepared sandwiches while Janie organised another dose of trilonite for herself. Took tuned the radio to the university station and watched the television screen for reports on the riots, and I retreated to the lounge room to join him while Janie completed her ritual.

"Here. There won't be any time to eat once we begin the search," I said, handing him the meat sandwich.

He accepted it and went directly to the ice-box for a can of beer.

"This search is going to take some time," I pointed out. "I think we ought to work ninety-minute stints and meet back here to report our observations. If you spot what might conceivably be the plant, don't make any move on your own.

Safety in numbers, remember."

To this Took nodded agreement while chewing on a particularly large mouthful of sandwich.

"Most of the factories are out of commission, but out of those still in operation I doubt we'll find any of them working on a Sunday. This makes our job easier. Anywhere showing signs of activity will be a possibility. Take note of the position and what they appear to be doing. Anything fishy and we'll get back to it, *together*, okay? Oh, and you better take the Luger. Janie and me will take the shotgun along."

When I returned with the Luger, he and Janie were paying close attention to the television. The screen showed footage taken around the suburbs: Supermarkets and shopping centres with doors and display windows smashed in, goods left strewn on the footpaths where looters had dropped their plunder and fled under pursuit of the police. Sporadic fires burned here and there; evidently Government offices and exotic cars drew the most attention from the roving mobs.

Footage taken in the city depicted more graphically the seriousness of the situation. I turned up the volume and we listened as an almost hysterical reporter prattled well-worn adjectives in describing the scene, while the camera focused on a pitched battle going on in the main shopping mall between police, rigged out in riot gear and wielding truncheons, and hundreds of rebellious citizens who appeared to be making a good job of it, repelling the attack with dust bins, pieces of timber and steel pipe. Doing so well, in fact, that the police were forced to retreat back to their own lines, whereupon a hail of missiles rained down on them, launched from the second line of rioters. In retaliation the police fired tear-gas canisters.

Quick on the uptake, the rioters utilised the dust bins to catch the canisters, which they immediately hurled back at the police.

The camera lifted to the city skyline, over which a pall of black smoke now hung. From this angle two tall department stores could be seen gouting smoke and flames from upper-storey windows. The reporter mentioned that public transport into the city had been cut. *Hoards of hellions*, as he put it, had been travelling into the city since first light, to swell the *riotous ranks.*

The unmistakable crack of small arms fire halted the reporter's effusive narration. The picture swung wildly as the cameraman ducked for cover, then steadied and brought the fleeing crowd into focus as they sought to scramble down alleyways or into the looted stores in effort to evade the angry hornets.

"Madness! This is madness," shrilled the reporter. *"Madness in the streets of our city!"*

I prodded the off button. "Come one" I said. "It'll be dark in another six hours."

Janie and I started our search at the edge of the two-thousand metre limit, while Took worked back from the outermost edge.

The combination of Took's information concerning wind direction together with our guess at a two-thousand-metre margin proved to be pretty well on the money. At the outer edge the amount of ash was markedly less, and I could only hope that the quantity of ash collected by the ute Guido's men had used at the warehouse was due to the amount of precipitation in the area it was usually parked in, rather than the amount of time elapsed since it was last hosed down.

This was an oversight on my part, and the idea that we might be concentrating our search in too small an area began to gnaw at my innards as we scoured through this industrial graveyard, searching for that something, that tell-tale sign which would say: *"this way to the bad guys!"*

There were scenes like this in plenty of other places around the land; stark reminders of the country's flagging economy. Factories which once employed hundreds of thousands of people now stood derelict and ramshackle under the blazing, non-ozone-screened, Aussie sun.

The whole locality stank: a mixture of decaying wood and iron, leaking drums of chemical toxins, long ago left to rust through and seep into the sterile earth; and the pervading stench from the rubber mill, whose smoke-stack it was that spewed tons of fine, grey ash over the whole ghastly scene. Many of the one-time employees of these factories, I fancied, were even now running through the streets of the city, venting years of pent up frustrations, tired of living abject lives with little or no hope for the future for themselves, for their children, or for their country.

"Why are you smiling?" Janie asked.

"I didn't know I was."

"Well you were. What are you thinking about?"

"I was thinking about the rioters in the city. I was thinking that they must be feeling truly alive for the first time in ages."

I felt her use that stare on me. The same penetrating stare she used the night I drove her away from the Old Coach. Was it only three days ago?

"You're meant to be watching the buildings," I reminded her. She watched me a while longer, then turned back to the task as I swung the bus onto the second street of our itinerary.

"They're united in a struggle," I added, attempting to clarify what I had said. "And that's important ... to be united against a common foe. No matter how insane it looks from the outside, at least they're not just voiceless, subjugated individuals any more.

Not as long as the fight lasts, anyway. They're a tribe, and the longer it lasts the stronger the bond will become. Maybe, as Joe Grummen said, some good will come out of all of this."

"Perhaps," Janie responded introspectively. "But people were probably killed in that gunfire."

We threaded our way through street after deserted street, at not much more than a jogger's pace, being careful not to miss a single possibility, keenly aware of what a lapse in concentration, a single clue overlooked, might cost.

Surprising how the need for alertness always brings on a bout of lassitude, especially when you haven't had a proper night's sleep, the mercury is hovering at around forty degrees and the drab scenery into which you're peering in search of minute signs rolls past your eyes with such monotonous regularity that it threatens to mesmerise. I remembered the radio and was happy to find UMRadio playing a cacophonous brand of music, ideally suited to dispelling soporific tendencies such as mine.

At two-thirty the disc-jockey uttered the warning Grummen had promised. A trite message:

"To all you angel wings freaks out there. Word has it there's a contaminated batch about to hit the streets. It's a killer, kids. We have the dope on the dope and the dope is that the dope is no good. If you've been thinking of kicking the habit, kick it now, before the habit kicks you! Pass the word, people, we don't want anybody harmed by this stuff."

Janie turned to me and said: "You realise, of course, that some users will still take the risk. Poison batch or not, the temptation will be strong once they start hanging out."

Three days ago I would have been incredulous of this statement, but having seen for myself the symptoms of trilonite withdrawal, I could well believe an addict might rather a game of chemical Russian roulette than face days of torment.

At three-thirty we returned to the squat, hoping that Took might have something to report. The only activity *we* had come across was a moving van, the driver and his offsider unloading furniture into a storage shed.

We shared a cold beer while we waited, and watched the news update of the situation in the city. But after fifteen minutes Took still had not arrived.

"I don't like it," I said, rising and moving to the window to peer out into the street. "He wouldn't be this late unless there was trouble."

"Maybe his bike broke down?" Janie suggested.

"Not very likely. That bike is in perfect running order. Come on, we're going to look for him."

There was nothing else for it but to cover Took's search area from the beginning. It was time-consuming and frustrating, but vital that we did so.

We headed out to the far north-east corner of the district and began the sweep more rapidly than before, not bothering to scan as intently the buildings and the sites they occupied.

The tone of the area was hardly distinguishable from what we had previously reconnoitred, except that here the depth of the ash was appreciably greater. This proved to be a boon; Took's tyre tracks were clearly visible at each street corner where spoon drains collected ash to a depth of a couple of inches. If mechanical failure was his problem, we would soon be there to lend a hand.

On Little Creek Street, the tenth of Took's itinerary, we passed a motley array of sheds and a water tower set way back behind a red brick wall, just low enough to see the layout from our elevated position in the bus.

My curiosity was immediately piqued when I noticed the ironclad gate, chain-locked between two concrete pillars, at odds with the apparent dereliction of the rest of the property. The paint-pealed letters on the wall read, BAGSHAW'S TANNERY, and I tried to take in as much of the premises as I could in the time it took to drive by.

At the end of the street I pulled up short of the corner, and there again were the tyre prints of Took's motorcycle. My retinae retained the images behind the tannery wall: three sheds, one large, two small; a water tower, very tall, concrete, windows up the trunk of it; the site was overgrown, mainly fennel, Scotch thistle and rye-grass; wheel ruts cut into the broken surface of the bitumen access road.

"What's up?" Janie asked.

"Did you notice the old tannery back there?"

"I did." She smiled and held up the map, pointing to where she had marked its position.

"What was your reason for marking it?"

"I don't know. It looks like the sort of place. Secure like. Most of the other places are more open and have that chain-link fencing. But that one is hidden. And that big iron gate..."

"Yeah, that gate got me too. Less than twelve months old, I'd say. We'll get back to that one."

I swung left, then left again at the next corner after crossing a small bridge which traversed an open concrete drain; what was once known as Little Creek, I imagined.

We covered a further three streets. At the end of the third there were no motorcycle tracks in the spoon drain as we had come to expect. I halted the bus and we swapped bemused looks. Janie spoke first.

"He didn't double back. I've been watching closely and there's only the single set of motorcycle tracks on every corner we've come to."

"Yeah, I know. Then he must have left the road somewhere between here and the beginning of this street."

I made a three point turn and drove back the way we had come, extra slow, paying close attention to the verge for any sign of Took's point of departure. Halfway along the street, Janie called, "There! Alex, stop." I complied. "What is it?"

"There."

She pointed to the middle of the road in front of us. How had we missed it? Black skid marks, and a few small pieces of red plastic. I yanked on the lever to open the door and we climbed out to get a closer look.

Up close, we could see that the bitumen was scored just after the black line of rubber, where the footrests, exhaust pipe and handlebars had scraped the surface.

"He came down here," I said, pointing to the marks. "But he was tail-ended here. This red plastic is from the tail-light. Someone knocked him down from behind then cleared away most of the evidence."

"Could it have been an accident?" She looked down at the incriminating signs.

"On a straight road in perfect visibility? Not a chance." She looked up round-eyed and spoke quietly. "Then they have him, don't they."

I didn't answer, but looked up and down the street. There was nothing to distinguish between this and all the others we had searched. I looked away, north, my eyes searching among the drab hulks and roof-tops of the silent factories. My gaze drifted of its own volition and came to rest on the most prominent feature of the area... the water tower. Its grey, solid dominance among the surrounding tumbledown structures seemed to speak to me on the subconscious level. *BAD GUYS HERE!* it said. It was the tannery. I knew it in my bones.

Janie followed my line of sight. "I think so, too. He couldn't have failed but take an interest in the place, as we did. Maybe he scaled the wall to get a look inside. He made someone nervous, and when he moved off they sent someone out to run him down?"

"The timing would be about right," I concurred. "By the time they got a vehicle and caught up to him..." I looked back to the scrapes on the road surface. "I don't think the impact was great. I doubt their intention was to do any more than disable him. They'd want to question him, find out what he knows and who else knows."

Suddenly there came a *CRRUMP* and *BOOM* of a distant explosion. We both spun round in time to see a huge roiling mass of smoke and flames spouting skywards, some ten to fifteen kilometres away to the south. The sound came again, reverberated from the escarpment of the line of hills east of the city.

Janie reflexively clutched my arm in fear. "What's happening, Alex?"

Bewildered for a moment, I couldn't answer her question. Then it dawned on me... the only thing in the area which could produce such an explosion. "It's the oil refinery. Sabotage, no doubt."

"Shit!" Janie exclaimed, then she started to laugh --- a little too easily, I thought. "For one crazy moment I thought war had broken out."

Her laughter grew ragged. She pushed her face into my shoulder and I instinctively held her to me.

"War?" I tested the word, allowed for a moment a few longsuppressed images to emerge from the past.

Nineteen

There was only one course of action to be taken; with no reinforcements to call in, Janie and I were the sole reserve. I had to enter the tannery grounds unseen, and ascertain if it really was the manufacturing plant we were looking for. If so, the onus was on me to devise a strategy to effect Took's escape and destroy the plant. Easy, I told myself sardonically. How the hell was I going to do this in broad daylight? But there was no time to waste, we had no way of knowing Took's plight. We had to move immediately and find out at least if he was still alive. Pushing this thought aside I set my mind to the logistics of the problem.

I broke open the padlock securing the gates of a disused compound. On site there was a shed large enough to drive the bus into. With the bus safely out of sight, I emptied the tools I wouldn't be needing from my bag and we headed off towards the concrete culvert we had crossed earlier.

The open drain ran along back of all the sites north of Little Creek Street, including the tannery, and it was a safe bet that storm water from these premises was carried through subterranean pipes directly into this drain, in which case I would make like a sewer rat and gain entry from underground.

At the bridge Janie slid down the side of the culvert. I tossed down the tools and the shotgun to her, then slid down beside her. She handed me back the shotgun and, thus concealed from view, we strode off along the floor of the drain which was covered with the ubiquitous grey ash and littered with debris such as engine blocks, mattresses, timber and tangles of fencing wire. Janie carried the tool-bag, leaving me free to wield the shotgun, should the need arise.

From down here I could see the top of the water tower some three hundred metres along, and we made our way towards it, occasionally having to climb around a pile of filth or a tangled mess of sheet iron which some cretin had seen fit to dump there. As expected, storm water pipes emptied into the drain from every factory site we passed. They were concrete, a metre wide with two divisions of two metal bars at their opening; one set horizontal and the others vertical.

"Why are they barred like that?" Janie wanted to know.

"Security against would-be thieves and vandals," I explained.

"And to stop kids from playing in them, I suppose. There are sumps inside which a kid could easily fall into and drown."

Janie snagged her jeans on a coil of barbed wire and ripped open a triangular-shaped flap high on her thigh. We were both already covered in the ash we kicked up as we trudged along the floor of the drain, which pleased her not at all, but now she let fly a string of oaths few beer-swilling ockers could hope to rival.

She stood holding the flap of denim with a forlorn look on her face. With her other hand, which also held the tool-bag, she brushed ineffectually at unruly strands of hair, which only served to smudge grey ash across her cheek. My smile was met with a defiant glare.

"Laugh and you're dead, mister." She slung the tool-bag up to her shoulder and stalked off in a huff. I followed up the rear... and a lovely rear it was, too!

The storm water pipe protruded from the concrete wall about three-quarters of the way up. Janie sat astride this with the shotgun across her lap, keeping peg while I hack-sawed away at the halfinch steel bars at its opening. Not an easy job when you're standing on a forty-five degree incline and it's forty-plus degrees in the sun.

Inside the first minute I was soaked with sweat and the saw began squirming in my wet grip. The blade snapped as I pushed hard to finish the first cut, and I skun my knuckles on the adjacent bar, providing me with the opportunity to show that I was no slouch, myself, when it came to malediction, as I scurrilously cast aspersions on the sexual proclivities of whoever it was chose to use high tensile steel bars and, likewise, question the lineage of the manufacturer of such poor quality hack-saw blades. When the pain subsided, however, and I removed the broken blade, I realized my mistake.

I looked up to find Janie smiling down at me. "Would you pass me a high-speed blade from the bag, please? One of the brown ones."

I sawed and sweated and grunted for the next twenty minutes, until I had removed enough of the bars to allow access. By this time my arms were leaden and my shoulder muscles burned, but my ankles, which had been cocked at forty-five degrees for the duration, were merely numb. "Some holiday."

"What?"

"Eh," I replied, not realising I had spoken.

"You said something about a holiday."

"I'm supposed to be on one, now. It's why I came to Monarto."

"Why on earth would you want to take a holiday here?"

"Long story," I said, tossing the last bar into the drain and passing the hacksaw up to Janie. "Hand me down the torch, will you."

I took it from her and shone it into the opening, the beam disappearing into the gloom. Straight for at least thirty metres, beyond that I couldn't tell.

"Okay, let's go."

"You're kidding. I'm not going in there." She affected a look of disgust.

"Suit yourself," I said, shrugging.

I reached up and relieved her of the gun, shoved it into the drain and climbed in after it. It was a snug fit, just high enough to assume a crawling position. I crawled in about ten metres, then turned off the torch and waited. It wasn't long before I heard her climb down off the top of the pipe, and shortly afterwards her head appeared, silhouetted at the opening.

"You can't leave me out here, alone!" (I remained silent) "Alex?"

I aimed the torch at my face and switched it on. "Oooooo-oooo."

I saw her flinch.

"You bastard."

"Coming or not?" I chuckled.

She climbed in, pushing the tool-bag in front of her.

"You can leave that here for now. We won't be needing it."

She left it just inside the opening and crawled up beside me. "It stinks in here."

"Yeah... does pong a bit. Here, you take the torch and try and give me some light up front from time to time. I'll keep the shotty, so's I don't get my butt shot off."

"It would be a definite temptation," she rejoined.

We set off along the pipe, the movement of the torch sending my shadow lurching around the interior in a dizzying fashion, and the clacking sound of gun and torch, as they bumped against the concrete with each crawling motion, resonated up and down the narrow pipe.

"You really know how to show a girl a good time, don't you."

"I suppose you had a better idea?"

"I don't have to enjoy it. I just hope Took is all right. This had better be the right place."

"If it isn't, it should be. And if it is, it might be beneficial for both of us if you wouldn't talk so much. Sound carries a long way in a confined space like this."

She lowered her voice. "I know that. Places like this frighten me, is all. I can't help thinking how horrible it would be to get trapped... you know, like entombed, and never get out. So excuse me, mister fearless wonder, if I try and take my mind off it. Some of us aren't quite as at home crawling through sewer pipes as others."

"This is a storm water pipe," I reminded her. "And who says I'm enjoying this? And even if it was a sewer pipe, there'd still be no other option. Maybe I should have left you back there to sun yourself like a lizard on a rock ... *Yow!*" She hit me on the ankle with the torch.

"Who're you calling a lizard?"

We continued to argue in whispers for the next couple of minutes until I noticed a peculiarity a short distance ahead. I squeezed over to one side to let Janie come up next to me with the torch, illuminating a two-way junction.

"Which way do we go?" she asked.

"It doesn't matter. We're going to check them both, anyway. You choose."

"That way." She shone the torch down the right hand fork.

We hadn't travelled far when we came to another branch, heading off at right angles to our left. Along its length were three openings through which sunlight streamed in from above. And I could hear a rumbling noise.

"Hear that?" I asked.

"Yeah. Where's it coming from?"

I listened more intently, and it sounded more like a gurgling, rumbling noise now. "From back the way we came, I think." We turned left at this new branch and crawled up to the source of light, almost blundering into a water-filled sump beneath the grate, our eyes dazzled in the brightness.

I straddled the sump and tried to raise the grate in order to ascertain our position, but it was too well wedged in for me to lift, and all I could see was the water tower and the roof of one of the buildings. I was aware that the gurgling rumbling noise was now a gurgling, *splashing*, rumbling noise... and it was getting louder!

Something fell onto the grate above my head, partially blocking the sunlight. *My tool-bag!*

There was a rush of foul-smelling air about us and my stomach turned to lead as I realised what was going on.

Janie turned the torch back along the way we had come, in time to illuminate the first gush of water passing through the junction and begin to spill into our section.

"Quickly," I snapped, and dragged her over the sump, causing her to drop the torch into it. The outside light caught her face – deathly white and terror-stricken. Even as I drew her along behind me, I worked out what must have occurred. We had been seen entering the storm water drain. They plugged up the pipe somehow, and were now flooding it, probably from the water tower, judging by the speed with which the pipe was filling.

Janie screamed and crashed into me in a desperate attempt to get past; the reason for this became apparent when I sprawled forward and was washed along by cold, putrid water. Panic surged in me like a demented thing and threatened to overwhelm me, but I beat it down with all that I could muster ... perhaps there was still time.

It was only the initial surge, I realised; there was still a lot of pipe to be filled before it began to back up and rise to the top. The water was at chest level.

"We can make it!" I yelled to Janie. "The next grate, come on."

She was sobbing. Her worst nightmare had been realised, but she had the guts to regain control and fight the urge to scramble over me.

The water had risen to my chin by the time we crawled to the next grate. I heaved with all my might to lift it and felt a bolt of white hot pain shoot along my spine, and I knew then that we were in real trouble. Did they really intend to drown us like rats?

Laughter came from above. Then a voice. "If you can get to the next one, you've made it."

The water was at my mouth, now. Janie was trying to scream but couldn't. She gasped for air and stared at me with wild, desperate eyes.

"We're going for it." I screamed, in order to penetrate the panic I knew was overtaking her. I turned her on her back and dragged her past me, then continued to propel her towards the last grate, still some twenty metres distant.

Before we made the first five of them, there was not enough room between water-level and the top of the pipe for me to breathe, not in the position I needed to maintain in order to continue pushing Janie along. I rammed my lungs full with what I expected was going to be my last breath of air.

Janie began thrashing about violently. She had taken in water and was beginning to drown. I pushed, scrambled, clawed my way along in the darkness beneath the vile water, grappling with Janie's thrashing limbs.

My lungs were caving in ... Janie had stopped struggling ... consciousness was slipping away ... it was out of my hands now ... *I'm sorry, Janie* ... I breathed water ...

Twenty

Limbo. A foggy, grey whirlpool where I drifted in and out of consciousness several times before my mind began to accept messages from the nether regions of my body. Something pressing against me ...cool and hard. A low hum. An ache stretching across my back, shoulder blades and the back of my head.

A fit of coughing seized me and I rolled onto my back and opened my eyes. A face. Whose face?

"Rest for a bit. You'll be all right. You've got a cut on the back of your heads and you've been bounced around a bit, but nothing serious."

I heard the words but they didn't seem to mean anything to me. Rest a bit? Yes, that's right. Rest a bit. I'll just lay here awhile. A pressure I hadn't noticed released my shoulder. A shuffling sound. The cloud began to lift. I remembered. . .

"Ja–" I spluttered and coughed some more. "Janie," I managed, then pushed myself up to a sitting position.

I was in some sort of cage, under bright lights, and I noticed for the first time I was soaking wet.

"She's okay," came the voice, behind me now.

"Took?" I twisted around, causing a bolt of pain to shoot along my back.

Took was on his haunches beside Janie. She rested with her back against the chain-link wire of our cage, bedraggled and pale, but alive. Her hand moved feebly towards her face in an effort to brush tangled hair from her cheek. Took assisted her with this then looked over to me as I tentatively climbed to my feet. I teetered precariously for a moment before finding balance, then took my first step.

"I thought you were both dead when they brought you in."

"How is she?"

Janie let her head fall back against the wire. "If I look half as bad as you, I've got problems." Her voice came hoarsely, but she managed a wan smile.

Laughter gagged in my throat, resulting in another bout of coughing. I felt thoroughly unnerved.

I staggered sideways, not the direction I had intended, and had to catch hold of a set of steel shelves to keep from falling.

"We're in the tannery, right?"

"Yep," Took replied.

I looked around at our surroundings. We were in a caged area of about two and a half metres by four metres. The humming I had heard came from a diesel-powered generator nearby, toward the nearest end of the shed which terminated just beyond it, in green painted corrugated iron and a set of large sliding doors. Batteries of bright fluorescent lights shone down, suspended from high rafters. I moved from behind the steel shelves and looked along the greater length of the building.

Within the outer walls stood a separate enclosure. It was built of clear perspex panels between aluminum framework. Inside it white-coated, white-capped people worked with sophisticated-looking apparatus, and partitioned off to one side was a well equipped laboratory.

Looking through the clear partitions to the rear, I saw what appeared to be large, stainless steel vats, *cookers*, the fumes from which were being drawn off by overhead exhaust fans; and suspended above the whole enclosure, on heavy, steel framework, a monstrous air-conditioning plant connected by wide, concertina type ducting. The whole show, it appeared, was being run in a strictly controlled environment.

The cage in which we were confined was part of the storage area where scores of canisters, no doubt containing chemicals used in the production of trilonite, were stacked in groups along the wall. Janie got up, a mite groggily, and came over to join me at the wire.

"You okay?" I asked.

She nodded. "So this is it. The big banana. Excuse me if I don't shout eureka, won't you."

Took came over, too. "You were seen from the moment you turned onto the street, you know."

"The tower?"

"Yeah. There are lookouts stationed up there. I saw them when they brought me in. Take a look down the side of the shed."

I did, and noticed gun-toting guards standing at two exits along the walkway between the outer wall and the manufacturing enclosure.

"Two more on the other side," he said. "And some more positioned in and around the other buildings, I imagine."

"How long have we been here?"

"About ten minutes"

"What I want to know," said Janie, backing away from the mesh and wringing the water out of her blouse, "is how did we get out of that drain? The last thing I remember is swallowing that putrid water.

"I guess we were spat out at the last sump." I remembered, vividly, the disembodied voice telling us we would make it if we got to the last one. "The water pressure must have pushed us the last few metres." I continued to search the interior.

There were drums of diesel fuel standing behind the generator. There were containers full of chemicals, electrical wiring along the walls, water pipes along the rafters to supply the air-conditioning plant, cooking vats, and an oxyacetylene unit, not ten metres away. Among all these things were the ingredients of destruction. But, first, we needed a viable escape plan. The gate of our cage was bolted and secured with a padlock, I noted with some amusement. But how to get out of the grounds without being dropped in our tracks?

"I heard an explosion a while ago." Took commented.

"The refinery," I replied, while I searched the roof. "The shit has really hit the fan out there." I bent down and extricated a piece of heavy gauge wire which had lodged in a crack in the concrete floor. "This is one crazy city, Took."

Behind the generator the sliding doors rattled open, and in walked two men, each carrying army issue SLR 7.16mm rifles. Close on their heels followed a smallish man with dark hair and dressed in a sharply tailored blue suit.

"I wonder who that is?" Janie said softly.

"That," I replied, "is Vincent Zendell, Guido's playmate nephew and probable pretender to the throne. Monarto's equivalent of haemorrhoids."

The goons marched up to the cage and halted by the gate, with rifles levelled threateningly. Zendell came right up close and gloated for a moment. His lips parted in a smile suffused with rancour.

"Enjoy your swim, Jaeger, you and your whore? And where did you scrape up this one from?" he said, meaning Took.

In a sudden lapse of decorum, I spat through the mesh and managed to hit his highly glossed shoes, and gave him a look which made words unnecessary. "You come within reach and I'll snap your neck, you jumped-up little twerp," I said, in case he hadn't got my drift.

My venom stunned him for an instant, but when his hand darted behind his lapel and withdrew holding the Luger I had last seen in Took's possession, I had to wonder if I hadn't acted unwisely. There was a measure of relief on my part, therefore, when one of the goons wrapped his paw around the weapon and pointed it skywards.

Zendell glared at him. "Let go!"

"Mr Spinoza wants them alive."

Having said this, he released his grip, which had encompassed the weapon and Zendell's hand.

Zendell struggled to contain himself, ambivalence temporarily staying any positive action.

"You'll keep," he said, turning his beady eyes on me. Then: "You low-lifes will be buried here before the night is over." And with that he stalked off, taking the other goon with him.

I watched the remaining man. His eyes displayed contempt as they followed Zendell's retreating back. "What an arse-hole," he growled.

I resisted the urge to thank him. After all, he was only following Guido's instructions. I turned instead to Took and Janie.

"Sorry about inciting the dramatics."

"It was *you* he was going to shoot," Took said dryly.

Janie shot him a sideways look. "How can you joke about a thing like that."

He ambled over to the corner and sat himself down. "None of us are out of it yet, Janie"

There was nothing caustic about the way he said it. He had simply pointed out that if we didn't get our act together, the future held little for any of us. Zendell's parting words had underlined that point very nicely.

While Janie went over to sit beside Took, I regarded our unwanted guest standing at the gate.

"You want to come in here with us?"

"I'll be here until Mr Spinoza arrives."

"Oh? And when will that be?"

He reversed back a couple of steps and seated himself on a pile of hessian sacks. Resting the SLR across his knees, he said: "When he gets here."

I was in no particular hurry to see Guido; I had a rough idea what was in store for us when he got here, and with this guy watching over us, there wasn't too much we could do.

While Janie and Took talked quietly in the corner, I paced the floor, as I sometimes do to help me think, searching for anything we might turn to our advantage.

Our watch-dog pulled a packet of cigarettes from his pocket and lit one up. "Cigarette?" he offered.

I eye-balled him suspiciously for a moment, without breaking rhythm.

"I'll have one," Janie said, coming up to the gate.

He tossed the packet, sliding it under the gate, followed by a book of matches. "Keep them," he said. "I've got some more."

Then: "If it wasn't for me, you two would have perished in the drain. Zendell was all for letting you drown."

I stopped pacing. "What is it with you? You trying to score brownie points or something?" I turned to join Janie and Took against the wire, but our watchdog was persistent.

"Alex Henry Jaeger, infantry, seven brigade, third battalion. Graduated Royal Academy, Duntroon, Lieutenant first class. First tour of Nam, February '68. Busted to Warrant Officer for striking a fellow officer. Decorated for bravery later that year for retrieving vital intelligence behind enemy lines. Busted again, to Sergeant, for refusing a direct order from an American Army Major during Operation Pinnaroo. The Major was later found in a ditch with his neck broken. Nothing was proved.

"1969, Tet Offensive, Nui Dat, citation for valour, offered reinstatement to the rank of Lieutenant, which you refused. 1971, you led a special unit into Cambodia, a highly classified mission from which no one ever returned. Last sighted, 1974, San Vicente, El Salvador. U.S. intelligence wanted your skin for the role you played in organising military resistance against U.S. troops in Nicaragua, namely, selling your knowledge of weapons, tactics and explosives to the Samosa regime, but you somehow got wind of it and vanished before you could be captured. Since then, whereabouts unknown." He took a long draw on his cigarette.

"Welcome home, Mr Jaeger. How long have you been back?"

He certainly had my attention now.

"What is this crap and who the hell are you?"

"I'm a fan of yours, Mr Jaeger." He looked around furtively. "Jozef Kosciusko, special agent." I continued only to stare at him. ASIO? ... was it possible?

"It has taken many months for me to infiltrate Spinoza's organisation," he said, when it became clear I was going to make no reply to his bizarre claim. "We have been trying for years to build a case against him. One which will stick. He's a slippery bastard, but we have him now." He waved the rifle muzzle to indicate the plant, then glanced at his watch. "In two hours time this place will be swarming with Feds." He smiled broadly. "Your troubles are over, Mr Jaeger, and your part won't go unrewarded.

"Oh? What about my part?"

"There's no need for modesty, Mr Jaeger. We know you've been molesting his operations. I have no doubt you intended destroying this factory ... a man of your capability. And the books you stole from Zendell. You still have them, don't you?"

Bingo! So that was it ... that was the hook.

I gave him my best sneer. "You know, you really had me going for a minute there. If you're ASIO, I'm the Dalai Lama. Everything you've told me is well within Guido's scope of knowledge. Much of it I told him, *myself.*"

He was about to protest his innocence but I was sure of myself now. This was just the sort of thing Guido would try on: the man's deviousness never failed to amaze me.

"You don't sucker me that easily, especially with that good guy/bad guy routine. Zendell tries to put the frighteners on us, then you ride up on your white charger, pretending to be ASIO, and I'm supposed to spill my guts? Come off it Kosciusko, or whatever your name is. I've been 'round too much to fall for that old routine. Guido's idea, right? Vinnie the viper doesn't have the mental capacity of a flatwom."

Our bogus special agent seemed only slightly put out by my seeing through the audacious charade. With a shrug, he said: "It was worth a try." Then, with a chuckle: "Vinnie the viper. The boys will like that."

Over the next three hours we either paced the confines of our cage or sat, taking turns to rub flat against the concrete the piece of wire I had discovered in the crack in the floor. It would make a fine lock-pick once it had been narrowed and shaped, but it looked as though our keeper was not going to give me the chance to use it.

After yet another stint of ambulatory contemplation, I sat down to face Janie and Took. "I've been thinking," I said, softly, so I couldn't be overheard. "There's no doubt we'll be questioned when Guido arrives. I'm surprised it hasn't already begun, but it seems he intends conducting the proceedings himself. In any case, he'll be primarily concerned with three things. How much do we know? Who else knows, and where are the ledgers and diary?

"The first two are related. If he knows we know about the planned massacre of thousands of drug addicts, this ingredient X thing, he'll want to know how we know, in which case he won't cease until he makes the connection to Mainwaring, and we sure as hell don't want to land him and his wife in the same predicament as we find ourselves. Obviously the same applies to Jim and Pat."

"Have you forgotten about the radio broadcast?" Janie asked.

"No, I haven't. If he knows about that, he'll pin it to us, naturally. We'll just have to hope he and his goons don't tune in to the university station, or that they don't find out by other means. We might be lucky on that score.

"As far as the books are concerned, to save ourselves any needless discomfort," and my eyes were focussed on the floor as I used this euphemism, "tell him anything he wants to know, barring one thing... the whereabouts of the originals. We'll say they went to the Attorney General's office in Canberra. If things don't turn out so well for us," and I managed to look them both in the face, this time, "at least those books might prove to be his undoing. The newspapers are good at that sort of thing."

"It's some consolation," Took said.

Poor consolation, I mused bitterly, but better than none.

"But it's not going to come to that," I said, trying to sound confident. "We're getting out of here one way or another. I've been in worse-"

"Alex," Janie cut in. A grave look clouded her face as she sat, hugging her knees against her chest. "It was my decision to come along," she said after a pensive moment. "I know it was against your better judgement to let me get involved, but just remember, I'd probably have been killed two nights ago at the Old Coach if you hadn't come along. So don't go putting yourself on some sort of guilt trip, okay? I sometimes imagined myself dying alone in some sleazy room somewhere, with a needle stuck in my arm. I can face this." She looked away momentarily then engaged me again with her dark eyes, almost coyly. "I just wanted you to know, that's all."

How could she say something like that to me... at this time, in this place, after I had nearly gotten her drowned and with the threat of death still looming over us all? I think I was ashamed at that moment, truly ashamed for the first time in my whole, selfish, rotten, misguided life. If she would just stop looking at me as though I were so goddamned blameless ... with those eyes! I reached across and put my hand on her knee. "Thanks, Janie, but we are getting out of here."

She delicately placed her hand over mine. Electricity flowed between us as though a long-open circuit had finally been closed, and I knew then more than ever that I had to succeed in getting us safely away from this place.

Took ha-hemmed. "If we weren't locked in this cage," he said through a silly smile, "I'd do the decent thing and make myself scarce."

With renewed vigour I set my mind to the task. Rudimentary fragments of a plan circled one another in my thoughts, disjointed elements randomly trying to fuse together into one workable scenario. Too few options, too many unknowns and no second chances: this was the refrain my mind continued to throw up at regular intervals. The ingredients just were not there yet, but I stayed with it, doggedly plunging back into the problem to sort and correlate information in search of the right pieces, in proper sequence, finally to discover the flaw in their defences and turn the smallest chink into a gaping fissure through which we could escape. *There is always a way.*

I paid close attention to the men and women at work inside the perspex enclosure. Eight in all, two women and six men, all working steadily at their designated tasks.

The section nearest to us appeared to be the central monitoring station. Cables ran into it from each of the other three areas, connected to a computerised system where a number of display screens were being closely watched by a tall, middle-aged woman. While the rear two sections looked to me like high-tech kitchens, the section adjacent to the monitoring station at the front of the enclosure, looked to be responsible for a particularly delicate process... possibly the final stage of the complex operation.

Here, wide but shallow ceramic receptacles containing a raw version of the trilonite, a viscid, blue-black substance, were trollied in from the adjoining cubicle and deposited on a large bench-top hotplate. What I thought was an over-developed range hood suspended above the bench, with heavy, rubber hoses and insulated fine wire cables attached, was then lowered over the bench and locked into position. I realised they were forming a pressure-resistant chamber, and the rank of gas bottles on the walk just outside the cubicle, to which these hoses were connected, suggested that it was to be pressurised rather than vacuumised. Other hoses and cables were then connected to the chamber, and some system-testing was done in concert with the computers in the monitoring station.

The meticulous attention being paid to detail suggested to me that, not only was this operation a delicate and sophisticated one, but that it also involved not a small element or risk. Having had a smattering of laboratory training, I knew that the most common reason for conducting such a procedure (*outside of normal atmosphere*) was to avoid explosions, and what I had learned from Mainwaring about the structure of trilonite, tended to support the notion that there would be a stage in its production when it was unstable. No doubt this was that stage.

The gas or mixture of gasses within the chamber probably served a fluxing role, and because heat was being applied, the gasses would also need to be inert to combustion - or so ran my line of reasoning. The upshot of all this was that if someone were to pump the wrong gas into that pressurised gismo, the result might be very surprising.

As the day wore on, Janie became more and more restless; an indication that her last dose of trilonite was wearing off, and that before too long she would again be suffering the miserable effect of full-blown withdrawal - an added torment to an already untenable situation, and one neither Took nor myself could share the burden of.

I attempted to cajole our guard into acquiring a small amount of the drug, but was met only by a terse and bigoted remark about useless junkies, and at Janie's intervention I ceased my remonstrations.

I had just resumed my pacing when, half-way along the length of the shed, a door opened, admitting a large, bull-necked man I immediately recognised as one of the goons who had met me at the bottom of the steps outside Villa Vulgar, the day I had visited Guido. It was about to begin.

He strolled towards us, ostentatiously twirling a set of handcuffs before him, and came around the side of the cage to stand before the gate.

To our guard, he said: "We'll take one at a time. Jaeger first." Then to me: "Back up against the gate, hands through here." He indicated the space where the padlocked bolt was located. I complied and was handcuffed behind my back before the gate was opened.

Twenty One

The ape following then directed me to along the narrow space between the manufacturing enclosure and the outer wall, as far as the first exit. The armed guard stationed there opened the door and we stepped out into the twilight of evening.

The building we emerged from was the largest of the three, the one to my left being the second largest, and with its doors swung open I saw that it housed a minibus and two cars, one of them being the beat up old ute I had loaded at the dockside warehouse. The other was Guido's Rolls Royce.

My escort turned me to the right and headed me in the direction of what I decided had once been the factory offices, located at the end of a gravel surfaced road and about fifty metres away. No building showed any light from within, and the one towards which I was being steered had its windows blacked out, no doubt to avoid attracting attention.

Looking up to the water tower I was unable to see whoever might have been behind the stairwell windows keeping watch. Ahead I saw the grate which had been lifted to allow our escape from the storm water drain, and I managed to discreetly veer towards it, enough to notice as we passed that the water-level was still at the top. I could scratch that as a possible escape route, I thought, as my sneakers squelched in the clayey bog created by the flooded drain.

As we drew level with the end of the factory shed, my heart sank when I saw Took's bus parked behind it. I had hoped it would remain undiscovered, ready for our escape bid, if I ever came up with a viable scenario. Guido's men had been quite thorough, it seemed.

We halted at the door of the office building while my escort knocked. Another armed guard opened the door and waved us in to the lighted passageway with an Uzi machine-gun. I was shoved toward a door on my right and again my escort knocked. After a short delay Guido's peevish voice called, "Come." My handler twisted the knob, pushed open the door and we entered a sparsely furnished office.

Vincent Zendell sat in a chair against the left wall. Guido, wearing a blue business suit with a white carnation in the lapel, leaned back in a swivel chair with his feet up on a desk on which sat a pile of paperwork. Behind his head stood a filing cabinet, in front of him a straight-backed wooden chair which he now gestured towards.

"Sit down. I think it is time we had another chat."

Although it was a hot and sultry evening outside, the ambience in here was decidedly frosty. Musclehead shoved me forwards and pushed me into the chair.

"So. . . What would you like to talk about?"

Guido folded his hands over his small paunch. "You've been busy since the last time we met."

"Yeah, well. Idle hands and all that. You know what they say."

"I could never understand why you refused to come and work for me. You could have done very well for yourself." He gestured to my somewhat compromised position, grinned smugly. "Certainly better than this."

"Why would I lower myself?"

"Morals, Alex? From you? I know you too well to accept that. Do you deny your own past?"

"Let's cut this *auld lang syne* bullshit, Guido, shall we? You want to know how much I have discovered about your sordid operations."

He smiled coldly and looked at me as one might look over a cut of meat in a butcher shop window. "I already know what you know. You know far too much, Alex, and you know what is the remedy for that."

I noticed Zendell's leering face at the edge of my field of vision, and turned to him. "You'll be having a fire sale later this week, Vinnie. It's a shame I didn't think to torch your club as well, with you in it."

The sneer stuck to his face as if frozen. He certainly wasn't used to being spoken to in this manner. After a moment's hesitation he lunged out of his chair and struck me an ineffectual blow to the side of the head.

"Vincent!" Guido halted him as he raised his arm to take another swipe. "That's enough."

Zendell looked from Guido to me, glaring petulantly. "You're mine," he spat. "When we have what we want from you, you're mine."

"Oooo, I am frightened," I mocked.

He straightened his jacket and waistcoat and sat down, still glaring.

Guido pulled his feet from the desk-top, dropped down to the floor and slid open the second top drawer of the filing cabinet.

Reaching into it --- it was head-high to him --- he withdrew my needle gun, realised he had grabbed the wrong article and tried again, this time producing the unit Jim had devised and attached to the phone lines at Villa Vulgar. He got back on his chair and placed the device on the desk.

"I hope you're not going to bore me by denying this is yours?"

"It made for some very interesting listening," I admitted. "By the way, your housemaid might appreciate a wage rise. She didn't do so well on the gee-gees this week."

"I want those tapes, Alex."

"And you and your bank manager have a cosy little arrangement going, don't you. What did you find out about that property developer. What was his name. . . McLaren?"

Guido glanced behind me, gave a curt nod. There was an explosion inside my head and the next thing I knew I was being dragged up off the floor and unceremoniously dumped back into my chair.

"This is not a game," came Guido's voice, beyond the loud humming noise in my right ear. I found it difficult to raise my head, so I replied with my chin resting on my chest.

"I thought you liked games? You and your idiot nephew seem to have quite an unusual game going at present."

This I immediately identified as a foolish remark, considering the force of the first blow. A second, I marked with considerable relief, was not forthcoming however. When my head had cleared somewhat, I looked up to meet Guido's dispassionate gaze.

"And what game are *you* playing now?" he asked.

"No game. I know too much. *We*," I corrected, "know too much." I had the germ of an idea. Guido would get what he wanted, if not from me then from Janie or Took. "So what have I got to bargain with, and what can I hope to bargain for?"

I hadn't really meant to express this question aloud, but Guido was already considering it and I would have to follow through.

"You do accept that you and your friends cannot be allowed to live?"

I nodded. "It appears to be the logical conclusion."

"I *will* have those tapes, *and* the books, one way or the other. I see no basis for any form of bargain."

Neither did I. I was up shit creek and desperately in need of a paddle, but I knew I was on the verge of finding a way out of this maze. The thought processes were at optimum now; surprising what a little stress can do. Pieces of the puzzle were beginning to topple into place in orderly fashion. I was willing to trade anything, say anything to deliver my companions from the brutal treatment this maniacal midget meant to deal out. We needed more time, and unbroken bodies.

"Time," I blurted out, hoping something lucid would follow.

"You want to bargain time?" Guido looked puzzled. He withdrew a cigar from his pocket, lit up and assumed a relaxed pose. "Go on."

"Time is what neither of us have enough of. Naturally we knew from the beginning what the price would be if we were captured. We took that risk and lost." (*A little ego stroking never hurt.*) "We pay with our lives, Guido, but we will endure any punishment you can mete out over the next few hours to ensure that you pay for everything you've done. Any one of those items are evidence enough to lead to a Governmental inquiry, and ultimately to your conviction. Combined, there will be enough evidence to have you arrested, which by my estimation ought to be around Tuesday afternoon. You'll soon be a number in a Corrections institution, or, at best, a fugitive."

Guido was dour-faced. "You've mailed them," he said tonelessly.

"I have. I mailed them yesterday, and I'm the only one who knows which mail-box. It's Sunday, Guido. Mail pick-up in the city is at around nine o'clock. I only have to hold out for a couple of hours and then. . .*pfft*, off they go to the places where they'll do you the most harm."

I saw Zendell check his wrist-watch. "Eight o'clock," he said. "Well, well. Time really does fly, doesn't it?" I permitted myself the luxury of a bitter smile.

"I'll kill your friends," Guido said.

"We're dead anyway. You said so yourself."

"I'll beat it out of them, then."

"If you want. I don't care. I'm the only one who knows and beating takes time anyway. It's a half hour drive to the city from here."

He wasn't looking nearly so relaxed, and I was beginning to feel solid ground under my feet, the first in some time. I had a plan now, the last piece of the puzzle had finally fallen into place. It would take some doing, but it was a chance. Immeasurably more than we had until now.

Guido was an intelligent man, albeit an evil intelligence. He was looking for a loop-hole, a flaw. There was none, not if he believed everything I had told him. A cold fish like him had no way of knowing I would have spilled my guts, there and then, to protect my friends. I wouldn't have believed it myself, a year or so ago. In this instance my past worked *for* rather than against me.

"You're lying," he said.

I looked him straight in the eyes, an icy stare aimed at the heart of his twisted being. "You think so, do you?"

He didn't like this one bit. I knew he believed me.

"I'll make him talk," Vinnie the viper hissed.

"Shut up, Vincent," Guido snapped, slamming his palm against the desk-top. "Damn it, he's right. You *are* an idiot. If things were different. . ." He let it hang. "Never mind."

He turned to me, blowing cigar smoke into the air between us.

"There's no way out for you, Alex. You know that." (*Was it possible I detected a note of regret in his voice?* "What kind of a bargain did you have in mind?"

I felt light-headed. A pin prick of light had just appeared at the end of the tunnel.

"In return for my handing over the goods, all I ask is enough time to prepare ourselves. My companions deserve it. A simple military style firing squad at dawn would be acceptable."

For one terrible moment I thought I was going to break into laughter. Guido, on the other hand, appeared to be lapping this up.

"And there's just one other thing. Janie is addicted to that stuff you're making here. She's starting to go into withdrawal. Give her enough so she doesn't have to suffer the last few hours.

"Effectively, I suppose I've just sold out our cause. But what the hell, we'll be dead, right? Why should I care what happens in this lousy world after I'm gone?"

Guido extricated the cigar from his mouth, arranged himself squarely in his too large chair. "You're all right, Alex. I always thought so."

Recalling the burnt out ex soldier crack from the tapes, I had a momentary pang of doubt, but I was going to commit to this.

"It's a deal," he said. "And no hard feelings, eh?"

"It was a good game," I replied.

At this remark he laughed heartily, then regarded his nephew.

"You hear that, Vincent? If you were half the man. . ."

Vinnie didn't seem to be warming to me in the slightest. If it was really possible for a person to spontaneously combust, I'm sure he would have done so at that moment. I had a strange compulsion to poke my tongue out at him.

"All right, Alex. Where are they?"

Too late to turn back, I jumped in with both feet.

"The tapes are in a derelict house not far from here. Thirteen, Anderson Avenue, Monroe. The books are in the post-box outside the city library, addressed to the State and Federal Attorneys Generals' offices, the Federal tax office, and to the Monarto Daily News."

"Good," said Guido, obviously relieved. He turned to Zendell.

"You got that? Take Neeson and McNally with you."

"And the trilonite for Janie," I added.

Guido nodded. "See to it, Vincent."

When Zendell had left, Guido shook his head. "My sister's boy. He will never make it to the top." He consulted his watch. "You have until midnight, that's all the time I can give you. It'll be dawn maybe on the west coast of America at least."

I shrugged. It was enough.

"I expect you want to get back to your friends." He was about to signal the guard when I interrupted.

"You could grant me one last courtesy, Guido. I never figured it all out. I know about the game you have going with Vinnie, or training program, perhaps, and how you set me up against him by letting me think it was him who was responsible for that phoney assault against me at the White Horse. I traced the drug racket back to you and I got to wondering why the authorities hadn't done the same thing, but I soon learned you had them in your pocket. And then the water got deeper, murkier. There's some underlying skulduggery going on I haven't been able to fathom. . . not entirely. I'd hate to go out not knowing, and there can't be any harm in satisfying my curiosity at this stage of the game?"

This he considered this for a moment while I tried to will him into compliance. I was sure he wanted to. Guido loved nothing better than to talk about himself, about how big he was, but did he know the identity of Cassandra? I doubted it, but if we succeeded in avoiding the sticky end Guido had planned for us, there would be no better time than right now to acquire some vital information.

Finally, he looked up to the guard. "Parker. Wait outside the door until I call for you."

"That's not wise, Mr Spinoza." Parker protested. But Guido's penchant for basking in his own light had gotten the better of him, as I had hoped.

He reached into a desk drawer and pulled out a small pistol with pearl inlaid handle. "Does this reassure you?"

"Yes, Sir." He came around beside my chair and scowled down at me. "If I hear anything at all, Jaeger. . ." and he waved the barrel of his SLR under my nose to illustrate the point. Such a faithful servant, this *nosy* Parker. I would have said as much, but the ringing noise in my ear was only just beginning to abate. I smiled pleasantly instead.

"All right, Parker," Guido said in dismissal, and he left us to take up his post outside the door.

It was an odd feeling to be alone in the room with the person who had complicated my life to this extraordinary degree, and so arbitrarily, merely to satisfy his lust to control everything he saw.

Now it was his intention to kill Took, Janie and myself. A mere peccadillo, though. He was also going to kill every junkie in the city! How many people was that?

"Why did you come back to this country, Alex? What is there here for a man like you?"

"What is there anywhere?" I answered, surprised as hell that he should ask such a question. "One place is as good as another. This is my country. It's where I was born."

"But what sort of country is it? With all the untapped resources, the wealth of minerals lying wasted in the ground while a cowardly government talks about Aboriginal land rights, ecology and conservation. All this while more than three million parasites sap billions of dollars annually, in the form of unemployment hand-outs. Three million people who could be serving this country, as you did, in military service. This could be a great nation. With the right government we could become the most powerful nation in the Pacific region."

I was beginning to get the picture. "And we have the uranium and the technology to make our own nuclear weapons. That'd give us some clout."

"Of course, yes. That's exactly it. *Clout!* We could be a significant world power inside of ten years."

"And so killing every junkie in Monarto will move us one step closer to this wondrous dream. Now I get it. Why didn't I see it before?" I couldn't help myself, this was the most ludicrous thing I had ever heard.

"That's right!" Guido flared, contemptuous now. "You have no idea of the enormity of the situation you have stumbled into. We're going to clean the refuse from the streets of this city. Monarto is the proving ground for a most powerful social tool. With it we can control, totally, the drug trade in this country, or any other for that matter, raise huge amounts of revenue or even eradicate part or all of the addicted population. It's both a tool and a weapon. A world-wide market will mean world-wide control."

The mental image I held as he described this insidious dream made me shudder. The proposition was madness. . . *Inhuman!*

A fervent light shone in Guido's eyes as he said, "This is the reality, Alex. Whole governments held to ransom while we strengthen this country on every level. Politically, industrially, financially, militarily."

"We?" I prompted.

"The Organisation."

"An organisation of nutters, headed up by some chap with a girl's name. Cassandra. . . Right?"

Guido suddenly sobered. "Ah, yes, the tapes."

"And what is he, a disgruntled politician? Some top brass quietly retired on psychiatric grounds?"

Guido was silent, dangerously so. He toyed with the pistol for a while, then looked up, a crooked smile growing on his face. "That information is of no importance where *you're* going." And with that, he terminated out chat.

Twenty Two

As my escort shoved me out into the muggy night air a narrow beam shone down on us from the tower; a spotlight I fervently hoped was being powered by the compound generator and not a power cell.

There was another source of light. It came from the near end of the factory, beside the parked bus, where an articulated tanker had been backed into a loading bay, its nose protruding beneath a big roll-up door. I was near the verge of the gravel road and closing on the clayey bog I had stepped in earlier when I slowed to peer in at the activity. Two workers feeding a fire hose into the back of the tanker. For my curiosity I received a poke in the back with a rifle.

"Get a move on, Jaeger."

"Push me one more time, *mutton-head*," I cursed over my shoulder, and naturally he did just that.

I tried to make the fall look convincing by letting one foot slip out from under me. I spun as I went down and landed on my back in the wet clay.

The guard stood over me, looking pleased with the result, while I managed to sit up. What he didn't know was that I had scooped up two hands full of thick, sticky clay, and as I struggled to my feet I pushed as much of it as I could into my back pockets, working on one pocket at a time as the handcuffs held my hands too close together to fill them simultaneously.

I continued to face him as I worked at it, covering my actions by telling him I didn't think he was a very nice fellow for pushing me in the mud like that. By the time he had spun me around by the collar and shoved me onward, I had ample supply, and with the coating of clay I had plastered on my backside, I doubted he would notice.

When I was brought to the cage Took and Janie both stood and came to the wire to check my condition. Kosciusko ordered them back from the gate as he unfastened the padlock and swung open the gate for me to enter.

"You want another one?" Kosciusko asked my escort.

"No. We've got what we need." He turned to leave.

"Hey, the cuffs." I reminded him.

He extracted the key from his pocket, threw it to Kosciusko and stalked off towards the exit.

"So you spilled your guts, hard-man?" Kosciusko sneered. I was backed up to the gate, but I knew he was sneering. Janie and Took were looking at me kind of funny, too.

"Alex, they gave me some trilonite," said Janie, holding up a brown paper bag. "How did you get them to do it?"

Out of earshot from our watch-dog, who had settled back in his nest of hessian bags, I described, with frequent interruptions from Janie, what had transpired during my audience with Guido.

"What? Are you nuts!"

Took, being of a more patient nature, remained silent, allowing me to attempt to finish the story, which I never did; I was harried into defending myself against Janie's accusations.

"Look, Janie, I did it to get us out of here. He would have had his goons beat it out of us. And even if we endured the beatings, we certainly wouldn't stand much of a chance of escape in the condition we'd be left in, would we? We'd be easy meat."

She thought for a moment, and replied sullenly. "I thought we were going to make him pay?"

"And pay he will. I've managed to buy some time, that's all."

I glanced at my watch and saw that it was a quarter past eight.

"We've got almost a whole four hours, and I've got a plan."

I wondered if that sounded as feeble to the two of them as it did to me.

She shot me a doubtful look. "You're not going to get us drowned again, are you?"

I tried to ignore this remark and set about explaining the escape plan I had devised, doing my best to sound confident in the telling. When I had finished, I sat back and looked at two blank faces.

"That's your plan?" This from Janie.

"What's wrong with it?"

"You're kidding. What's right with it, you mean. What do you suppose our chances are?"

Took, God bless him, intervened on my behalf. "I don't think either of us could come up with anything better. I like it. It covers everything. If it works we're out of here and we achieve everything we set out to do. Besides, he's had a lot of experience at this sort of thing."

Janie nodded her head forward and scratched her nose. "*If* it works."

"Stoned," Took replied to my inquiring expression. "She made rather a piggy of herself when they gave it to her."

"You can hardly blame her," I said, watching her loll forwards.

"It's a hell of a situation."

"Hey, who's a piggy? What are you talking about?" she said, straightening up suddenly.

I went over the procedure twice more.

The first thing to do was to get our guard away from the cage for a while. Just a couple of minutes would do. According to Took and Janie he had not shifted from his position since arriving. We waited half an hour, hoping perhaps nature would call. . . Not even crossed legs.

Janie lit up a cigarette.

"Last one," I reminded her. "We need the matches."

I waited until she had finished the cigarette and went to the gate.

"Hey, Kosciusko. The lady wants to use the bathroom."

"Tough."

So much for that idea. I gave it another ten minutes and tried again.

"Kosciusko."

"What?"

"I've got a news flash for you. Something I figure will spoil Spinoza's whole day."

He leaned forward in his nest, moved the rifle from beside his leg and rested it across his knees. "What are you on about, Jaeger?"

His manner was saturnine, I observed with some satisfaction. The boredom of his post was getting to him.

"I'm on about the fact that I've known about his plan to poison the drug addicts of this city for some time. There has been a warning broadcast over the radio since the middle of this afternoon. Your mission is compromised.

"Take me over to see him, Kosciusko. I want to deliver this personally. I want to see the look on his dial."

He was alert, now. "I don't know what you're on about, but you aren't going anywhere."

"You'd deny me this last, small victory?" I feigned dismay, then changed to thoughtful amusement. "Yeah. Actually, it'll be better that way." I turned away, chuckling.

"Hold it, Jaeger. What poison? What warning?"

"You don't know? Never mind." I moved to the corner to sit with Took and Janie, gave them a wink as I eased myself down.

"Hey, I'm talking to you. A warning on the radio, you said." He was up on his feet and at the gate now.

"Yeah, that's right. I know all about that poison moth-ball stuff. I was at the docks this morning when your pals picked them up."

He hesitated for only a moment, then marched off in the direction of the nearest exit, as expected, to report to Guido.

Janie handed me the crude lock pick we had fashioned during the hours of our incarceration, and I set to work on the padlock while the others kept watch.

We had done a good job, it slipped neatly into the key-way and I counted six tumblers as it slid in. . . the standard number.

Picking locks is not so much a skill as an art, and I had spent many hours in my self-training as a professional thief, practicing on every conceivable type of lock. My hands knew instinctively what to do, and in very short time the lock popped open.

"Okay?" I asked over my shoulder.

I got an *"Okay/Yep"* reply, and went for it.

The steel shelves inside the cage afforded me good cover from the guard at the near side entrance. The guarded door on the opposite side was, fortunately, just around the corner of the manufacturing enclosure, so the converging angles of the perspex obscured visibility until I had cleared the hessian sacks. The sacks provided further cover if I stayed low. I crawled the remaining distance to come up beside the generator, the fuel tank directly above my head. I would have to stand in order to reach the filler cap.

I dug my hands into my pockets and scooped out the clay I had collected from the roadside, squeezed it into two good sized balls, then raised myself high enough to take a peek over at the far exit. The guard there had just turned to watch a trolley being pushed along the walkway. I was clear.

Standing, I reached over to the screw cap, almost directly over the feed line at the bottom of the tank, while keeping an eye on the guard. He was still looking away, following the progress of the female trolley pusher. The cap came free in my hand just as he shifted his balance, and I had to duck down again as he began to turn his head in my direction. I stayed down for a few seconds before risking a peek above the level of the sacks.

When I did, I found him stretching, tilting his torso from side to side. Then he turned away again, leaned against the side of the shed and pulled a packet of cigarettes from his shirt. Clear.

The filler spout was sufficiently large for me to put my hand through while holding the first of the clay balls. I gave it a bit of a tweak as I released it, enough for it to fall, I hoped, directly over the fuel line at the bottom of the tank, its spherical shape enabling it to travel perpendicularly through the fluid. I repeated the performance with the second ball of clay and replaced the cap, wondering as I did so how long it would be until the particles of clay were sucked through the lines to clog the injectors. Or, indeed, if this is what would happen.

I offered up a silent prayer to Huey, amorphous god of reckless souls, and bobbed up to check if the coast was clear. The guard was still leaning against the wall, smoking his cigarette. Urgent movement in the cage caught my eye. Janie was at the gate, making rapid beckoning gestures. Kosciusko was on his way back!

I made it, barely. By the time I had snapped the padlock closed and assumed a suitably innocent pose, Kosciusko rounded the side of the cage; and judging by his countenance, his tattle-tale errand had sparked a response.

"Back up to the gate. Mr Spinoza wants to see you."

I complied with alacrity. "From ASIO to Judas in such a short time?"

"Shut up," he snapped, clamping the handcuffs tightly about my wrists.

By the expression on their faces, Took and Janie showed that they were primed and ready to act upon my return. There could be no second thoughts or refinement of planning from this point.

The moment I left the factory with Kosciusko at my back, the spotlight beam leapt down from the top of the tower and began tracking our course along the gravel road. I felt for the keyholes in the cuffs and located them, one facing outwards, the other facing inwards. I commented on the clouds, the first for days, passing across the face of the moon; and guessing Kosciusko would glance up, I plucked the lock pick from my pocket and inserted it into the keyhole.

As we neared the office, Zendell emerged from the building and strode purposefully towards the open bay doors where the tanker was parked, followed by another man I had not seen before. The guard at the office doorway, noticing our approach, held open the door for us to pass within. I had not yet managed to unfasten the cuffs.

We entered Guido's office to find him filling his brief-case with papers, and on the desk were the opened envelopes which had contained the copies and the original diary and ledgers. The tapes were there, also, along with the micro-recorder from Took's living room.

Guido looked up while continuing to fill the briefcase. "What do you think you know?"

"Oh come on, Guido. You've had a listen to the tapes. I was there at the docks when your chaps picked up the last consignment, unloaded from the Eastern Star. I sampled the contents and I've learned that the stuff is deadly when combined with trilonite."

Guido bundled up the books and tapes, shoved them into the case.

"You're a clever bastard, aren't you. So what have you concluded from this?"

At that moment the ceiling light seemed to dim, then brightened again, and the damn cuffs were so tight around my wrists, I couldn't manipulate the pick properly. If the power failed before I could release them, well. . . it didn't bear thinking about.

"The conclusion is obvious," I said in answer to his question; and still struggling with the lock. "You mean to contaminate the drug with the stuff, and waste God knows how many people. But I've seen to it that a warning has been broadcast over the radio for the better part of the day. By now the news will have travelled throughout the drug community and your murderous scheme will come to nothing. Cassandra won't be too pleased with you, will he?"

To my considerable relief, the cuff released its biting grip and I held it in place. I looked down to the floor, noted Kosciusko's position, behind and a little to the left of me. The barrel of his gun was lowered.

"The number of addicts in this city," Guido began, and ignoring my last remark, "is around two hundred and ten thousand. A surprising number for a city this size, isn't it? This city alone represents a considerable burden to the economy of the country, if only in the areas of crime and social security."

Guido cocked his head. "Do you hear that?"
Beyond the blacked out window I heard the rumble of a diesel engine. The tanker, I supposed.

"What of it?"

He leaned forward with his small hands pressing on the desk, a thin smile slowly growing on his face. "What of it? I'll give you a hint, shall I?

"One part in fifty million of that stuff, when it combines inside the human body with the residual, active element of trilonite, triggers the growth of a crystalline structure between the cellular walls of the brain. The hypothalamus, actually, it controls vital functions. One part in fifty million, Alex, and we've been stockpiling the stuff for months. Am I getting through to you?"

My expression evidently reflected my inability to grasp exactly what he was getting at. He continued.

"The stuff is highly soluble, as you may have discovered, and absolutely undetectable in such small amounts. No amount of analysis of drinking water will discover its presence."

Realisation struck like a hammer blow. "You're going to contaminate the reservoirs?"

"No, no," he sniggered, obviously amused by my consternation.

"Too large a volume." He paused, giving me time to try and work it out for myself.

He looked up as the light globe flickered, brightened, then died, plunging the room into total darkness.

I had run this situation through my mind at least twenty times. My actions within the next few moments would determine the success or failure of our escape bid, and as things stood, the lives of two hundred and ten thousand people depended on its success.

I had taken care to avert my eyes when I realised the power was about to fail. The others, I hoped, had automatically stared at the light bulb, covering their retinas with dappled images in the sudden darkness.

The second the bulb winked out I spun and aimed a kick where Kosciusko's crotch ought to be. With the impact he doubled over, and I was able to locate his head. Time was of the essence; I dealt with him quickly and severely, located the key to the cage in his trouser pocket.

I knew Guido would have reached for his gun in this time. I lunged beneath the desk, caught his legs and whipped his feet out from under him. I heard his head hit the floor with considerable force, and immediately afterwards, the clatter of the pistol against the floor-boards. If he wasn't out, he was stunned.

I fumbled for the filing cabinet, found it, felt for the second drawer, slid it open and located my needle gun. Its grip was cool and reassuring in the palm of my hand.

I had found it none too soon. I heard the office door open, and, shadow within shadow, I discerned the shape of a sentry in the open doorway.

"Mr Spinoza?" . . .I sent a needle in that direction and heard him fall to the floor soon after.

I grabbed the briefcase containing the vital evidence and for a second considered what to do with Guido. What *could* I do? I couldn't take him with me and I couldn't kill him in cold blood, even though I'd be doing the world a favour.

"Damn you, you little toad." I kicked his prostrate form as hard as I could and headed for the exit. There would be another time.

I hit the gravel at a sprint. How long had it been. . . thirty, forty seconds? Beyond the sound of adrenalin-charged blood pounding in my ears, I heard someone shouting instructions away to my right. I got off the gravel quickly and had to slow my pace a little on the uneven ground, but now my foot-falls were much quieter.

The compound was in total darkness; the cloud cover I had witnessed earlier had thickened to blot out the full moon. *Huey* was with me.

I was quickly closing on the far end entrance, beyond which Took and Janie were waiting, no doubt nervously, for me to show. I couldn't see it, but my army training and my ability to judge distances in situations such as this were as good as ever. I slowed to a walk, and my foot found the entrance path I was looking for. At the door, I halted, slowed my breathing and listened. To hell with it. I tapped on the door.

"Hey, open up. I can't see a thing out here."

The door swung open and I popped a needle into the black shape within.

All was darkness as I entered and made my way towards the cage.

I was almost there when a flashlight winked on, held by someone at the generator. The light spilled about and I hit the floor to avoid detection.

Another man appeared from behind the generator, carrying a toolbox. "Give us some light, here at the filter," he said to the other.

I crawled lizardlike along the floor, trying to keep the briefcase and loose handcuff from scraping against the concrete as I went. One of them hit the starter button, the motor chugged over without firing. I took aim and sent four needles in their direction. The torch hit the deck, along with the men. Time was a-wasting.

I was up and at the cage door. The padlock rattled against the gate as I inserted the key and popped open the lock.

"Alex?" It was Janie's anxious whisper.

"Yes." I swung open the gate and pocketed the padlock; I had a use for it at the front gate, if we made it that far.

Took and Janie knew what to do. The book of matches and a cigarette Janie would use as a delayed incendiary device, placing it over the spout of an opened drum of dieseline. The resulting conflagration would do considerable damage, but I wanted to certain of taking out the manufacturing area. To this end I stood watch with my needle gun pointed into the darkness while Took disconnected the acetylene bottle from the oxy-welding unit against the wall. As soon as he had done this, he hoisted it onto his shoulder and I led him across the factory floor towards the rank of gas bottles standing alongside the perspex enclosure.

I missed by only a couple of metres or so; not hard to do on an open factory floor in pitch darkness, and we had to edge our way along the outer wall until we found the bottles. Here we were within five metres of where there ought to have been another guard standing at the nearby exit, and when the acetylene bottle chimed as Took put it down on the concrete, I expected to be challenged, but this did not occur. Perhaps it was this fellow who had left his post to attend to the failed generator. A wrong decision, if so.

Took's experience served in good stead with the connection procedure. I heard a pop and a hiss as he disconnected a hose, then a snap as the hose was reconnected to *our bottle*.

"Done," he whispered, and we quickly headed to the opposite side of the enclosure where Janie would be lying low.

Arriving at the opposite corner I called softly. "Janie?"

"Here."

I turned in the direction of her voice, saw her dark shape rise from the floor. I reached out and found her hand, then led her and Took at a trot down the narrow walkway towards the other end of the shed.

As we emerged into the night, there was an almighty roar and a ball of orange flame which lit the interior with a ghastly light. The acetylene. We were lucky to have gotten clear.

There was an awful lot of screaming and yelling going on as we rounded the corner of the shed and piled into the bus. Took slammed the door shut and kicked over the engine. When she fired, he let out a triumphant laugh and turned to us. "The importance of preventative maintenance."

He gunned the bus out from behind the building, swung hard left where the gravel road should have been and only missed by a metre. With a bit of bumping and squeaking he found the road, and selecting a higher gear propelled us through the smoky surroundings at an increasing rate of knots. Automatic rifle fire shattered the rear window as we swung left onto the exit road and headed towards our final obstacle.

With a hundred metres to go to the looked gates I located my trusty wire lock pick and prepared to disembark, post-haste. We were travelling at a good fifty miles an hour when Took decided we were close enough and stood on the brake pedal, bringing us to a screeching halt within spitting distance of the ironclad gates.

He switched on the headlights and opened the door. "Do your thing," he called as I jumped out.

The gates were bound at the centre with a heavy chain, and secured with an equally strong-looking padlock. To my astonished delight, as I rammed the piece of wire into the keyway and gave a testing twist, the lock sprang open. I ripped the chain away and, with a flourish, flung wide gates.

Took quickly pulled out onto the street while I chased up the gates to swing them closed again. I had one in position and had just moved for the other when a lead hornet tore through the air beside my ear, followed an instant later by the report from the rifle which had fired it. There was a vehicle speeding along the access road towards us. The beaten up ute with two armed men standing in the back.

As I pushed the second gate closed, a volley of shots slammed into the cladding, exploding chips of rusty metal into my face and paining my ears with the resulting din. I slung the chain around the gates, pulled from my pocket the padlock I had saved from the cage and snapped it shut through the links.

As I ran to board the bus, the sound of exploding drums of dieseline reverberated in the warm evening air.

Twenty Three

Janie gripped the armrest with both hands in order to stay seated beside me while I worked on the remaining cuff. Took concerned himself with putting as much distance between us and the factory as possible, the resultant buffeting doing little to aid my efforts.

"What now?" he shouted over the noise of machinery being worked to the limit.

"There's a small matter of a tanker-load of a particularly nasty substance being put in the city's water supply."

He leaned over the wheel to make eye contact with me. "That mothball stuff? But I thought. . ."

"Yeah, so did I. We thought wrong. It goes into the domestic water and the poor bastards don't know what hits them. Guido says they've been stockpiling the stuff for some time. Extremely virulent, enough to take out every addict in the city. Cassandra's idea of a marketing campaign."

"That's insane," Janie gasped. "He can't expect to get away with it."

"No? Well maybe someone ought to tell *him* that."

"Moot point," Took observed, taking a left and directing us toward the main road. "The immediate problem is catching the tanker. Where's it headed?"

I shrugged. "Damned if I know. The generator failed before I was able to get an answer to that one. But it isn't the reservoir, he did give me that much. Too big a volume of water, he said."

"Into the pipeline, then," Janie suggested. "Like they do with the chlorine."

I stared at her in admiration. "Of course, yes. That has to be it. Janie, you're a genius. The *chlorination plant!*"

"Did I do good?" she said, feigning childlike innocence, and I realised she was still high on the drug.

"You did good, Janie."

"I don't like to be a killjoy," said Took, scratching under his beard, "but there are three reservoirs supplying this city, each with its own chlorination plant on-line."

"Which is the closest? I'm willing to bet they'll lighten the load at the nearest one before moving on to the next."

"That would be Mary Vale," said Took, thoughtfully. "How much head start do they have?"

"About five minutes. Do you think you can catch it?"

"Good chance. A fully-laden tanker, they'd most likely take the freeway to avoid steep gradients. I know another route. It's steeper, but we ought to make up a five-minute lead, easy."

At that moment a chirping sound started up beneath the seat.

"If it's for me," said Janie, "tell them I'm washing my hair and can't come to the phone."

I located my cellular phone amongst a collection of rusty tools which Took had stowed under the seat: screwdrivers, spanners, tomahawk, tin snips and other assorted miscellanea.

I pressed the *receive* button. "Yes?"

"Mr Jaeger?" It was a woman's voice.

"Yes."

"Exec Message Service, Mr Jaeger. Mr Harris has asked that we contact you and relay any message you might have."

"Just a second." I turned to two pairs of inquiring eyes. "Jim's message service. He and Pat will be worried." Into the receiver I said, "Tell him everything is under control. I'll contact you when one or two loose ends have been tied up."

She gave me the company's number and I stowed the phone in the glove compartment.

"Under control?" Janie stared at me incredulously. "Would you mind telling me what we do if we catch up with this tanker, or has it escaped your notice that we are unarmed?"

No, this unfortunate situation had not escaped my attention. Since we had no weapons on board other than my needle gun, which I doubted would be of much use in the event of overtaking Vinnie and friend, I was locked in personal debate about the advisability of taking the time to procure the appropriate fire power. But we simply didn't have the time, and I bitterly rued my oversight in not having picked up one of our captor's rifles at the factory.

"If we catch them on the road," I began, and Janie pounced before I could finish. ". . .we can martyr ourselves under the wheels of a forty-ton truck. You know what you can do with that idea."

"Nothing quite so dramatic," I replied defensively. It was, in fact, almost exactly what I had in mind, but I wasn't going to tell *her* that. I would have to think on it some more.

Traffic was light. We cut eastwards, headed towards the foothills which skirted that side of the city, passing through one sleepy suburb after another, with barely any sign of activity to be seen anywhere.

Clouds of tiny, winged insects circled crazily beneath the orange glow of street lamps. A milk bar owner stood patiently behind the counter of his shop, perhaps waiting for one last sale before closing up for the night. Television sets flickered behind the curtained windows of the dreary, red brick houses that we passed.

Onward we rolled, leaving in our wake row after identical row of the miserable dwellings the State had conceived and built. Lowrental housing for low-income earners and those who maintained a frugal existence on government handout in lieu of paid employment. A spiritual vacuum, I mused; exactly the environment I had existed in until I'd become old enough to enlist.

I attempted to shrug off such thoughts and concentrate on the task before us. From the snatches of conversation which reached me above the noise of the droning motor, I gathered that Janie and Took were swapping stories from one another's past. What *bonhomie*; what a familiar little group we had become, an army deserter turned thief, a fringe-dwelling drop-out with vague dreams of an idyllic life in a foreign land, and a drug addicted girl with only the thief and the drop-out in whom she could place any trust. How jolly.

We had left the easternmost suburb of Mitchell behind and were beginning to climb, the road cutting diagonally across the escarpment so that the city now stretched out below, a panorama of coloured lights fanning out over the plain between the hills and the gulf-waters. Like tapestried fairy lights they appeared to me, belying the mayhem which had, and probably was *still* taking place down there. . . The sound of distant thunder rolled across the night sky.

Looking down at the city like this, it was a simple exercise to divorce myself from those who existed there; my fellow man, struggling and striving for what? There were over three million people under my gaze, and every individual's life consisted of joys and dramas unique to themselves. It was what mystified me so much about mankind. A single person could be many faceted, interesting, good company, but a great many people took on the personality of a single, dumb animal, concerned only with exploiting its environment in order to satisfy its crude urges. A case of the sum of the parts having greater worth than the whole; and there was going to be a few less parts to this whole if Guido had his way.

A social tool was how he had described it. No doubt the Nazi propaganda machine had churned out similar phrases in their heyday. The more I thought about it, the more diabolical the scheme appeared.

Drug-running was one of the most insidious and profitable rackets going. It was self-sustaining in that the number of consumers always grew, there was never any shortage of willing distributors to foist the product onto the populace in exchange for a lucrative cut, and only a small proportion of the profit needed to be ploughed back into production. The network would spread quickly, the prices would be pushed up and huge sums of money would begin to flow back.

Countries held to ransom, Guido had suggested. How? An undetectable substance introduced into the water supply. A specially concocted batch of the drug which would trigger thousands of addicts to violence? Guido's words came back to me: *This city is a proving ground for a most powerful social tool ...control the drug trade ... raise huge amounts of revenue ... eradicate all or part of the addicted population.*

On the other hand, it was *"social cleansing"* for sale. How many despotic rulers might consider this as a means to solving the embarrassing problem of urban poverty and growing slum areas? The image of death squads operating under the cloak of night in South America sprang instantly to mind. Conceivably, a major portion of the world might take to trimming back what it regarded as *"dead wood"*, thus relieving the strain on dwindling purses and overburdened resources. Many governments were ripe for seduction, exploitation or extortion, depending on their particular bent. What fiend had set this insidious concept into motion?

Code name Cassandra. The spider at the centre of the web, tugging at the strings. He had managed to recruit Guido to oversee operations here in Monarto, but how many other Guidos were there, and how many other factories churning out this poison?

Lightning flickered across the sky and illuminated a roiling mass of thunder-heads sweeping in from the west.

"Storm brewing," Took called above the engine noise, and as if to lend support to his words, a brilliant series of zigzags tore through the darkness.

"Yeah. There certainly is."

"It might put a dampener on the riots," Janie said.

"Or stir them up," added Took. "They sure looked as though they were having some fun this afternoon, on the tele."

"Those were real bullets being fired," Janie reminded him.

By the time we turned onto the Mary Vale exit, the weather had overtaken us, beginning with a few large drops of rain splattered on the windshield and a noticeable fall in temperature, followed soon afterwards by a vicious wind and a torrential downpour. The bus took a buffeting as we rolled on, our speed reduced, necessarily, due to poor visibility and the added risk of washouts on the road.

The road we followed cut into the hillside, winding as it climbed to the summit, and there, joining at right angles with the Mary Vale road, a slender strip of bitumen which continued to climb for a further kilometre before steeply descending to the valley floor.

As we crested the rim of the valley and looked down the slope before us, awash and strewn with debris, it occurred to me that this section would require extreme caution if you happened to be handling a heavily laden tanker. And the steep incline prior to the crest had reduced our speed quite considerably. The tanker would manage little more than a walking pace.

Spotting a *"private road only"* sign on our left, I called to Took to swing onto it. Reacting instantly he smoothly brought us to a halt, twenty metres off the main road and parked before a white gate, above which, in letters large and ominous, a sign read: *RUSHBROOK HOUSE.*

"Well I'll be damned," declared Janie, staring at the entrance of the hospital where Mainwaring had arranged for her treatment.

"I wish you wouldn't say things like that," I said, getting down on my knees to rummage beneath the seat. "But it is quite a coincidence."

"What are you looking for?" Took asked.

I withdrew my arm from under the seat, my hand grasping the rusty tomahawk I had discovered earlier. "This."

I tested the edge with my thumb and found it to be suitably sharp.

My companions' faces exhibited puzzlement. "The tanker has to pass this way, doesn't it?"

Took gave me a nod. Janie said, "You're going to stop a juggernaut with that weeny little chopper? Are you mental?"

"I'm going to try to disable its brake system. We haven't got much time and it's the best I can come up with. When the tanker goes past, pull out and follow it."

"And if it has already gone by?"

I was at the steps, waiting for Took to pull the lever and let me out when she asked this question.

"All right, you two go ahead and check. Come back for me if you find anything, or even if you don't find anything. How far is it to the chlorination plant?"

"About five or six kilometres," Took answered.

I was locked in debate with myself. What if we had gotten it all wrong, that the chlorination plants were not the targets; or only half right, and the poison was heading to the Carrington Creek pipeline to the north?

"Go ahead," I said, escaping my bout of ambivalence. "There's nothing else we can do."

I was nearly at the top of the hill by the time Took had reversed out and headed off for the chlorination plant. The red tail-lights dwindled to obscurity through the surrounding mist, and the engine noise was lost to the din of driving rain and the wind rattling through the dense bushland on either side of the road.

I crested the hill and continued on down for a distance of about fifty metres, where a gum tree near the verge of the road offered itself as a perfect place for concealment. There I waited, soaked to the skin, standing in a stream of muddy water, tomahawk in hand like some Hollywood Apache indian lying in wait to ambush a pale-face wagon. I remembered the ever recurrent fate of that hapless indian and dismissed the image.

A lightning bolt struck not far away, and the resulting crash of thunder sent a rush of adrenalin through my system. And when the already heavy rain stiffened to a teeming downpour, I couldn't help thinking that someone up there was having a marvellous joke at my expense. This was patently stupid. While I stood behind a tree in the pouring rain, Vinnie and company were well on their way to achieving their objective. We had gotten it wrong!

No sooner had this thought emblazoned itself across my mind in giant-sized flashing letters, than the white beans of powerful headlights threw long shadows across the ground. From a distance, the roar of a diesel engine broke through the heavy air as the driver worked down through the gears to negotiate the steep gradient.

It could have been any heavy vehicle carting any of a thousand different things, but my adrenal glands refused to listen, and my attack of the collywobbles gave way to keen anticipation as I peeked out from behind the tree trunk to see, climbing steadily up the hill, two sets of headlights casting brilliant cones of light into the slanting rain.

Behind the field of illumination I couldn't see, but the driver continued to shift down through the gears as momentum was lost and the prime mover continued to labour. I pulled my head in and pressed my back against the trunk, readying myself for a fiftymetre dash.

The light grew more and more intense and the roar grew louder and louder until, taking me by surprise, the cab drew level, then passed me by, Zendell's unmistakable profile framed in the passenger side window.

Breaking cover, I urged my legs to find top speed and realised at once that the standing had stiffened my joints, and my soggy sneakers had put on weight. I had fallen back to halfway along the length of the tanker before I was able to match its speed, and there just ain't nowhere to climb aboard one of these things from that position.

Giving it everything I had, I found I was making some ground, but would it be enough? The crest was drawing ever nearer and the organism was already complaining bitterly at this sudden and inexplicable desire for speed. I was desperately close to the bogie drive over which the tanker coupled with the prime mover, but in no man's land, failing either to gain or loose ground. Then fortune smiled. The driver shifted down a further gear to compensate for the last, small rise, and in that time I gained the necessary distance to draw level with the wheels. I grabbed hold, and, with flagging energy, managed to haul myself up onto the wheel guard as we made the crest. It was all downhill from here.

My intention was to sever the air hoses which operated the trailer's braking system; the trick being to do this at the critical moment, when the vehicle had reached sufficiently high speed to ensure that control could not be maintained, and slow enough so that I wouldn't break my neck as I abandoned ship. Or in this case... truck.

One thing I hadn't reckoned on. It was pitch dark behind the cab and gallons of muck was flying up from the road surface, stinging my eyes and making it almost impossible to see. I reached out for the edge of the chassis and pulled myself towards it. Through the darkness and flying muck I discerned the brake hoses suspended over a T-bar arrangement, running from the rear of the cab to the underside of the tanker. And with every passing second we were accumulating speed.

I figured we were travelling at around sixty to seventy kilometres per hour and nearing the first bend on the downhill run, as I shimmied along a cross-member and found purchase enough to facilitate a precarious standing position.

This was it ... *Christ, what was I doing?* This was tantamount to climbing high up in a tree and sawing off the very branch you happened to be sitting on; and even that sounded more reasonable than this!

As I procrastinated in this way before executing what now appeared to be an obviously stupid act, the truck's brakes were applied. We were approaching the bend.

I chopped down on the hoses where they rested across the T-bar, managing to slice through one and halfway through the second. There was an immediate lurch through the chassis as the whole inertial force of the load pushed forward on the bogie. The shift sent me reeling, and I copped an eyeful of muck as I threw myself in the direction of the wheel guard, where I landed flat and grasping for any available handhold.

The driver's first reaction was to apply greater braking pressure. Bad move. The trailing weight imparted further force, now sideways on as we entered the corner. The tyres on the prime mover broke traction with the wet road and the vehicle instantly jack-knifed, sending us gracefully and ponderously gliding towards the precipitous drop just a few metres from the verge of the road.

Through those sickening moments of time dilation, where everything went to slow motion, two things occurred. The organism dumbly refused all commands to release its grip and bail out, and delirium struck. I could have sworn I saw Jim's father standing in front of me, dressed in battle fatigues, smiling one of his enigmatic smiles. "Alex," he said to me. "You sure are one crazy soldier."

Twenty Four

From the hospital verandah, where I sat with one leg plastered and jutting out ridiculously, I looked out over the garden where other patients strolled about or sat in the warm afternoon sunshine. It looked like one of those perfectly inane scenes from a 1940's British war film where Biff Jones, ace fighter pilot and all-round good chap, convalesced after losing all his arms and legs in a *Spitfire* crash.

Beside me sat one of my three constant companions, Harry, the eight-to-four shift; undoubtedly an employee of the Government, but totally averse to divulging anything whatsoever on the subject.

They had been with me throughout the past nine weeks, which was six weeks longer than *I* had been with me, because during that time I had been in a coma; nature's own little time capsule. One apparent function of these reticent guardians was to see that I didn't talk to anyone, evidently this extended to talking in my sleep. It was not exactly a great mental feat, therefore, to deduce that there was a cover-up going on; and

I figured these guys as ASIO or ASIS, both of which spelled trouble in anyone's language. One glance at my file, with *DESERTER* stamped across it, and I was for a military prison and court-martial.

This rather unpleasant thought was interrupted by the appearance on the verandah of a grey-suited man of about fifty years of age. He was a big man, square-shouldered and a head which might appeal to a television network in the market for a distinguished, believable type to read the six o'clock news. His arrival caused my man Harry to drop his crossword puzzle and scurry over to meet him beneath the potted jasmine where he stood.

So... it was about to hit the fan, I thought, while I watched them talking surreptitiously. I began weighing my chances of escape with my leg in plaster and wearing a lilac pink dressing-gown and hospital pyjamas. Very poor, I imagined.

When the six o'clock news guy disappeared back into the building, Harry came sauntering towards me.

"Who was that?" I asked, feigning indifference.

"You ought to be flattered, Mr Jaeger. One of the bigwigs, flown all the way from Canberra to meet you."

"Flattery is for fools, Harry. He hasn't come over all that way just to massage my ego."

He got behind my chair and pushed me towards the door. "There's some others waiting for you, too."

Others! I had a sinking feeling. I just knew it was the State police, over the insurance company heist, or the Law Society ripoff, maybe even the car-yard fire or the hire-car or ... to hell with it. My goose was microwaved anyway.

We entered the building and he pushed me along the polished linoleum floor of the corridor leading to the staff rooms. At a door marked "CONFERENCE ROOM" he halted and knocked.

The *bigwig* opened the door, pulled it wide to facilitate the wheelchair.

"Do come in, Mr Jaeger."

But I wasn't paying any attention to him. At the polished wood table sat Janie and Took, smiles wide on their dials. Took gave a sideways wave. Janie got out of her chair and came over to greet me.

"Hello Alex." She dipped down beside my chair. "How are you? They wouldn't let us see you before now, and I was ever so worried about you."

"I'm okay, Janie. Really. Hunky-dory as soon as this leg mends. How about you?"

"Great. I spent two months in the clinic. It was horrible at first, but they got me off that rotten stuff. I'm clean," she said with obvious pride."

"That's great, Janie. Terrific. I'm very proud of you."

She flushed a little at this remark, and I sat there looking at her. How well she looked. She wore new blue jeans, a white blouse and the same silver jacket she had bought the morning after I had rescued her from the Old Coach motel. Her eyes were bright and clear --- clearer than I had seen before.

"What's going on?" she whispered.

Our host cut in. "If you will both come to the table, you will find out."

She brushed my man Harry aside and wheeled me to the table to sit beside her. Took gave me a comradely slap on the back as I passed by, and nearly dislocated my shoulder, the big lug.

"My name is Jackson," said the bigwig, taking his place at the head of the table. "I've been sent here to, ah, *resolve* one or two things."

"Hey, Jack," Took interjected. "Have we done something wrong or something? Because, pardon me if I'm wrong, but didn't we like save thousands of lives?"

"That is true," said Jackson, unfazed, "and your government is duly grateful."

"Then why," Took continued, "is our friend being kept here without being allowed visitors, and why have Janie and I been under constant supervision?"

Took shot me a sly wink. He wanted his two bob's worth.

Jackson looked to me. "Perhaps Mr Jaeger can answer that. He has experience in these matters. Alex?

I was rapidly learning to dislike this guy. "Cover-up," I stated flatly.

"National security," he amended, his complexion darkening somewhat. "Our government does not need it to be known in the international arena that a plot of this nature could come to such a stage of maturity without being detected by our law enforcement agencies. You do, of course, appreciate the expediency of this."

"You can't keep something like this hushed up," Janie said, her voice rising in pitch. "You have to warn the rest of the world of the danger."

"That is true," said Jackson. "But there are appropriate channels for disseminating delicate information like this. We can't have the press getting hold of it and starting a panic, now can we? Which brings me to the point of my visit."

"Just a moment, Jackson." I didn't like the way he was attempting to control these proceedings. "I know where you're going with this, but before it goes any further I think there's a couple of things we deserve to know. Firstly, Zendell and Spinoza. . . do you have them?"

"We have them." He chuckled deep in his throat. "Zendell is in slightly worse condition than yourself, but he will survive.

And thanks to the documented evidence you provided, in the form of the books and tapes, both their fates are sealed."

"And Cassandra? You must have nabbed him by now."

"I'm afraid that is classified information," Jackson said dourly. "Highly confidential."

I sat looking at him. He didn't look nearly so cocky now.

"You missed him, didn't you. You damn well let the bastard get away."

Jackson sat there, stony-faced. "Confidential," he repeated feebly, and there was silence in the room. He leaned down and lifted his brief-case to the table, opened it and produced three documents which he placed before each of us.

"Please sign these."

I knew very well what these were, but neither Took nor Janie would ever have seen one before.

"What's this?" Janie asked indignantly.

"Official Secrets Act," I explained. "Once you put your moniker to that, you're bound, under penalty of imprisonment, to not utter a word of what you know."

"No way," she exclaimed, and stubbornly folded her arms. "I'm not signing it."

"Neither am I," Took agreed. "People have a right to know the danger, what sort of animals are running around loose, and how incompetent the police are at catching the *real* crooks. Man, I once got busted for a tiny bag of grass, and I had coppers climbing all over me for months, like I was *Mr Big* or something. And you let this guy get away?"

"And you, Alex? Do you concur with your *friends*?"

The way he emphasised the word made me angry enough to want to slug him, and maybe I would have, had I not been aware of the dossier he had in his case, with my name on it.

"I fully concur with my *friends*, you pretentious son of a bitch. My *friends* and I have been out risking our lives, doing the work you and your colleagues should have been doing, only to see you come in at the last and screw up by letting the real brains of the operation skip the country. And don't bother denying it, I know that's what happened, otherwise we wouldn't be going through all this bullshit. So if you ever try casting aspersions on my *friends* again, I'll climb over this table and tear your goddamn head off your shoulders. You got that?"

I was up on my foot and angry enough to explode when Took jumped up on the table. I thought he was going to attack Jackson, and I think Jackson thought the same thing, judging by the way he pushed himself back into his chair. But, no, to everyone's amazement the big galoot started into a gravel-throated rendition of Instant Karma:

"Instant karma's gonna get you," he pointed to Jackson, *"it's gonna knock you right on the head. Better get yourself together, brother, 'cause pretty soon you're gonna be dead."* Now he started with the freaked-out hand movements. *"Instant karma's gonna get you. Better get yourself together, sister,"* he pointed to Janie, *"join the human race. Why in the world are we here? Surely not to live in pain and fear. Why in the world are you there?"* and he pointed to me, *"when you're everywhere."*

Janie was in tears by this time, covering her face with her hands but peeking through her fingers, and I was laughing so hard that my leg began to throb. Jackson was astonished to the point of immobility, and could only watch as Took collected up the papers and began tearing them into tiny pieces... *"And we all shine on, like the moon and the stars and the sun. And we all shine on, everyone, come on"* . . .and he threw the pieces above his head like so much confetti. "No way, man. We ain't signing no draconian establishment contracts."

He climbed down off the table to a well deserved and rousing ovation. Jackson, still somewhat flummoxed, remained silent in his chair until the congratulations were over with - which took a little while. We were still struggling to regain composure when he stood and, for a time, regarded the three of us in a serious manner.

"Very well," he said, gaining our attention. "As free citizens, I can't force you to sign." He pulled another document from his brief-case and turned to me. "Alex Jaeger, I am arresting you on the charges of desertion from the Australian army, insurrection against an ally in a time of war, sedition, grand larceny, burglary, tax evasion, arson and, ooh, this one looks bad. . . driving without a licence."

There was a nasty silence. Took started gathering pieces of the shredded paper. "You got another one of those form things? Mine seems to have got torn up, somehow."

"Yeah, mine too." Janie chimed in.

Jackson remained silent and stony-faced. He fixed me with a practised stare, which probably set his young subordinates to trembling in their shiny shoes. Then the edges of his mouth began to curl.

"You are one lucky son of a gun, Jaeger. There must be someone up on the hill who remembers you from your army days – someone who made it to the top of the heap – because what I'm about to do is beyond my comprehension."

From his case he pulled out replacements for the forms Took had shredded, and placed one before each of us. "As from the moment you sign this document, you are off the hook, which avails you of all the rights and privileges afforded to any other free citizen of this country. Congratulations."

The three of us signed in turn and handed the papers over to him. He stowed them in his brief-case and snapped it shut.

"Remember your obligations," he said, moving towards the door. "The Government is entrusting you with the security of this country. Not many people have that honour." He halted in the doorway. "You're all free to go, and remember," he said, putting a finger beside his nose, "not a word."

We watched him leave, and there was an odd sense of *so that's it?* in the room.

Took was shaking his head in disbelief. "I don't believe that dude. What an arse-hole. He just blackmailed us out of our constitutional rights."

I slapped him on the back. "Hey, Took, where'd you learn to sing and dance like that? I know a couple of night-club owners who might be interested."

"It's the only song I know the words to," he said, grinning hugely.

"I thought he was going to have a conniption or something, didn't you? Him and that fore-dude at the docks ought to get together sometime."

Out of the corner of my eye I caught Janie gesturing to Took.

"Oh, um, Alex. I've got to go check the bus or something. The, ah, thingy is loose and I've got to, you know, check it out. Hey. You are coming with us, aren't you?"

"Just as soon as I get some street clothes on," I replied.

We watched him leave by way of that peculiar bouncing gait of his.

"He is something, isn't he?" I said, turning to Janie.

"He sure is. Oh, I just remembered, Alex. I spoke to Pat-"

"You did? That's great. I've been going nuts worrying about them. I couldn't use the phone and . . . are they okay?"

"That's what I was about to tell you before you interrupted. They're fine, and guess what?"

I knew by the smug smile on her face that I wasn't going to be able to guess. "Okay, what already?"

"No, come on," she said playfully. "You have to have at least one guess." Her eyes sparkled with mischief.

I struggled to think of something. . . *anything*. "Jim's selling up and they're moving over west?" I tried.

"Pat's pregnant," she said, her face splitting with a wide smile.

"Hey, no kidding? That's terrific. I'll have to send them on holiday more often. Do you suppose that makes me an uncle or something?"

"I bet it does," she replied cheerfully. "Boy, I really envy those two. They've got it all, and now a baby on the way. That's got to be the greatest." She had a funny look in her eye.

"Maybe we shouldn't keep Took waiting."

"He won't mind," she said dismissively. "Do we need to take this thing?" she asked, meaning the wheelchair.

"No." I got up out of the contraption to demonstrate. "The plaster will be off in a week or two. A walking-stick will get me around for now."

When I had stood, Janie was right in front of me. Close. She didn't back away. We were staring at each other, the room was unnaturally quiet and, suddenly, there didn't seem to be anything to say. Her face was beginning to flush, but her gaze held mine unwaveringly.

Now that it was all over there was no further need for pretence; I had known I was attracted to her since the morning after the night we met, and since then the condition had worsened.

A faint smile crept slowly across her beautifully formed lips. "We made it," she said, just above a whisper.

"Yes. We did, didn't we."

The distance between us was gradually diminishing, yet I wasn't aware of moving. As we slowly, inexorably drew to one another, her face tilted up to mine, graced with smile which betrayed just the merest trace of apprehension. Her brown eyes bright and clear.

Without quite knowing how it happened, we were embraced. She kissed me, hard and hot, like I had never been kissed before; and, curse whatever indolent god whose role it is to look after reckless fools like me, I kissed her right back.

end

Also by the Same Author

ISBN: 0 646 40490 3

A selection of unusual short stories

ISBN: 0 957 85860 4

Two novellas in the same cover

ISBN: 0 957 85861 2

A fast-paced crime novel
with a sense of humour

ISBN: 0 957 85862 0

Two damaged lives
One destiny

www.ingramcontent.com/pod-product-compliance
Lightning Source LLC
Chambersburg PA
CBHW020651120726
47906CB00001B/226